D0180503

Books by Carol Lea Benjamin

FALL GUY
THE LONG GOOD BOY
THIS DOG FOR HIRE
THE DOG WHO KNEW TOO MUCH
A HELL OF A DOG
LADY VANISHES
THE WRONG DOG

And coming soon in hardcover

WITHOUT A WORD

CAROL LEA BENJAMIN

THE WRONG DOG

A RACHEL ALEXANDER MYSTERY

AVON BOOKS

An Imprint of HarperCollinsPublishers

This is a work of fiction. Names, characters, places, and incidents are products of the author's imagination or are used fictitiously and are not to be construed as real. Any resemblance to actual events, locales, organizations, or persons, living or dead, is entirely coincidental.

AVON BOOKS
An Imprint of HarperCollins*Publishers*
10 East 53rd Street
New York, New York 10022-5299

Copyright © 2000 by Carol Lea Benjamin
Excerpt from *Without a Word* copyright © 2005 by Carol Lea Benjamin
ISBN: 0-06-076236-5
www.avonmystery.com

First Avon Books paperback printing: August 2005

Avon Trademark Reg. U.S. Pat. Off. and in Other Countries, Marca Registrada, Hecho en U.S.A.
HarperCollins® is a registered trademark of HarperCollins Publishers Inc.

Printed in the U.S.A.

10 9 8 7 6 5 4 3 2 1

For Dexter and Flash, semper fidelis

Everyone is in the best seat.

—JOHN CAGE

ACKNOWLEDGMENTS

For the generous sharing of information, my gratitude to Urs Giger, D.V.M., and Sheldon A. Steinberg, D.V.M., of the University of Pennsylvania Veterinary College; Bonnie Wilcox, D.V.M.; Joel Davis and his seizure-alert dog, Alex; Deborah Dalziel of the University of Florida Seizure-Alert Dog study; Scott Redstone; Liz Palika; and Conan the iguana.

I am grateful to Helma Weeks, director of communications, the University of Pennsylvania Veterinary College; to Beth Adelman; Stephen Solomita; and Marshall Mintz, good buddy to this writer and her dogs.

For the loving care every book needs to make the journey from idea to the hands of readers, I thank George Gibson, Michael Seidman, Cassie Dendurent, Chris Carey, and Krystyna Skalski at Walker & Company; and at Brandt and Brandt, Gail Hochman, Marianne Merola, and Meg Giles.

And, as always, I take the occasion of a new book to send written notice of my love to Stephen Lennard, my sweetheart; and to my daughter, Victoria; her husband, Stephen; and my grandson, Zachary.

THE
WRONG
DOG

CHAPTER 1

You Can Say That Again, She Said

I was doing the acrostic when the phone rang. I let the machine pick up. The dog on the tape barked three times. Someone sighed. I knew what that meant.

"Alexander," I said into the receiver, turning the puzzle sideways so that I could take notes in the margin.

She said her name was Sophie Gordon and that someone who knew someone had given her my name. She waited then. I did, too. I turned the puzzle back the right way and filled in the answer to G, a four-letter word for the thread Theseus used to find his way out of the labyrinth.

The line was still silent. She seemed to need help getting started.

"Who's dead?" I asked.

"Sorry?" she said. "My dog was shoving her leash onto my lap and knocked the phone out of my hand."

I repeated my question.

"Oh, no one. This isn't that sort of case."

"What sort is it?"

"I need you to find someone."

"A relative?"

"It's a rather long story, and complicated, but Bianca will drive me crazy if I don't get her to the run. I was hoping I could tell it to you there."

"The one in Washington Square Park?"

"Yes, that one."

I asked if fifteen minutes would be too soon. She said it wouldn't, it would be perfect, and told me she'd be sitting on a bench on the east side of the run.

"How will I know you?"

"You can't miss me," she said.

"Why is that?"

"I have red hair."

That narrowed it down. Half the women over forty in the city had red hair. The other half were blond.

I thought that was it, but the line was still open.

"Sophie?"

"I never thought I'd find myself hiring a private investigator."

"That's the thing about life. You never know."

"You can say that again," she said.

She must have put the radio on before she hung up the phone because suddenly I heard someone playing the piano, a haunting melody I couldn't place. Then the line went dead.

I didn't know much when I left to meet her at the park, just that her dog was probably white and that this wouldn't be one of my usual cases. It wasn't about someone dying. I'm sure Sophie believed that. She seemed sincere. Unfortunately, she was mistaken.

The park was pretty empty for a Saturday. Maybe it was the unseasonably chilly weather, the wind knocking leaves off the trees and making them eddy in great circles on the paths. Or perhaps it was simply too early for the weekend crowds, couples who might have decided to have brunch before strolling in the park, fathers reading the paper before taking their kids to the playground, bums still sleeping in doorways before convening on the benches at the south end of the park, hoping to snag a beer, a cigarette, whatever they could. And it was way too early for the drug dealers and their clientele. They wouldn't be open for business for another few hours.

A young white bull terrier bitch met us at the inner gate of the dog run, spiriting Dashiell away the second I unhooked his leash. I looked around for Sophie.

She would have looked pretty ordinary, sitting there alone, diagonally across from the gate, her skin as pale as 2-percent milk, her eyes hidden behind small, round, tinted glasses. Except for the hair. This red didn't come out of a bottle; it was the real thing. With the sun hitting it, it looked as if it were on fire. If a hundred people had been at the run, with a hundred dogs running and playing, I still would have noticed Sophie.

"It started two years ago, right here on this very bench," she said immediately after I introduced myself. I put out my hand to shake, but she left hers where it was, resting on her coat which, despite the chill in the air, was bunched up and lying to her right on the bench. She'd just nodded instead. I sat at her left, turning on the tape recorder that was in my jacket pocket.

"I'd come to the run to exercise Blanche. Shortly after I got here, a young woman, early twenties I'd guess, sat down next to me and unhooked her dog's leash to let her go and mix, only the dog, a black mutt, a little bigger than Bianca but not as big as . . ."

"Dash."

"And not a purebred either, some terrier and God-knows-what-else, cute but sort of sad looking, too, well, she just sat there, not doing much of anything. It was almost as if she didn't know how to play with other dogs, poor thing. After a few minutes, she'd backed up to my legs and was sitting on my shoes, just watching the other dogs, as if she thought she'd been dropped on some alien planet. That was the first strange thing that happened that afternoon, but not the last, not by a long shot."

She turned to look at Bianca, who was giving Dashiell a run for his money. I looked at them, too. Bianca was young, as tall as she would get, but not yet as wide. I figured Blanche had died and now there was Bianca. But I didn't interrupt the story to ask.

"After taking a pack of cigarettes out of her pocket," Sophie said, "the woman began to talk, just dog-run talk at first, same as any other conversation you'd have here, how nice it was that the Parks Department had put in the run, how important it was for city dogs to be able to socialize and run around safely off leash, how beautiful the day was. Then she noticed Blanche's cape folded and lying on my lap. She asked me what it was and seemed *really* interested.

"I told her that Blanche wore her cape most of the time, except when she was playing with other dogs. I told her it was a service dog cape, and I held it up and let it fall open so that she could see it, so that she could read the round patch I'd sewn on the left side.

"She read it out loud—Please don't pet me. I'm working—then asked if it was for real.

"I told her it was. I tell everyone who asks. And they all do.

" 'A service dog?' she asked. She started to bite the skin next to one of her ragged nails. I remember wondering what was making her so nervous, or if that was just her type—high-strung, one of those people whose motor seems to run too fast.

"I pointed to the other end of the run, saying that Blanche was the white bull terrier who was teasing all the male dogs and then running away to get them to chase her. I said she was a seizure-alert dog and asked if she knew what that was?

"That's when she told me that I was the person she'd been looking for.

"I don't know why, but for a minute there, I got scared. I thought something was wrong, that somehow I was going to lose Blanche."

"Why did you think that?"

"I don't know. It was just a feeling that came over me. But it passed quickly. When I asked her what she meant and she started to explain, well, what she told me was so fascinating that I forgot everything else. Even caution.

"She said she didn't have my name, that The School for the Deaf wouldn't give it to her when she called, but that they said they would give me her number, and that it would be up to me if I wanted to call her back."

"The School for the Deaf?" Was she lip-reading?

"I work there. I'm a teacher."

I nodded, wondering when she was going to tell me who'd gone missing.

But Dash was racing back and forth with Bianca and the sky was the kind of blue I'd always thought you'd have to live in Montana to see. So what if she took her time?

"I'd never gotten any message," Sophie told me. "Maybe they just forgot to give it to me. Sometimes they get really busy." She shrugged. "She told me her name was Lorna West. She even introduced her dog, Smitty. I thought it was a funny name for a girl dog, but the way she was sitting, with her legs straight out in front of her, her belly exposed, I had no trouble seeing she was a female. She'd turned her head then, right when Lorna said her name, and I remember how big and round and dark her eyes were, how she'd looked first at Lorna, then at me, with this astonished expression on her face.

" 'Here's why I was looking for you,' Lorna said, scooting closer to me and lowering her voice. 'I work for Side by Side. Did you ever hear of it?'

"I told her I hadn't. She smiled and said she wasn't surprised. She said that the man behind it was very rich. But very private. She nodded for emphasis.

" 'But what *is* it?' I asked her. 'What's it for?'

"And she said it was a charitable organization that supplies service dogs to disabled people who need them.

"I wondered why she was whispering. For a minute, I thought she was going to hit me up for a contribution, but I didn't say anything about that. Instead I asked her if it was like the Seeing Eye or Canine Companions for Independence.

" 'Not exactly,' she said, and she took a cigarette out of the pack and lit it. I moved away a little, to get away from the smoke. It must have bothered Smitty, too. She sneezed, then moved right with me. But Lorna didn't seem to notice."

"Did she explain?"

Sophie nodded and then looked toward the part of the run where Bianca and Dashiell were rolling around, both grinning and in dead earnest, the way bull and terrier dogs love to play.

"She told me she'd called The School for the Deaf because Side by Side was looking for service dogs with gifts, you know, an inborn ability to do something."

"As opposed to dogs that are trained to help with a disability," I said.

"Exactly. She said she thought she'd find dogs like that there, dogs who knew to inform their deaf owners when someone was knocking at the door, the phone was ringing, or the alarm clock was going off. She told them Side by Side was doing a survey, some public-service thing, tracking how the owners had discovered their dogs' abilities. And whoever she spoke with told her that only a few of the kids used dogs, but that hearing-alert dogs are trained at special schools and that not every dog, but a great number of dogs, particularly lively ones, could be trained to do the work. It was a matter of education, not a matter of talent, as it were.

"So she said she thanked the woman and was about to hang up when the woman told her that one of the teachers, meaning me, had a seizure-alert dog, that seizure *response* could be taught to a variety of dogs but that no one had yet figured out a way to teach seizure alert. Once someone began to seizure, you could get the dog to stay with them until it was over, no problem. But as far as alerting prior to the onset of a seizure, either a dog knew when one was coming and warned his owner or he didn't.

"She said she'd gotten all excited and said that that was just what they needed for their survey and could she talk to me, and that the woman she'd spoken to said no, that I was teaching, but that she would give me Lorna's name and number and I could call if I wanted to. It would be up to me. But then Lorna said, 'That was a lie.' "

"What was?" I asked her.

"That's exactly what I asked. 'About the survey,' she said. 'The real thing we're doing, it's top secret and we don't want it to get around.'

"That's when I got that funny feeling again. But what she told me then, well. You see, Blanche was nine at the time, and she had some arthritis in her elbows. 'Crepitus,' the vet called it. What it meant was that on rainy days, and when it was cold, she limped pretty badly."

Sophie stopped and pulled a wad of tissues out of her coat pocket and blew her nose. She wore her long red hair loose, the bangs so long they covered her eyebrows, touching the frames of those small, round glasses. She looked across the run at Bianca and began shaking her head.

"Is she . . . ?"

"Blanche? Oh, no. She's right here."

That's when I realized that Sophie's coat wasn't bunched up. It had been spread out under and over her old dog, to keep her warm.

"She's eleven and a half," Sophie said, dropping her voice to a whisper as she peeled back a corner of the coat and showed me a glimpse of her sleeping bull terrier before carefully covering her face again. "All this running around is much too much for her, but Bianca can't get through the day without serious exercise. On workdays, it's worse, because Blanche is with me at school, so I have a dog walker who brings Bianca here for an hour or two of roughhousing. Without that, she'd keep annoying Blanche when we got home, trying to get her to play. Well, she still does, but not as much."

Dash and Bianca were standing up now, face-to-face, paws on each other's shoulders, all but breathing fire at each other. When their front feet hit the dirt, Bianca took off, Dash in hot pursuit, his tongue lolling out to the side. I thought I might have to hose him down before the afternoon was over.

"So what did Lorna tell you next?"

"Well, it got pretty amazing. She said that the founder

of Side by Side was after a dog like Blanche. She turned slightly away then so that she wouldn't blow smoke right in my face. Smitty sneezed again, I remember, and I was thinking about how bad it would be for a seizure-alert dog to be around cigarette smoke. No one's one hundred percent positive, but it's thought they work on scent, you know, from chemical changes in the brain, that that's how they can tell trouble's coming."

I nodded.

"Then Lorna asked me how old Blanche was. The longer we talked, the more businesslike and less nervous she became.

"Nine, I told her, almost nine and a half. Then I'd looked at Blanche and she was limping over to the water bucket. All that running, getting the boys to chase her, her favorite game, but she was getting too old for it, even two years ago.

"Lorna said, 'Nine. Getting on, for a bull terrier.'

"I turned back to her then and watched as she dropped the cigarette and didn't bother to grind it out even though we were at the dog run. Her face was hard, almost masklike. For a moment, I wanted to leave, not even say goodbye, just get up and go. But when she looked back at me, her expression had changed. Her face was full of concern. It threw me. And I stayed.

"She went on. She said that what they'd like to do is make sure I always have a Blanche when I need one. She leaned toward me, talking softly, reaching out and touching my arm. She said her employer, who is a very charitable man, would like *other* people with epilepsy to have a dog as skilled as Blanche. 'You'd like that, too,' she said, 'wouldn't you?'

"I didn't say anything right away. I just looked at her, those gnawed nails and her nicotine-stained fingers, her scowly little face, trying to look all warm and concerned now; the way she seemed hunched into her coat, as if it was too light for the weather; and the dog, how Lorna never paid attention to her, never touched her and how Smitty sat there all that time, just watching and not playing. Maybe they're just two of a kind, I'd thought, feeling, whatever it was she wanted, I didn't want any part of it.

" 'A Blanche,' she'd said. What an odd thing to say. I started thinking of some excuse I could make to get away from her. But once again, I didn't leave." She shook her head.

"What did you do?"

Sophie shrugged. "I asked her to elaborate. So she did. She asked if I'd read about some of this in the paper, about Dolly, the sheep that was—'

" 'You mean, you want to clone Blanche?' I said astonished to hear those words coming out of my mouth.

" 'We do,' she said. Just like that. 'And what's more, we can.' "

I turned from Sophie to look at the dogs. Dashiell was at the water bucket where he'd tanked up and then laid down on the wet earth, his big mouth open, his big tongue hanging out. Bianca was leaning on him, as if he were a cushion.

When I looked back at Sophie, she was nodding.

I should have gotten up then, told her I wished her luck with whatever it was she needed me to do, but that I wasn't interested. Clearly, I should have said I wasn't the right person for this job.

Hell, I'd just gotten my arm out of a cast.

I had to get my winter clothes out of mothballs, too.

Or, at least I would have, had I bothered to put them away in the first place.

Still, who had the time?

Cloning? No way. If someone was cloning dogs, I didn't want to know about it.

That's what I should have said.

But I didn't.

What was the problem? I kept asking myself. My arm was healed, I certainly could have used the money, and, at the time, things seemed benign, not the usual scenario in my business. Most of my work comes shortly after someone's life has been snatched away, often brutally, and always before it was time. Of course there are those who would argue with that statement, who would say that if life ends, then it is time. Is is, my former employer Frank Petrie used to say. But in this case, I disagree. When a life should end is not a decision one human being should be making about another, especially when that decision is informed by vengeance, hate, possessiveness, or greed.

This was different.

Or so she said.

So I didn't walk away. I said, "Tell me more."

And she did.

Then, later, I said, "Tell me what you need me to do."

She told me that, too.

We sat there so long that dozens of dogs and their owners came and went, the dogs having run around, gotten into mild squabbles and made up, and finally gotten tired enough to leave, Sophie talking all the while, me listening and changing the tape several times so that I wouldn't miss recording anything. After a long while, even Dash and Bianca quit playing. For the last hour of our conversation, they were asleep in the space between the bench and the fence, Bianca's head on Dash's side as if they'd known each other forever.

Two more times during that long afternoon, as I sat and listened, I wanted to excuse myself and leave. It was the weirdest story I'd ever heard and one, I had the feeling, I would regret, more than once in the weeks to come, having listened to. Even then, right there at the dog run, I began thinking about issues that made me really uncomfortable, that shook me to my very soul and threatened to alter everything I ever thought I knew before this conversation took place, before I met Sophie Gordon. As she talked and I listened, I told myself it would be smarter to not get involved, to just plain quit. But, like Sophie, I couldn't walk away from it. And curiosity was only one of the reasons why.

I'd been only seven and a half when my father died. He had gone to work that day as he always did, and come home right on time. After dinner, he'd played chess with me and listened to Lili read a story she'd written for school. Later he'd come to my room to kiss me good night. Then he'd gotten into his own bed to read before going to sleep—*For Whom the Bell Tolls,* which he'd taken out of the library the weekend before. When his eyes had grown tired, he'd kissed my mother and turned off the lamp. In the morning, she couldn't wake him.

For several weeks, the book my father had been reading lay on his nightstand, just where he'd left it, an empty envelope holding his place. When my mother finally returned it to the library, I'd cried and cried, as if the continued presence of the book on his nightstand meant death was only a temporary condition. For the longest time, nights when I refused to let myself fall asleep for fear that, like my father, I'd never wake up, I imagined my father miraculously returning, looking for his book and feeling disappointed to find he couldn't finish what he'd started.

So now, all these years later, even if my client is dead, and there's no one to answer to, and no one to pay my fee, I'm doing what I was asked to do. Despite the fact that part of me doesn't want to know the answers I'm risking my life to find out, I have trouble leaving things unfinished, even things that, God knows, I never should have started in the first place.

CHAPTER 2

We Know Everything We Have To Know, She Said

"It was a good thing Smitty was leaning against my legs because, as you might imagine, I felt as if I might float away without her weight there to ground me. I was flabbergasted."

"But intrigued enough to stay."

"Yes. I was. You see, once Blanche had been diagnosed with arthritis, I was forced to face the possibility of losing her."

I raised a hand to interrupt, but Sophie went right on.

"Oh, I don't mean I was contemplating the ultimate loss. I had every reason to believe that was years away. It was the loss of her ability to help me that worried me. If the day came that she was in a lot of pain and I couldn't help her feel better, I figured her own troubles would fill her consciousness and she would no longer be able to concentrate on me enough to warn me when a seizure was coming."

"That makes sense," I said.

"Before Blanche, I used to just black out, no matter where I was. Some epileptics get warnings, a feeling that something awful is going to happen. But I don't. I'm not aware of anything until I wake up, sometimes bruised and banged up, sometimes with strangers around me, staring at me with a mixture of concern and . . ." Sophie turned away for a moment. "Revulsion," she whispered. "Even fear, the knowledge that what they are witnessing might happen to them. You know how people are. They don't want to hear about—." She lifted one hand into the air. "But that was before Blanche. Now, in fact, I can avoid most seizures because she lets me know they're coming, so I can take a pill. And if the medication doesn't work—it doesn't, always— because Blanche has warned me, I can almost always take myself out of harm's way. When I wake up, instead of a bunch of strangers, there's Blanche, lying next to me and licking my face." She slid her fingers under her glasses to wipe her eyes. "She's the most beautiful thing I've ever seen in my life, Rachel. I could never put into words how much I love my dog. Nor how grateful I am to have her in my life."

I looked over at Dashiell for a moment, then nodded at Sophie.

How could she have turned away from Lorna and gone home?

How could she have said no to such a tantalizing offer?

On the other hand, what exactly would Side by Side give her?

I tried to remember how long ago I'd read that article in the *Times,* the one about the wealthy couple who had agreed to pay 2.3 million dollars to Texas A & M University, to the scientists who had promised to clone their dog, Missy, a part Border collie mutt. At first, like everyone else, I guess, I thought the whole idea was crazy, either a joke or a scam to get a ton of money from some very rich, very naive people.

But then the *Times* was full of news about cloning, news that made the idea of cloning a dog not only seem plausible, but inevitable. There'd been the piece on the successful cloning of stem cells, the stuff of life. And then the disturbing piece about a human nucleus growing in a cow egg whose own nucleus had been removed, inspiring thoughts of half-human, half-animal monsters when, in fact, the cow egg was merely a cheap and easy way to harvest a host for the human nucleus, which, as it grew, displaced all signs of cowness. Still, it had gotten President Clinton's attention, and that of ethicists all over the nation. There was already a ban on using government funds for research on cloning. What else would be banned, and done anyway with private funding, was anyone's guess.

After this later news, I'd wondered again about the "Missyplicity Project," as the attempt to clone the pet dog had been called. With each article in the paper about other attempts at cloning, the plan to clone Missy seemed less like science fiction and more like science.

But what would those anonymous rich people think when they got their cloned dog? They loved their pet enough that they were willing to spend a fortune for a carbon copy of her, something, I thought, a surprising number of pet owners might do, if they had the means. But weren't they bound to be mighty disappointed when they got what they'd paid for? No matter what they did, the clone would never be the real thing. She wouldn't be Missy.

With sheep, it wouldn't matter. The scientists in Scotland were funded by a pharmaceutical company that wanted to clone sheep that were able to produce a certain drug in their milk. You could say it had to do with profits.

Or you could say it was altruistic, that the company wanted enough of a supply of a necessary medication to meet the demand. Either way, no one gave a damn about what Dolly's personality would be, if she'd have the same little quirks and endearing habits as the original, all the things that had made her separate, different, and better than any other sheep around.

Dolly wasn't a pet. No one shared their bed with her, loved the sound she made chewing her food, told her what was in their heart.

That wasn't true for Blanche. True, she was a service dog and performed an important function for her owner. But she was family, too. Who she was counted for as much as what she did.

Was that what all this was about, I wondered as I waited to hear the rest of the story—Sophie's disappointment, that despite the fact that Blanche had been cloned, Bianca was simply her own dog?

And if so, what was I supposed to do about it? But I wouldn't have the answer to that question until it had turned dark and almost everyone had taken his dog and gone home.

"Go back to when you met Lorna," I said. "Tell me exactly what the deal was. Tell me how they got the cells, how long it took, what they told you along the way. Tell me how you felt when they gave you Bianca. Tell me everything."

Sophie smiled. "Then you'll help me?"

I didn't say. But when I reached out and touched her hand, we both knew what my answer to her question was likely to be.

"Lorna said they'd need a blood sample and some cells they'd scrape from the inside of Blanche's cheek, no big deal and far less stressful than her annual checkup. She said they wanted to clone three puppies. Three little Blanches. She said I'd get one, and the other two would go to people who needed a seizure-alert dog but didn't have one. She asked if I'd agree to that and I nodded, too stunned to speak. Then she asked if I'd meet her the following Sunday, at a veterinary office on the corner of Horatio and Washington, at ten in the morning. I said I would. I didn't know that part of the Village well, but Lorna said she'd be there. She'd meet me and take me in, no problem."

I took exception to the wording of that, but didn't say so.

"I was so happy all week. You know the feeling. It was like when I decided to get Blanche. Even before I found her, I was happy all the time just thinking about it."

"Did you get her from one of the schools that provide service dogs for people with disabilities?"

"No, that's the interesting thing. I'd never heard of seizure-alert dogs. Besides, the schools usually can provide only seizure-response dogs. I mean, that was the whole point of the cloning, wasn't it? To reproduce an ability that can't be taught, that's inborn. But I just wanted a pet. I was lonely. When I wasn't at work, I was staying in more than most people because when I went out, there was always the danger of a seizure, anywhere, at any time, with no notice at all. I thought that if I had a pet dog, I'd feel safer and better just having her with me, or knowing she was waiting for me at home."

"But what about at work? Weren't you in danger of having seizures there?" I was wondering how she held a job, especially a teaching job.

"Yes, but the amazing thing is, it's happened only once. And that time, it wasn't in front of my class. I think it's because I'm so happy teaching. I love the kids and I love the work. I feel so useful and appreciated. Of course, that's hardly scientific."

"But it's your experience."

"It is."

"Go back to the puppy."

"Oh, I couldn't get a puppy. I was gone too much of the day. I got in touch with a bull terrier rescue organization, because I knew I wanted a bully, I always had, ever since I can remember. And three months later, I got Blanche. She was two years old when I adopted her."

"Did she alert right away?"

"No. Well, yes, but I wasn't aware that anything unusual was happening. I didn't get what she was doing. It wasn't until the third time that I understood. That's when I realized that having Blanche was going to change my life entirely."

She put her fingers to her lips, as if she was thinking about what to say next.

"I didn't realize quite how depressed I'd been, not until it was nearly over. Once I understood what she was doing and that it would give me the freedom to come and go almost like an ordinary person, I let myself see how limited my life had been before Blanche."

Sophie's face had changed as she talked about Blanche. She'd even brushed her bangs away and was holding her head up higher. I heard the tape recorder stop and asked Sophie if she'd wait a moment while I turned the tape over.

"It's just for me," I told her, "so I won't forget any detail."

She nodded. People will say astonishing things to virtual strangers, but some clam up if you're recording them. Not Sophie. She was so into the story by now that I'm not sure she gave any thought to the fact that I was taping.

"Once I knew that when a seizure was coming, Blanche would let me know and I could take a pill and often ward it off, I became so euphoric, there was no stopping me. I decided I deserved the one other thing I craved besides a dog. A garden. I thought life would be perfect if only I could plant things, and if Blanche could be out of doors whenever she wanted to, even if I wasn't feeling so well.

"It took me nine weeks to find the new apartment, almost as long as it took to locate Blanche. It's just a block and a half from here." Sophie smiled proudly. "We have a small bedroom with a weird little bathroom off it, a tiny kitchen—but big enough for us—and a living room, everything facing the garden. It's perfect for us, exactly what we need. The garden is actually bigger than the apartment, with an ivy-covered brick wall in the back. Oh, it's just beautiful. I knew I wanted it the moment I saw it.

"And then the agent said no dogs.

"But by then I'd had Blanche registered as a service dog with the Department of Health and it's not legal to deny an apartment to someone with a disability because they use a service dog, so after a couple of tense days, they told me, yes, I could move in, the apartment was mine."

A smooth fox terrier was trying to get involved in Dash and Bianca's folie à deux, but they wouldn't give her the time of day. They were too busy digging to China, as my father used to say when my sister, Lili, and I would dig at the beach. I'd have to fill in the hole before I left, but they were having much too much fun for me to stop them then.

"So," I said to Sophie, "when the week passed, you walked over to Horatio and Washington and met Lorna?"

I knew that part of the Village well. It was the cusp of the meatpacking district, the favored area for the late-night parade of transvestite hookers and denizens of the popular motorcycle bar Hogs and Heifers. I'd once poked my head in there to see their famous bra collection, one of them supposedly slipped off and tossed onto the rack over the bar by Julia Roberts. I'd seen the meat markets, too, carcasses hanging outside like clothes at the dry cleaners, and the new galleries and restaurants opening along Fourteenth Street, signifying a neighborhood in transition, but a vet's office? No way. Sure, there were men in white coats, but they were butchers. Maybe the office was less obvious than the one on Washington and Perry, which had big glass windows with oversize paw prints on them and a prominent sign, or the one on the corner of Tenth Avenue and Twenty-second Street, animals painted on the side of the building, where I take Dashiell.

"Lorna was waiting for me when I got there, smoking a cigarette and doing a little dance to keep warm. I didn't see any sign outside, but I followed her in and in the back of the first floor there was a sign on the door that said Horatio Street Veterinary Practice on it.

"It looked more like a doctor's office. You know how they're always on the ground floor." She shrugged. "But Lorna said, 'Here we are,' and took out a bunch of keys and unlocked the door. So I figured it was the right place. There was no one in the waiting area. Well, there wouldn't be. It was Sunday. And she'd already told me this was top secret. She'd stressed that."

"Did she say why?"

"Yes—because people are so negative about cloning. Side by Side is trying to do a world of good for people in need, but if the story got out, you can imagine the press. They'd never be able to raise another dime."

"I thought there was this one rich guy behind it."

"In the future, Rachel. Even the Seeing Eye does fundraising now. Endowments can't last forever, not with something *this* expensive. They had to think ahead if they were going to be able to continue with the work, if they were going to survive."

"So, the veterinarian came out and explained the procedure to you?"

"I didn't actually get to meet the veterinarian. As soon as we were inside, Lorna locked the door behind us, then took Blanche's leash out of my hand and headed for the door on the other side of the waiting room. 'Wait here,' she said. 'This will take only a minute.'

"I'd never allowed anyone to work on my dog without me being there, unless it was surgery, like when Blanche was spayed. But I was . . ."

"Hooked?"

Sophie nodded.

"And it was so fast, the way she took her and walked away, but also, what she'd said was true. She and Blanche were back in no time and Blanche didn't look any the worse for wear. She put her paws on my legs, then up on my shoulders, and laid her big face against my cheek. I could feel her tail slapping against my legs. Everything seemed normal."

"And then?"

"Lorna took me out, locked the door, and said I'd hear from her when my puppy was ready. I wanted more. I wanted to know where the cloning was going to take place, was it there, at that office, or at some lab, and who the surrogate mother would be, what kind of dog, what breed, and I wanted to know when the pregnancy took so I could count the weeks until my puppy was born and then count the weeks until I got her, but I just stood there on the corner, dumbfounded by it all. I thought, Be quiet, be grateful, don't look a gift horse in the mouth."

I wondered why she hadn't thought, If it looks too good to be true, it probably is.

"Lorna lit a cigarette and then gave me a little wave. 'See ya,' she said. And walked away. I didn't have anything, not a piece of paper, not a phone number—nothing. In fact, Lorna'd said she'd call me, but she'd never asked for my phone number. And it's unlisted. So I began to think it was some sort of scam. But what? They hadn't asked me for any money. And whatever they'd done to Blanche had taken only a few minutes and Blanche appeared to be fine. So I just stood there, long after Lorna had left. And then, disheartened, I went home.

"Seven and a half months later, I got a phone call from Lorna."

"At work or at home?"

"At home. Don't ask me how, I don't know. Maybe she has a relative at the phone company." Sophie shrugged. "She said, 'When are you going to the run next?' But she didn't wait for an answer. She just said, 'I can meet you there with your puppy.' "

I leaned forward, literally as well as figuratively drawn into Sophie's story.

"I was so stunned," Sophie said, "all I could think to say was that she shouldn't bring the puppy into the run. 'Too many germs,' I blurted out. 'Meet me at the fountain instead.' She agreed and we made a time. When I hung up, my heart was pounding so fast that Blanche came over, her forehead crazed with wrinkles, then she backed up and barked, as confused, I guess, as I felt.

"That was a Sunday, too. I got there first, looked all around and didn't see her. So, of course, I began to think it was a gag, a pretty elaborate one, and that she wasn't coming at all.

"But then I saw her. She was carrying Bianca in her arms. As she approached, I looked down at Blanche, then back at Bianca. She was like a miniature of my dog, the same in every way."

Wouldn't any white bull terrier look pretty much like any other white bull terrier? Isn't that the whole point of having a standard? But I kept that thought to myself.

"She handed me the puppy and took a pack of cigarettes out of her coat pocket, scowling at them before taking one out. 'Will you need me to report to you? Or to anyone?' I asked. I felt foolish. I was acting as if I was in a spy movie. Maybe she'd hand me a tape with my instructions and it would self-destruct after I played it. I didn't know what to think. Or what to say.

" 'We know everything we have to know,' she said. She put the cigarette in her mouth and began to fish around in her pocket for matches. 'Under the cellophane,' I told her. Isn't it weird that I remember that? But I do. I remember everything—what the sky looked like, how there was a guy on Rollerblades in the dry fountain, headphones on, singing and dancing, his arms up, his eyes squeezed closed. And this homeless man with torn rags wrapped around his feet, his skin all encrusted with grime, staring at me and the dogs. He looked so poor and I felt so rich.

"Lorna lit her cigarette and inhaled deeply, as if she was hungry—like that poor man must have been—and the smoke would fill her up. She blew a long stream out toward the center of the fountain. 'Anyway, we know where to find you if we have any questions.'

" 'There were three?' I asked her. She didn't seem to hear me. 'There are two more Blanche puppies?' 'Yeah, sure, two more,' she said. 'But you only get one.' She was one strange lady. She just turned to go. 'How old is my puppy?' I asked after her. 'Eight weeks today,' she said without turning around. 'Has she had shots?' Lorna turned back, dug around in her pockets, and handed me a piece of paper. Before I'd unfolded it to see the list of inoculations and dates, she'd started to walk away again. 'Thank you, Lorna,' I called after her. 'Thank them for me, will you?' She raised the hand with the cigarette and gave a little wave. That was the last I saw of her."

"No phone calls? No nothing?"

"Uh-uh. Nothing."

"And when was that, the day you got Bianca?"

"Fourteen months ago."

That made Bianca sixteen months old. No wonder she had so much energy.

"I believed her. I believed all of it, at least once I got Bianca I did."

"And now?"

She didn't answer my question. "Now I have to locate Side by Side," she said.

"How come?"

"When a seizure is coming, Blanche will get real close to me with this concerned look on her face. First she licks my hand, almost frantically. If I'm sitting—at school, or on the bus, or at home—she'll crawl up onto my lap and start that frantic, worried licking on my face. Then she jumps off and starts pulling on me, to get me to my bed, or just down on the floor. I always have the pills with me, on me, in a pocket or a little pouch. So I take one out and as soon as Blanche sees the pill, even before I put it in my mouth, she calms down, sighs, and waits for me to lie down. Then she lies down next to me and waits it out. If a seizure starts even though I've taken the pill, she gets on top of me and licks my face until I wake up again."

"What if you're out walking?"

"She'll stop. It's like trying to get a building to move.

She just won't go. And when I tug, or turn to look at her, she starts to whine and pull toward home. If I'm not close enough to get home and lie down, I take a pill and find a place to sit down until it passes."

"What about Bianca, how does she alert you? The same way?"

"That's just what I was about to tell you, Rachel. She doesn't. She doesn't alert me at all. For a while, I thought they'd given me the wrong dog, just any white bull terrier, not a clone. But for the life of me I couldn't think of why someone would pretend to clone my dog and then hand me a free, uncloned purebred bull terrier pup. It's not as if I *paid* to have this done and they had to produce a pup to keep my money."

"There was never any question of that, any suggestion that you pay or contribute, nothing like that?"

She shook her head.

"Did they talk about your estate, about mentioning Side by Side in your will?"

Sophie laughed. "Estate? You've got to be kidding. There is none. I only have what I earn and I spend every cent of that by the time the next paycheck is due. I only teach for three hours a day, Rachel, because of . . ." Her voice trailed off. "When my kids take art and gym, I get to eat a snack and lie down. If not, there'd be no way I could do what I do. What I get paid, it's barely enough to live on. When I can, I do little extra jobs, mostly for the dogs, for special food for them and to pay for Bianca's walker. He's much, much cheaper than all the other Village walkers, but still, by the end of the month, it adds up."

I nodded. "So, no money up front and no request to bequeath them anything."

What was the catch?

"After a couple of months of worrying, I decided I needed some answers."

"Did you try to find Lorna then?"

Sophie took off her glasses and rubbed her eyes, then put them back on quickly. I'd heard that light bothers some epileptics, but she apparently spent a lot of time outside with the dogs. Maybe she was just tired.

"No, I didn't. I took Blanche and Bianca to a vet and asked for a DNA test."

"A vet?"

Sophie exhaled. "I didn't want to go to our regular vet, just in case."

"In case what?"

"I didn't want to be laughed at. I didn't want someone I had to deal with thinking I was crazy. Even with the new vet, I lied. I didn't ask him to please have my dogs tested to see if one of them was a clone of the other."

"What *did* you ask?"

"I said I'd gotten both girls from the same breeder and that his practices were being challenged by the AKC, a question of parentage that might put Bianca's papers in jeopardy. I said I'd been told that Blanche was Bianca's mother, and I wanted to know for sure."

"And?"

"He asked me what difference it made now. He said, 'Don't you love your dogs?'

"I said I did, but that I was thinking of breeding Bianca and I wouldn't get a fair price for her puppies if she lost her registration. I said I had to be sure of her parentage before I bred her, that the test would give me something to take to the AKC.

" 'Or it wouldn't,' he said.

" 'Exactly,' I told him. 'Either way, I have to know.' "

"Did he do it?"

She nodded. "He shrugged and took cheek swabs. He said he had to send them to Michigan State, to their DNA lab. He said it would take a few weeks and that he'd call me. Then, as an afterthought, he said he hoped I got the results I was after. I was glad he wasn't my regular vet."

"And?"

"The report came back saying, gee, this is very rare, but it appears that Blanche and Bianca have identical genetic markers."

"So she is a clone."

"That's not the conclusion the vet came to. He said the lab must have made a mistake. He said the markers couldn't be identical. Then he explained the facts of life to me, as if I was an idiot. 'The offspring gets fifty percent of its genes from the mother—that would be Blanche—and fifty percent from the father,' he said. The pattern is random, which genes each pup will get from its mother and which from the father. But in this case, it appears your dog has no father.' Before I could say anything, he said, 'Oh, sure, it's possible to have all the markers identical, but so rare as to be suspect.' He said they must have tested one dog's samples twice. He apologized for the lab's error and the delay it would cause and suggested we run the tests again."

"And you said?"

"I told him it wasn't an error. Then I made the mistake of telling him why."

"And he said?"

"That's not the point. The point is that I need you to find the people at Side by Side for me, Rachel, this Lorna West person and whoever she works for. They're spending God knows how much money on this project and the seizure-alert ability doesn't come through. They ought to be told that, that it's probably not an inheritable ability. They're going to break the hearts of whoever they gave those other puppies to. And their own as well. I have to find them and tell them. You *will* help me, won't you?"

I sat there for a while, saying nothing. Then I turned and looked at Bianca, asleep behind the bench, so hidden in shadow that she looked like a gray dog, not a white one. Or was that just dirt?

Sure, scientists had cloned a sheep, some mice, and some cows. And the South Koreans claimed to have produced the first stages of a human embryo, then they'd halted the experiment for ethical reasons. Still, this was all too fantastic to believe, that someone would be willing to spend millions to clone dogs for other people, out of the goodness of his heart.

Or did he think that once he'd accomplished this, cloning dogs with special abilities would be worth money? Was he planning on, let's say, cloning Morris the cat, Lassie, Benji? A triple-crown-winning racehorse? Was that it? Was it about money after all?

"Can I think this over?" I asked, the only sensible idea I'd had all day.

"Well, sure." She stood and picked up Bianca's leash from where it lay next to her on the bench. "If you feel you have to."

When she turned to look at me, I saw there were tears in her eyes.

"Sophie, I . . ."

"No, I understand. That vet didn't believe the story either. He had a good laugh at my expense. When he pulled himself together, he told me cloning dogs was not commercially viable. You lose a lot of embryos, he said, and it's very expensive. He said that either the dogs were from totally inbred strains or there was a mix-up at the lab."

She gently unwrapped Blanche, who I could now see was wearing the red service-dog vest. She was stiff when she stood, but her tail began to wag as soon as she was up. She was a fantastic-looking dog, that great egg head with a flush of pink along the slope of her nose where the fur was nearly negligible. The only other color, aside from the black of her nose, the dark area right under it, and her small, deepset, dark eyes, was a single black spot at the lower-outside corner of her right eye, like a smudge of mascara.

"I'll call you tomorrow with an answer," I said. "I promise."

Sophie blinked. One tear fell.

She called to Bianca, and when the pup lifted her head, I got to see her up close for the first time, the wondrous stand-up ears, the great, broad Roman nose, the no-frills dark eyes, and the big goofy mouth, open in a smile. And the single black spot, like an ink blot, at the lower-outside corner of her right eye. The spot was pinched in near the eye and rounded at the bottom, exactly like the one under Blanche's right eye. They both had smudges of black under their noses, too, square mustaches that made them seem even more comical than they already did, looking at me with their small, pig eyes, both their heads cocked toward their left. Except for girth, which reflected their age difference, they surely seemed to be identical.

Not knowing what to think, I glanced over at Dashiell, who was grinning, as if he knew a secret. Then I looked back at the two bullies, sitting hip to hip, waiting for Sophie to get her coat on.

Well, isn't that what took the seven and a half months, I thought, finding a puppy with just the perfect markings?

I looked at Blanche, then at Bianca. Then back and forth again.

"Let's go get some food," I said. "I'm starving."

Sophie just stared at me, puzzled.

"I get five hundred and fifty a day plus expenses, with a week's fee in advance," I told her. "I know it's steep, but I'm worth it. Besides, it includes Dashiell's services."

I bent down to pet the dogs and take a closer look while she thought it over.

She said, "That's okay. I figured it would be around that. I've been saving up."

For the first time, there were no questions about Dash's fee. If anyone knew how valuable a partner a dog could be, it was Sophie Gordon, my new client.

CHAPTER 3

Would You Do It? Chip Asked

I didn't get home from dinner with Sophie until eight-thirty and Chip was due back from teaching at the New York State Veterinary Convention within the hour. After feeding Dashiell, I ran upstairs to shower and change. As I passed my office, I saw the light on my answering machine blinking. As much as I would have liked to know who'd called—even if they hadn't left a message, now that my brother-in-law had gotten me caller ID—I had something more important to do.

I could hear the phone again from the shower, but my mind was on other things, and once again I ignored the impulse to put business ahead of pleasure. In fact, to help maintain my resolve, on my way past the office to get dressed, I turned the ringer off on the office phone, and later, between opening the bottle of red wine so that it could breathe and having Dashiell help me collect the clothes that had been tossed in various places around the house, I did the same thing on the downstairs phone.

Dash, hearing the car as my sweetie circled the block, hoping by some miracle he'd find a legal spot, was at the door, head cocked, a full ten minutes before Chip arrived. The way he tore past Chip to join Betty, Chip's Shepherd, you would have thought he hadn't been to the dog run in weeks, that he hadn't fallen madly in love with another bitch earlier that same day.

Chip set down his bags and put his arms around me.

"That's better," he said into my hair.

"How'd it go?"

"I had a good crowd, seventy or eighty. And I've been invited back for next year. They finally understand how much they need me." He pulled back and looked at me. "Did you miss me so much you could hardly stand it?"

I nodded.

"That's my good wench."

We never made it upstairs. We never even closed the door. At first, with the sounds of the dogs mock-fighting as mood music, we did okay. But when they decided to join us, hopping up on the couch and continuing to wrestle there, we began to laugh at all the wrong times.

"Sex is no laughing matter," Chip told them. But they just ignored him and went about their business. We had no choice but to do the same.

"That wasn't half bad," he said afterward as we sat outside on the top step drinking wine.

"Which half wasn't bad, mine or yours?"

He started to laugh all over again.

"So what else have I missed by being away?"

"I got some work."

I took a sip of wine before I began to fill him in on the

details, watching his expression change, as mine must have hours earlier as I heard the story I was now telling him.

"That was the big topic at the convention, at least at the dinner it was, arguments about cloning—could they, would they, should they? And a surprising amount of nervous joking to go along with the serious issues."

"It makes a lot of people nervous. You know something, Chip, it makes me nervous."

"Oh, come on, Rach. You don't believe that, do you, that the younger dog is a clone? It's so impractical. Can you imagine what it would cost to do that?"

"They look exactly alike." Lame, I told myself, not waiting for Chip to say it to me. "Well, they're both white bull terriers, so I know what you're thinking—why wouldn't they look alike? But they have identical black markings." I pointed to the outside corner of my right eye. "Here."

He sighed. "Rach. That's fairly common in bullies. You know that."

I decided not to mention the little Hitler mustaches, or the strip of pink running up their snouts. Those things were far more common than the black smudge under an eye, looking like the remnants of a healing shiner.

"You don't think it's *possible?*" I asked.

"It's preposterous," he said. "The work that's been done in Scotland and Japan, there's big money behind it because it's about making money, not about doing good. Rachel, Mother Teresa's dead. There's no one doing good anymore."

"Then someone's gone pretty far out of their way to pull this woman's leg, wouldn't you say?"

He didn't answer.

"What if what Sophie was told was a lie, Chip? What if this *is* about money?"

"How so?"

"Well, once they have the technology, couldn't they clone, say, animals that do commercials?"

"So that Morris the cat could go on forever?"

"Precisely. There's a lot of money tied up in those images."

"Why not the top-winning show dogs?"

"Right."

"But then why not just do that? Why the whole seizure-alert business?"

"Because even though they'd be able to prove they're producing clones with impartial DNA testing, if they can also show that a particular talent translates, then they'd be able to say, 'Okay, the clone will not only *look* like a winner, he'll *act* like a winner.' Now you're talking big money."

"Except . . ."

"Except what?"

"When you add up travel, handlers' fees, advertising, entry fees, and incidentals, it costs one hundred fifty to two hundred thousand a year to get a dog to Westminster. Then add the cost of the cloning. Even if the clone did look and act like a winner, you'd never make money. No way."

"Okay, suppose the rich guy's an epileptic himself. Or he has a close relative who is, his wife or his kid maybe."

"Could be. Still, he'd have to be *stinking* rich to try something like this."

I nodded. "Probably is."

"Rach?"

"What?"

"About the seizure alert. I wouldn't think you'd have to go through all this. You get a bright dog with a willingness to take on responsibility, it could be taught. I'm sure of it."

"Me, too. But that doesn't mean the stinking-rich guy

would know that. No one's saying it's so, that it's just an issue of focus and training. Sophie says the medical profession doesn't even recognize that there is such a thing as a seizure-alert dog. They say the evidence is anecdotal."

"That's exactly the sort of stuff I heard at the convention. And the sensible rejoinder—how could anyone run a study to test seizure-alert dogs when it would mean preventing the epileptic subject from taking the appropriate medication after the dog had alerted? To know if it was legit, you'd have to do just that, and watch to see if the person had a seizure."

"No one could be that cruel."

"Hence the notion that since it can't be proved, it's not real. So you end up with an underground of people who, despite what the doctors say, claim their dogs do indeed alert them prior to the onset of a seizure."

"Hence Bianca."

He leaned back against the door. I did, too. The sky was blue-black, the air crisp. As if he knew that I'd gotten cold, wearing just an oversize T-shirt and sweat socks, Chip put his arm around me and drew me close.

I was tired, but I had no desire to go to sleep. Even with Chip at my side and our protection-trained dogs just yards away, I had a sense of foreboding, a feeling there was something treacherous in the night, something that required vigilance to keep it at bay. I had told Chip that my new job would just be a matter of research. But I wasn't convinced of that myself. I was sure he wasn't either.

Over dinner, I'd even asked Sophie why she didn't do the work herself instead of spending a small fortune to have me do it. It was a logical question in this case. At first, she'd said she was too busy, and too tired after work to do much else. "The medication makes me sleepy," she'd told me. "I'm lucky to get through the day."

When I didn't respond, she'd gone on, telling me how stressful the whole idea was to her, that millions of dollars were being wasted on this project, money that could be used, one way or another, to *really* help people who needed help. She'd taken my hand then and told me that stress and exhaustion were the two major factors that triggered her seizures. She'd said she hoped I wouldn't change my mind. That's when she'd reached into the inside pocket of her coat and counted out my advance, in cash, thinking if all else failed, money might do the trick and persuade me to stay on the case.

"Would you do it?" Chip asked.

"What?"

He didn't elaborate.

"Oh, you mean, would I clone Dashiell?"

He nodded.

I shook my head. "It wouldn't be him. It would only look like him," I said. "What about you?"

"It sounds like an expensive way to get your heart broken."

"I've had it done for very little."

For a few moments, neither of us spoke.

"I'll have him as long as I can," I said into the night yard. "When he's gone, I'll cry my heart out and get another dog."

Chip nodded and tightened his arm around me.

The dogs were lying down together, chewing on each other's faces.

We sat there for a long time with nothing else to say. We both knew what was inevitable. For people like us, the life span of dogs is the world's dirtiest trick. When we finally went upstairs to bed, we called the dogs to join us and held the blanket up so that they could come underneath, Betty burrowing way down to the foot of the bed and Dashiell laying his head on my pillow, stretching out along my side, sighing as he did so.

"You'll be careful," Chip said right before we fell asleep, a statement rather than a question.

"It's just a missing-person case," I told him. "Well, a missing organization, actually." I snuggled closer. "Yeah, yeah," I said, "I'll be careful."

He left early to see a client with a destructive golden retriever. I showered and dressed, then turned the phones back on and went to check the blinking answering machine.

There were no messages, only hang-ups. Eleven of them, all from the same number. It looked familiar. Then I realized why. It was Sophie's, the one she'd written down on a napkin, along with her work number, at the end of dinner, the one that had appeared on the caller ID box the morning before, when she'd first called.

What was so urgent that she had to keep trying to reach me all through the night?

I picked up the phone and dialed her number, but all I got was her answering machine. Odd, I thought. It was too early for her to leave for work. But then I remembered she'd said, whenever possible, she took Bianca to the run before work in the hope that she'd use up enough energy so that she'd just sleep until the walker came at two.

I left a message saying that I'd wait for her call, but it never came.

CHAPTER 4

I Handed Dashiell's Leash to Mel

       After looking up Lorna West, the Horatio Street Veterinary Practice, and Side by Side in the phone books and finding nothing, I spent the morning making notes from the tapes I'd made talking to Sophie. At one, the phone finally rang. I figured Sophie must have been late for work and would call me during her lunch break, but caller ID told me that this call, like all the others, was coming from her home phone.

"Sophie?"

I waited, then asked again. The line was open, but whoever was there never said a word.

I pressed reset and called Sophie's work number, which was at the top of the first page of the notes I'd just made. The woman who answered told me Sophie hadn't come in.

"Did she say why?" I asked.

There was a pause.

"I can't—"

"Ruth?"

Another pause.

"How do you know my name?"

"Sophie told me about you last night, about her friendship with you."

"She did?"

"Yes. And, Ruth, I wouldn't ask this of you if it wasn't urgent. I'm working for her now and it's imperative that I reach her."

She was quiet again. Thinking it over.

"You're working for her? I don't understand. Are you the new cleaning lady?"

"No. Sophie hired me yesterday to check into some things for her."

"To check into some things for her?"

"That's right. So, can you help me out here?"

I waited.

"Ruth?"

"You're the detective? She actually did it?"

"That's correct."

"She never called in," she whispered. "Look, when you talk to her, please ask her to let us know about tomorrow. This isn't like her. She's always so responsible. She's never—"

"I'll be sure to tell her."

I grabbed my jacket and Dash's leash and headed for West Third Street, that feeling of foreboding I'd had the night before tagging along.

When we crossed Sixth Avenue, Dashiell pulled toward the park.

"Not now," I told him. "We have to go to Sophie's."

An old woman with a shopping cart full of used-up-looking clothes and deposit bottles turned toward me and stared. Great, the homeless were gawking at *me*.

Dashiell was gaping, too. He couldn't believe I had something more important to do than take him to the run.

The address I'd been given was a modest, six-story, red-brick building with a leather-goods store ground-floor front. I ran my finger down the list of names until I found Sophie's and rang the bell. No one asked my name or buzzed me in. I tried again, also to no avail.

First I heard him, the jingle of all those keys. Then I saw him, heading my way, the key ring looped over his belt, bouncing against his hip as he bounced along the sidewalk. His hair was standing up as if he'd stuck a fork into a live outlet. Perhaps he'd been out in the wind a long time—too long, if you asked me.

But there was no wind. It was one of those perfect fall days we have too few of in New York, ideal for sitting at the dog run and letting your thoughts roam while your dog reenacted the ancient rituals of his forebears, even better if, like the guy approaching, that's how you made your living.

He was oafish looking, tall and thin with the kind of posture that makes you wonder if there are any bones inside his insubstantial-looking body, all arms and legs flipping around like overcooked spaghetti with each step he took in my direction. But then he stopped and just stood where he was, at the far side of the leather-goods store.

"Are you Sophie's walker?"

He nodded, but he wasn't looking at me. His eyes were on Dashiell. I ignored his unsaid question. I had other things on my mind.

"She didn't go to work today and she never called in sick," I said. "I've been unable to reach her here."

That's when he looked up. "And your point is?"

"Are you here to pick up Bianca?"

"I am."

"I'd like to go with you."

"Into the apartment?"

I nodded.

"I can't do that."

I would have liked to have taken a step forward, to be, literally, in his face. But Dashiell was between us and I thought that would do.

"You can. And you will," I told him. "I'm really worried about Sophie and I'm not going to stand out here arguing with you about this."

He stood there staring, those skinny arms flapping at his sides as if he were trying to get airborne, probably trying to figure out who the hell I was to give him so much attitude.

"Rachel Alexander," I told him. "And Dashiell. Now open the fucking door."

"Mel Sugarman," he said, the key already in the lock.

He turned around twice to see what Dashiell was doing, then held the door so that we could go first. I don't think it was chivalry, which, as far as I can tell, is resting in peace back in the Middle Ages. He probably thought he'd be in a better position if Dash and I were ahead of him, if he could keep an eye on my pit bull. Sometimes I don't mind the fact that my dog's breed has the worst PR of any breed in history. Sometimes it's expedient to let people think what they will.

I stepped aside at the back of the long hall and watched as he unlocked both of Sophie's locks, then knocked. He tried a second time before pushing the door open.

He stepped inside and said her name with so much alarm that I pushed past him until I could see what it was that he had seen.

She was lying on her side on the far side of the couch. From the doorway, we could see only her legs, the knees pulled up as if she was in pain. But when we walked into the apartment, slowly, and very close to each other, as if we were attached at the hip, we could both see that Sophie Gordon was no longer feeling anything.

I couldn't see if her eyes were open or closed because her glasses were all smudged and covered with dust and dog hair. Her mouth was open, as if in a scream. The carpet looked wet near her mouth, as if she'd been drooling. One arm was over her head, the other out in front of her, the knees drawn tight to her stomach, as if she'd been thrashing around before she'd died and had then just frozen in that position. Lying against her back was the bigger of the bullies, Blanche, who had never lifted her head to see who was there. Lying near her face was Bianca, the baby, looking at us, then licking her dead mistress, still trying to wake her up.

I handed Dashiell's leash to Mel and felt around for a pulse in her neck, though it hardly seemed necessary. She was ice-cold.

Even then, when I was kneeling next to her, Blanche's head stayed down, her chin on the floor, her cheek pressed tight against Sophie's back.

I stood up and looked at Mel. "You better call nine-one-one." He pulled out a cell phone and punched in the number, giving the information in a voice so dry I thought he would choke.

Afraid to touch anything that would compromise the information available, we stood exactly where we were without moving, waiting for the police to arrive. Dashiell waited, too, standing at the side of the couch, his muzzle high, testing and retesting the air. And Bianca, though she whined from time to time, stayed right where she was, with Sophie. It was Blanche who broke my heart. In all the time we were there, she never once picked up her head to look at us. It was almost as if, with Sophie gone, she'd died, too.

I did talk to Mel. I knew there wouldn't be much time, that the cops would be there in minutes.

"Did Sophie explain about Bianca's relationship to Blanche?" I asked, cutting right to the chase.

"Well, she told me a pretty weird story one day, after I'd been walking Bianca for quite a few months. She was home because she wasn't feeling well. But she hadn't canceled the walk. She said Bianca still needed her time in the run and that she wouldn't be able to take her. She had to stay in bed. But she wasn't in bed. She was on the couch. Same difference, I guess."

This was one weird guy. "Right. So, what did she tell you?"

"It had started raining. She asked if I'd wait, to see if it would let up, even though Bianca didn't mind the rain and Sophie never cared if Bianca got dirty at the run. She said that's how she knew Bianca had had a good time."

"What did she tell you about the dogs, how they're related to each other?"

He was looking at his feet now, trying to think up something he could tell me other than the truth.

"The cops will be here in about two minutes. Listen to me, Mel. Sophie hired me to check into this."

"She told you?"

"Uh-huh. She did."

"Do you believe it's true?"

"I don't think that's the point now. Sophie hired me to do a job, and I'm going to do what she asked me to."

"Still?"

"Still. But she can't help me anymore, so I'm going to need your help."

"But—"

"I can't do this without you, Mel. For one thing, these

dogs are going to need care. For another, I'm going to need access to this apartment and you've got the keys."

"What are you, like, a private eye?"

"Mel?"

"I thought it was all guys that did that. I didn't know that women—"

"Will you help me?"

"Oh, I don't know—"

"Take your time. Think it over. You've got about a minute."

His too long arms moved without any purpose I could detect, as if he were a marionette and someone was untangling the strings. He bit his lip, stretched his neck from side to side, switched Dashiell's leash from hand to hand, and rolled his strange hazel eyes.

His skin was pale, which was odd, I thought, since he was out-of-doors all day long. But I noticed a baseball cap sticking out of his pocket. Maybe that did the trick. His hair was still sticking up, and it added to the frightened look in his eyes.

"I know this isn't easy," I told him. "But we can't just walk away from it, can we?"

"What do you want me to do?"

"Good boy," I said. "What I want you to do is keep your mouth closed. And don't give up those keys."

"Oh, no problem. I have another set. I never take a chance I'll lose my keys and leave a dog without a walk. I have a mailbox on Hudson Street. That's where I keep the spare set."

"Great."

"I never thought . . . ," he said, his neck immediately turning a splotchy red.

"Me neither," I said.

"She seemed really . . ." He bobbed his head. "Special," he said.

Dashiell turned toward the door and barked once. Bianca and Blanche were as still as concrete. Mel walked over to the open door to Sophie's apartment and buzzed the detectives in. I saw two uniforms there, too, but, for now, they stayed outside, one on either side of the glass door to the street.

"Just answer what they ask you," I said. "Don't volunteer anything. If we're separated, bring Blanche and Bianca and meet me at the run as soon as you can. Okay?"

He nodded.

"And Mel . . ."

The detectives had stopped a respectful distance from Dash. One of them was pointing to him, his way of asking if it was safe to enter.

"Mel," I said.

He turned to me, his back to the detectives.

"Sir," the shorter one said, "I need you to move your animal out of the way."

"Tell them we'll take care of the dogs until her family is located," I whispered to Mel. Then I took Dashiell's leash from his hand and made room for the detectives.

"She has no family," he said.

And then it was too late for us to say anything else, at least anything we didn't want overheard.

CHAPTER 5

We Sat for a While Longer

I got to the run before Mel and sat where I'd been the day before with Sophie. When I saw him approaching with the two bullies, I turned on the tape recorder but left it in my jacket pocket. Dashiell went to the gate to meet him, immediately running off to play with Bianca again. There was an intact black Shepherd at the far end of the run, watchful as Dash headed his way. I watched, too, grateful when I saw his owner jump up, leash his dog, and walk quickly toward the gate, someone else who knew that too many testicles in a small, enclosed area was not a good idea. I noticed that the Shepherd's hackles were up as he was taken past Dash. Boys will be boys.

Mel slipped off his faded denim jacket and laid it on the bench for Blanche so that she would be between us, but instead of lying down there, she came into my lap, curled herself into a knot, and, with her back tight against my stomach, fell into a fitful sleep.

I pulled the jacket up over her, watching her eyes twitch and blink as she wrestled in her dreams with the loss of her mistress.

"They said I could take care of the dogs, as long as I do it out of Sophie's apartment." He looked over at Bianca, then down at Blanche, and shrugged. "I can't take them back to Sophie's until they call me, in a day or two. They said they'd try to hurry it up, because of the dogs, but I don't think they will. I mean, dogs, why would they even care about them, or about us?" He glanced over at Bianca again, to make sure she was okay.

"What happens to the dogs until the cops release the apartment? Short-term, can you take them home?"

"No. Well, I can take Bianca. I've had her before, when Sophie and Blanche went to a conference, about six months ago. Margaret took to Bianca like a duck to Twinkles, but she'd be much too much for Blanche. It would be like having two Biancas to put up with." He smiled at the thought. "Blanche'd be miserable. You see how she is, don't you?"

I didn't have to look. I had fifty or so pounds of Blanche on my lap, her legs moving as if she thought she could run away from what must be the worst thing that had ever happened to her in her life.

That's when I remembered. Blanche had been a rescue dog. This wasn't the first time she'd been abandoned.

"I'll take her," I said. "Dashiell will be fine with her and I have a yard. It'll be like home."

Mel looked stunned and I felt my stomach knot up.

"I mean, she'll be able to go out as much as she wants to. I didn't mean that . . ."

"I know. It's just that . . ."

"Yeah."

I reached out to touch his arm, but Blanche started slipping off my legs so I put my hand back where it was, to brace her.

"Even when the cops release the apartment, then what?" he asked. "We can't leave the dogs there alone."

"No—not even if we walk them four times a day. They can't be left alone."

"Suppose I stay there with them. Well, with Margaret and Bianca."

"Thanks, Mel, but I need to get in there, to spend some time there. When the detectives call you, tell them you're going to stay there for a few days, to take care of the animals, until we figure out what to do about them long-term. But I'll be the one who'll actually be there."

"You're sure? I don't mind doing it. Or maybe we could both . . ."

I gave him a look, but he missed it. He'd apparently found something very important on the ground and was looking at that.

"Thanks," I said, "but I think I can handle it myself."

He didn't say anything. His neck was still a nice shade of red.

"But you can help by answering some questions."

"Sure. Anything."

I took a breath, wondering what planet this guy had landed here from. "Did Sophie ever say anything about any arrangements she'd made for the dogs, just in case?"

He shook his head. "She once told me you can have a fatal seizure, meaning *she* could have one. But she didn't say what would happen to the dogs. 'Who would I call?' I asked her. 'Who would take Blanche and Bianca?' I figured, as long as she'd brought it up, I ought to ask. My clients tell me things like that, the ones who live alone. There's a letter in the top drawer of the desk, one guy told me. It says who Pinky goes to, like you said, in case. But

Sophie never said. She'd had a really bad seizure and she looked really depressed. Not that I blame her."

"She never mentioned any relatives to you? Not even that time? Or in passing—you know—I won't be here next week, I'm going to Terre Haute to visit my sister? Nothing like that?"

He shook his head. "Look, I was her dog walker. I hardly ever saw her. Even the money—she just left my check on that table near the door. Sometimes she'd call me to say Bianca had diarrhea and could I come as early as possible, or that she didn't eat, her food was in the refrigerator, could I give it to her after I took her to the run. Except for one or two times when she was home, we never said a word to each other that wasn't about the dogs. So maybe she has a sister in Terre Haute, but if she does, I don't know about it."

"That's why I have to get into the apartment, to check her phone book, any diary she might have. I'll go over to the school, too, see what they know. I bet there are people here who know her," I said, looking around the run. "You know how people talk here. It's almost like airplane talk."

"What's that?"

"Um, movie-line talk."

He still looked confused. Maybe he didn't talk to strangers no matter where he was. Or maybe he wasn't playing with a full deck. Being a dog walker, as long as you didn't lose them, who was going to tell if you were spaced out half the time?

"You figure you're never going to see the person again," I said, "so you spill your guts."

He thought it over. "That doesn't make sense. The same people come here every day. You are going to see them again. And again. You're going to see them even if you're sick of them. And even if you told them the most embarrassing thing you ever did in your whole life."

"Right. But the dogs are here. So people talk anyway. Haven't you ever noticed that, when dogs are around, people open up more? That's why pet therapy works."

He nodded.

"Have you done that, too?"

"Yeah. I do it when I have the time. But sometimes, after the walking, I just need to be home, with Margaret."

"What breed is she?"

"I don't know. One with too much energy. I found her one day when I was walking dogs and took her home. I tried to find her owner, but I couldn't. So then I tried to find her a good home."

"And you did."

"Yeah. I did."

"We might have to do that with Sophie's two. Find them a good home."

He looked at Blanche, sleeping on my lap, and shook his head, as if to say, An eleven-year-old dog with bad arthritis? Good luck on that.

"First I have to talk to every single person Sophie knew. She must have thought about this eventuality. She must have. She was crazy about these dogs."

"More than you know."

"What do you mean?"

"Wait till you find out what you have to do to feed Blanche. A couple of times, Sophie asked me to go to the health food store for her, when she couldn't do it herself. She got tired easily and I didn't mind helping her out. I always told her that."

"The health food store?"

I raised my eyebrows, but didn't get an answer until

later, when he took ten minutes to write it all down for me. Finding a home for an old dog is always difficult. Finding a home for a dog on Blanche's diet, I thought, looking at the list of things I'd have to buy on the way home, would take a major miracle.

Dashiell came over to make sure I still smelled the same, then ran back to Bianca. Mel looked around, as if he didn't know quite where he was, as if he was still figuring it out on the spot—dogs, people sitting on benches, a water bowl, ah, the dog run.

"Did Burns ask you a lot of questions?"

"Who?"

He must have still been recovering from the shock of seeing Sophie dead.

"The detective who stayed inside with you."

He pulled a card out of his pocket. "He gave me this but I never looked at it. I was too nervous. Right. Dennis Burns. No, not too many, once I explained why I was there."

"You wouldn't think he'd have to ask, not with those." I pointed to the keys hanging from his belt. There must have been at least thirty on the ring.

"Could have thought I was the super," he said.

"Guess he could have. Burke asked me who you were, too."

Detective Burke, the smaller of the two detectives, a little guy the color of a walnut shell with muscles waiting in line to pop out. He'd taken me outside, to Third Street, to talk while Mel and Burke's partner stayed inside.

"Makes sense. They probably like to double-check everything. He asked me how long I knew you, too," Mel said, giving me a sweet, sad little smile.

"What'd you say?"

"I asked him what time it was, so I could be entirely forthcoming with him."

"So what else did Burns want to know?"

"What your connection to Sophie was?"

"And you said?"

He shrugged. "That I didn't know. That you said you were worried about her because she hadn't shown up at work today and she hadn't called to say she wasn't coming in. I told them you insisted on following me in, to see if she was home."

"Burke asked me the same question."

"What'd you say?" he asked, probably thinking he was glad he wasn't the one who had to talk to the cops about a cloned dog.

"I considered lying, for simplicity's sake. But I decided against it."

"Too immoral?"

"Too impractical. One way or another, you always get caught and then you're in worse shape than if you'd told the truth in the first place."

He pulled his nose out to an imaginary point in front of him.

"Yeah—that, too. Lie to the cops and you lose the chance to grow up to be a real boy."

Blanche was whining in her sleep again. I began to gently scratch the back of her head and neck.

"So you told him why Sophie hired you?"

"I did."

He whistled.

"Worse than you imagine," I told him. "Burke wrote it all down, then he looked at the uniforms who'd heard the whole thing. His smirk was a mile wide. 'You may hear from Officer Lamb,' he said, 'DOC.' "

" 'Department of Cloning?' I asked him. 'Yes, ma'am,' he said. 'Been through this before?'

"Then before I had a chance to answer him, he turned

to one of the uniforms, young, blond guy with a sparse mustache, probably thought it made him look older but it had the opposite effect. 'Joey,' he says to him, stretching it all out, you know what I mean? 'You know what the clone calls the original?' So this kid Joey, he shakes his head. Then Burke says, 'Ma-a-a-a.' I tell you, the way the three of them laughed, you'd think it was the funniest thing they'd ever heard. Watching them laugh, I thought, Good. If they think it's all a joke, they'll leave me alone and I'll be able to do what I've been paid to do without interference. Burns want to know anything else?"

Mel nodded.

"He made some phone calls. I'm not sure what they were about. You know how they talk, everything's a number—I got a six-oh-six, I need a three-nine-two, shit like that. Then he wanted to know if I knew the names of any of Sophie's friends or family. I told him I didn't, that most always when I came, only Bianca was home and she never said much. Did you ever notice, cops have zero sense of humor when they're interrogating you?"

"Unless you mention cloning."

"What else did they ask you, Rachel?"

"If we'd come together. I told him we met here by accident. Then I asked him if it would be okay for me to find the person who gave Bianca to Sophie, a woman named Lorna West, because Bianca was supposed to be a seizure-alert dog and wasn't doing her job."

"What'd he say?"

"He said he'd let me know. He said he wouldn't want me to waste my time *duplicating* any of the work they were going to do. Everyone's a comedian."

For a moment, I wondered if the vets' jokes had been any better. I'd have to ask Chip.

"There's nothing funny about this. Sophie's dead."

"You're right. I guess they do that . . . Well, they see this kind of thing a lot more than the rest of us."

"She loved her life as much as anyone does."

"Of course she did."

"She was looking ahead, that's why she wanted Bianca. You've got to look ahead."

I nodded, not sure where he was going with this.

"That's why she taught Bianca what she did. She figured it was better than nothing."

"What do you mean?"

"When she saw she wasn't alerting, she decided to teach her to fetch the medication."

"No kidding? I thought she always carried it with her."

"Not at home. She said Blanche would alert her and then stick to her like glue and not leave for anything. So she taught Bianca to get the pills from the top of the night-stand."

"That must have been something to see."

"Did you ever see her have a seizure?" he asked.

I shook my head. "Did you?"

"Once—a bad one. I was so scared. I thought with all that thrashing around she was doing, I'd get my teeth knocked out."

"Were you able to help her?"

He looked funny. Guilty, maybe. He'd probably stayed back until the seizure was over. Maybe he'd even thought it was contagious.

"I wrapped her in a blanket so she wouldn't get cold. Then I called nine-one-one. But by the time they got there, she was awake. She looked sort of stunned. I didn't know if she even knew who I was. In fact, when the paramedics came in, three men and one woman, they started asking her all kinds of questions, like who's the president of the United States, who's the vice president, stuff like that, to see if she was *compos mentis*. That's what the woman told me. Then she said Sophie was, but that she was temporarily disoriented. After they left, that was when she told me you could die from a seizure. I guess that's what she was afraid of, maybe all the time."

I nodded.

"She was right to worry about it."

"What do you mean?" I asked. "You can't be sure that's what it was."

"When Burns told me I could go, and asked me to take the dogs, Bianca wouldn't get up. When I went to pick her up, the vial of Sophie's seizure medication was under her. She'd been lying on it."

"Oh, god."

"No way of knowing if Sophie had the chance to take it."

"The ME will know. But even if Sophie did, it was too little or too late."

"He took it. Burns. He put it in a little plastic bag and shoved it in his pocket."

"An evidence bag."

He smiled. "Yeah. An evidence bag. I should know that from T.V., right?"

I nodded. "I'm surprised he did that."

"Why? Wouldn't they want to have it, you know, as evidence?"

"Yes, but they usually leave everything in place until the Crime Scene Unit comes and photographs the scene. You're not supposed to disturb anything."

"What about the dogs?"

I looked to see if he'd made a joke, but he hadn't. He was serious.

"That's different. It would be cruel to leave the dogs there. No one would follow the letter of the law to that extent. Anyway, he probably figured it was just what it appeared to be, an epileptic dying from a seizure."

"After he took it, he looked her over again, and then he said, 'Unofficially, she's been dead since sometime yesterday evening, pending confirmation by the ME.' Unofficially. Like I was a reporter or something."

He stood up so that he could get his hand into his pants pocket, then handed me two keys.

"I stopped on the way here," he said. "Don't lose them. The police took my other ones."

We sat for a while longer, watching the dogs play. Bianca, running with Dashiell, had apparently been able to put the past behind her. At least for now. Blanche was another story. She was moaning in her sleep, her eyes moving and looking as if they were going to open, her paws twitching, her tail beating up and down against my legs. I wondered if she'd need a new home after all, or if she'd just die of a broken heart.

CHAPTER 6

I'm Chopping Swiss Chard

I was scrubbing organic carrots, getting ready to feed them into the Cuisinart, when Chip called.

"I got your message. What's wrong?"

The light was gone from the garden. Being surrounded by buildings, it gets dark early.

"Sophie's dead," I told him.

"A seizure?"

"It looks that way. The meds were next to her. I don't know if she took them and they didn't work, or if the dog didn't get them to her in time."

"The dog? Blanche got the medication for her?"

"No. Blanche let her know what was coming. She usually had the medication on her, in a little pouch. But at home, she left it on her nightstand, and if she wasn't in bed, she'd send Bianca for it. My guess is, she did it as a step toward her alerting one day, you know, to focus her on how Sophie was feeling and have her respond."

Holding the phone in the crook of my neck, I put the Swiss chard on the cutting board and began slicing along the bright red ribs.

"I'm sorry, Rach."

"Me, too."

"So, you're going to work tonight, wrap things up?"

"It's not that simple. First of all, even if I chose to do nothing else, there are the dogs to think about. There may not be any relatives. At least, her dog walker doesn't know of any. Nor is he aware of any plans she made for the animals. So the very least I can do would be to find out if there are arrangements for the animals and if not, to try to place them. Blanche is here for a day or two. The dog walker has Bianca. He says his own dog is just like her, too much energy for Blanche or he would have taken both. But I don't mind having Blanche here."

"And what's that sound?"

"She hasn't eaten all day. Maybe she didn't eat last night. I'm getting her dinner ready. I'm chopping Swiss chard."

"Swiss chard? For Blanche? Don't tell me."

But I did. "Raw carrots and yellow squash, ground up small to imitate what would be in the stomach of a kill, cod-liver oil for essential fatty acids, vitamin E for a healthy coat and its antioxidant benefits, glucosamine and condroitin sulfate to help maintain and rebuild healthy joints, raw chicken, kelp—"

"And chard."

"For calcium."

"So homes for two bullies. The young one should be pretty easy. Blanche is going to be tough, though. She's how old?"

"You're way ahead of me, Chip. I can't place the animals until I'm sure that's necessary. Anyway, I said taking care of the animals was the very least I could do. Doing the least is not my intention."

I put the sliced chard in a pile and began to cut in the other direction.

"I'm going to do what Sophie asked me to do. Actually, *that's* the least I can do and live with myself. Sophie was concerned that Side by Side is cloning dogs that will not work as expected for their disabled owners and I'm going to do my best to find them and tell them that. I'm going to start by listening to the tapes again, see if there's anything I missed when I took notes. Tomorrow, after acupuncture, I'll go over to The School for the Deaf and see if I can talk to anyone who was close to Sophie. I know there's one person she was tight with, the receptionist. Then as soon as the police release the apartment, I'll stay there for a day or two so that I can take care of the girls in their own home and while I'm there, I'll check all Sophie's papers, bills, notes—whatever I can find. I have to see if she made arrangements for the dogs or if there are any relatives who might take them."

"Do you need my help with anything?"

"Maybe later, if I have to find the dogs a new home." I measured the cod-liver oil and dumped it into the bowl. "Chip?"

"I'm here."

"I wonder if it's the food."

"If what is?"

"Blanche. She's eleven and a half and still working. I thought service dogs retired by nine at the latest."

"Apparently Sophie didn't know that."

"And neither did Blanche."

She was sleeping on the couch, her face pressed into one of the pillows. It didn't look like much to most people, trotting along beside Sophie or sleeping under her desk while her mistress taught, but she'd taken on the responsibility of trying to keep Sophie from having seizures, and no matter what it looked like, it was a big job for a dog of any age.

"I'll call you tomorrow," I whispered into the phone.

"Rachel—"

"I love you," I told him. "Everything will be okay."

But looking at the old dog on my couch, I had trouble believing it would. What would become of her now that the rug had been pulled out from under her for the second time in her life?

I finished chopping the vegetables and mixed everything together, noticing how bright the colors were—the orange of the carrots, the deep green of the leaf and cherry-red rib of the chard, the yellow skin of the squash against its firm, pale flesh, and the paper-thin seeds, slippery to the touch and nearly as hard to pick up as a drop of water. When it was all blended together, I checked the list Mel had written out for me. I added a dollop of yogurt, the digestive enzymes, and kelp, putting the bowl down for Blanche, calling her to come and eat. I thought she might ignore me, or come and sniff at the food, then walk away. But she picked her head up from where she lay on the couch and began to slip down to the floor, front legs first, the hind legs oozing slowly afterward, rubbing against the couch as she left it. She trotted right over to her bowl and, legs wide, as if she was protecting her meal from competitors—and perhaps she was—she ate ravenously, not stopping until the bowl looked as if it had never been used.

When I began to fill a bowl with kibble for Dash, I couldn't help noticing that Blanche's meal had smelled like food and his did not. I might as well have been giving my own dog a bowl of pricey cardboard. I dumped the kibble back into the bag and began all over again, grinding carrots for Dashiell this time.

He looked up at me, hopeful, his tail wagging horizontally. As soon as I put the bowl down, he wolfed down every fresh, crunchy morsel. As I cleaned up, I could hear the sound of the bowl smacking hard against the kitchen wall as he made sure there was nothing edible left in it.

I thought I'd let the dogs out into the garden, wash a couple of raw carrots for myself, go up to my office to listen to the tapes I'd made, and try to figure out what to do next. Instead, I grabbed my jacket and took Dashiell for what I assumed would be a short walk, just to clear my head, ending up, to my surprise, but probably not his, in front of Sophie's building. I checked my watch. It was eight-thirty. Most people would be home from work and it was Monday, a dead night even in Manhattan.

Not counting Sophie's, there were five apartments in the building. After reading the names next to each bell, I used the key Mel had given me to get in, figuring I'd start at the top and work my way down. Dash headed for Sophie's but I called him back and pointed up the stairs, then followed him all the way to the top.

Bert Shore's apartment, larger than Sophie's because she shared the ground floor with a shop, looked like a greenhouse, a huge skylight over the back room to give him even more light than the front and rear windows afforded. I stayed pretty near the doorway so that Dashiell could stay in the hall, and told Bert part of what I was doing, that I was trying to find any information that might help me find a home for Sophie's dogs.

"I didn't know her, except to say hi at the mailbox or hold the door for her when she had both dogs. How'd she do that?" he asked. "They told *me* no dogs, no way, not even a Chihuahua. So I got Magnolia instead. But *she* had *two* dogs. It never seemed fair to me."

There were two little dishes just inside the kitchen doorway. One said, Kitty. I wrote "cat" in my little notebook. Born to the job.

"She's hiding." He pointed at Dashiell. "From him. Don't tell me you're moving in here now, with *that*."

I shook my head. "So you never really talked?"

"Not to speak of. Do they know *who?*" he whispered. "The coppers wouldn't say. You know how *they* are."

I shook my head again, handed him my card, and asked him to call if he thought of anything at all that might help me, even if it seemed "banal" I said. "Trivial. Don't be shy. I don't give grades."

I turned to go.

"There is one other thing I should mention, but I don't think it'll help." He took a pack of cigarettes from the pocket of his loose pants, hit the bottom, and offered me the one that popped out. When I declined, he just held the pack in his hand.

"She fed Maggie for me when I traveled. I'm a choreographer," he added.

"And you travel a lot?"

"A great deal."

"And Sophie would come up here and feed your cat?"

"Yes."

"That's pretty nice, from someone you hardly knew."

"It was business," he said. "I paid her."

"But you never—"

"I wasn't here when she came. That was the point, wasn't it? I'd call and tell her, 'Thursday through Saturday,' she'd say, 'Okay,' and I'd leave the money."

"She had the key?"

"Still does," he said.

"I'll look for it," I told him.

"It's a Medico."

I nodded. He thanked me. I thanked him. On the way down to the next floor, I looked at my notepad. It said "cat." I added, "Sophie fed it."

I was about to slip my card under the next door, with a note asking G. Pascal to please call me, when the door opened. There were two of them, arms wrapped around each other, Velcroed at the hip.

"Sorry to bother you," I said, which sounded lame, even to me.

But they were fixated on Dashiell and didn't seem to hear me.

"He's okay," I said. "I'm here about Sophie, your down-stairs neighbor, first floor?" If I was waiting for a look of recognition, I was bound to be disappointed. "I'm trying to locate friends of hers, or relatives. It's about the dogs."

"Cop?" He had a tattoo of a knife dripping blood on his free arm. He may have had a lot of calls from cops. Unless it was a fashion statement.

I shook my head. "I was hired by Sophie yesterday and now—"

"Bummer," he said.

The girl's hair was short and bleached nearly white. She watched him when he spoke.

"I'm trying to find out—"

"We just moved in," he said. "We told the police that. There's nothing we can tell you. We didn't know her. I mean, I looked down at the garden sometimes and thought, Wow, cool. All that green, when you're stoned, man, it's really something. But I never even saw her out there, just some dog. Was she very old?"

"Thirties."

"Overdose?" he asked.

"I don't know."

I handed him my card.

"Research?" he said.

"Yeah. I find answers for people who need them."

"Having any luck?"

"No one likes a wise guy." I wondered which of them was G. Pascal. But looking at them again, I doubted that either of them would have bothered to remove the former tenant's name from next to the bell and put their own name there. "Call me if you think of anything helpful," I said.

"About what?" he asked.

I shrugged.

They stayed in the doorway until after we'd disappeared. I never heard the door close. For all I know, they stayed there all night. No one was home on four. Three wouldn't open. He said he'd already talked to the cops and he didn't know anything. He said he'd be damned if he'd open the door for some stranger and then he asked how I'd gotten in the building in the first place. He was still talking through the door when I headed for two. Sophie's upstairs neighbor wasn't home either. Maybe Monday wasn't as dead a night as I thought it was.

There was no yellow tape across the hall leading to Sophie's door, but we didn't go that way. We headed straight out. The guy from the leather-goods store was closing up, pulling down the metal gate that covers the front of most small stores when they're not open for business. I asked him if he'd ever met Sophie. He said no. His English wasn't very good. At that point, neither was mine. I said it was the lady with the two white dogs. He nodded. Two white dogs, yes, yes, he said. So you knew her? I asked. He said, no, he didn't know her, but he'd seen her, and that she had had a nice bag, a green sling, good-quality leather, but that she hadn't bought it from him. He said he probably would have given her a better price. Then he shrugged and closed the four padlocks that held the gate in place.

We walked around the far corner but we didn't go into the park. By ten at night, the park belonged to the drug dealers and the dog run was closed anyway. We headed back on West Fourth Street where Dashiell suddenly began marking everything in sight. No wonder. West Fourth led directly to Washington Square Park. Lots of other males, hurrying to the dog run, had taken time out of their busy schedules to leave their stats. Dashiell did the same.

When I got home, instead of letting Blanche out and getting to work on the tapes, I surprised myself again. I hadn't really learned that much, so this time, taking Blanche along, I headed for the meatpacking district. If there was a veterinary office there where samples of Blanche's DNA had been harvested, perhaps *that* was the place to begin. I kept the notebook in my pocket, hoping I could add to the copious notes I'd taken at Sophie's building.

CHAPTER 7

What Brings You Here?

Blanche and I walked slowly north, passing the little shops, the ethnic restaurants, the pocket parks filled with flowers that tourists loved to come and see. With everything lit up, and couples walking arm in arm, heading for Da Andrea or La Ripaille, we might have been in Rome or Paris.

We turned west on Jane, the sort of street the neighborhood is best known for—Greek revival town houses, with high stoops and tall parlor-floor windows, set in two neat rows across a cobblestone street. When we got to Washington Street, we were at the cusp of the wholesale meat-packing district, now dotted with new or newly renovated luxury condos. Later in the evening, the neighborhood would also be dotted with black and Hispanic transvestite hookers with legs as long as flamingos, wide shoulders and narrow hips, and in case you still didn't get it, voices so deep the sound would reverberate in your stomach.

The indoor/outdoor contraptions on which carcasses of animals were hung on sharp, heavy hooks and moved into the buildings were no longer used this far south, perhaps in deference to the new residential buildings on the west side of the street. I was glad that Dashiell wasn't with me this time because the smell of the place bothered him; he took the plight of all those dead animals personally. Passing a trash can full of bones or even those ominous empty hooks outside each wholesaler's place of business made the hair on his back stand up and put a wary look in his eyes.

One block north was the place where Sophie had met Lorna West for the second and next-to-last time. Walking toward the empty corner, I wondered if before hiring me Sophie had checked the phone book to see if Lorna was listed. Once in a blue moon, all it took to find someone was trying the simplest and most obvious thing. But not this time.

When I got to the redbrick building on the northeast corner of Horatio and Washington, Blanche pulled to go in. But the building was locked up for the night. All the windows were dark, and if there was a cleaning staff that worked at night, after everyone else had gone home, they'd either not yet come or had already left. I let Blanche pull me up the steps so that I could check the names next to the bells. I went over all of them, even though Sophie had said the veterinary office was on the first floor. She hadn't given me the name of a veterinarian. Perhaps she was never told a name.

This building seemed an unlikely place for a veterinary practice. But I'd check again when the building was open and see who was on the first floor, and if there was no Horatio Street Veterinary Practice there, see if anyone remembered it being there two years earlier.

I felt Blanche's tail banging against my leg. When I

looked down at her, to see what was up, she began to pull hard in the opposite direction, away from the building and toward Bianca.

"What a surprise. What brings you here?"

"She was restless so I decided to take her for a long walk." Mel gestured behind him with one of those long wiggly arms of his.

"You took her for a walk along the river?"

He nodded. "But when I started thinking, this was where it all began. So I thought I'd come and take a look." He nodded again.

"You wanted to take a look at this building?"

"I never get to this part of the Village. My clients are all around Washington Square Park. So I thought I'd swing by, you know what I mean?"

"Yeah, I do. I had the same feeling."

"It's locked, huh?"

"Looks to be."

"You coming back tomorrow?"

"Maybe."

"Not definitely? Don't you have to talk to the vet who cloned Bianca? Isn't that what Sophie wanted you to do?"

"I don't think I'm going to find a veterinary office in this building."

"But didn't Sophie say that this was the place?"

"She did."

"That's odd."

"The whole thing's odd, wouldn't you say?"

He nodded. "But—"

"I doubt there ever was a vet's office here."

"How come?"

"They'd never have clients go through the lobby of an office building with their animals. It doesn't make sense."

"I guess not."

"You always enter directly from the street."

He nodded.

"Anyway, there's something more urgent I need to do."

He opened his mouth and lifted his arms, but that was all that happened.

"How long can we take care of these two, Mel? I need to find out if any arrangements were made for them and, if not, find them someplace permanent. And soon."

Bianca was licking Blanche's mouth, her tail wagging frantically.

"It must be very hard for them to be apart."

He looked at the dogs and smiled. "That's why I took Bianca out. Like I said, she was restless."

"Which way are you headed?" I asked him, realizing I didn't know where he lived.

He lifted a loose arm and pointed north. I stood there for a couple of minutes after he left, and then thought of someplace that would be open, even at this hour. So I followed in the same direction Mel had walked with Bianca, heading for Florent on the slim chance that someone who worked there would know if there was a veterinary practice a short block away.

When I got to the corner, I looked around for Mel, but he seemed to have disappeared.

CHAPTER 8

He Waved His Hand Back and Forth

"How you been?" Dr. Chen asked as he began to insert the slender needles in my arm.

"Pretty good," I told him. "Considering."

"Considering what? Broken arm? Arm almost one hunderd percent now. You come twice more, that's it. Arm good as new."

I shook my head.

"Ah. You start work again?" He shook his head. "No good. Arm still needs rest. Body needs rest to repair arm. Only two more weeks. You no can wait?"

"I need to work so that I can pay for acupuncture," I lied, not wanting to hear the rest of his lecture.

"Insurance pays for acupuncture. What you think, I was born yesterday?"

I shook my head. "No, but—"

"You no plan unpaid vacation. Unpaid vacation happens. You have no choice."

"Yeah, yeah, I go with the flow. But I have to pay the insurance premiums, Dr. Chen, not to mention rent."

"You wait two more weeks."

"I can't. I've already taken a job. This woman called me and told me a fantastic story, Dr. Chen. She said she was approached two years ago by someone with an offer to clone her dog—"

"Crone dog no good," he said; this was the only time I'd ever seen a hard look in his eyes.

"But the dog is a service dog, a seizure-alert dog—"

"No matter. You crone cells from great man, still end up with fool."

"What about all the positive, scientific—"

"No reason strong enough. Not God's will. Not healthy. No make strong offspring, only one parent." He waved his hand back and forth, as if he could erase the whole idea of cloning.

"I have better job for you."

"You do?"

He nodded. "Find homes for Chinese babies, no have families to take care of them. Girl babies," he said, "beautiful, rittle frowers, need roving American homes. This important work. Croning," he shook his head again, "take you no prace good."

He turned down the lights, slipped out the door, and closed it behind him. I closed my eyes, careful not to move anything. I had once tried to scratch my nose, after the long thin needles had been inserted in my hand, and the pain was excruciating. But lying still, I felt only pleasure, the gentle movement of energy flowing in my arms and legs, streaming down my torso, and sending chills into my scalp.

I lay still in the dark room for twenty minutes before the door opened and Dr. Chen reappeared.

"Arm feels good?" he asked, removing the needles and putting them in the red Sharps container.

"Everything feels good."

He nodded; wisps of hair covered the top of his round head, the skin of his face was as smooth as a baby's even though he was well into his eighties.

"You come ten in the morning next week, same as today. Okay?"

"No problem."

"Use arm, rest arm. Twice a day." He lifted his arm.

"Elevate arm. I remember."

"Good. One more week, no cook, no crean."

I nodded.

I lay there for several minutes after he left the room, my eyes closed, thinking about work.

The night before I had walked as far as Fourteenth Street, hoping to catch up to Mel, not sure why I wanted to do that. Was it merely curiosity? Did I just want to know where he lived for no particular reason? Walking past the giant-size pig mural, flat-looking pink porkers announcing in no uncertain terms that this was the meat market in case the rank odor and the hunks of animal fat and bones strewn around didn't get the message across, I had begun to wonder what I was thinking. I'd see him anyway in a day or two. Was there something I wanted to say, or to ask?

I'd stopped on the corner of Fourteenth Street and had stood looking around, aware that Blanche was breathing hard, that I'd been walking too fast for her. Across the street and west of where I stood was Moishe's Mini Storage, New Yorkers' answer to not having an attic or a basement—rent someplace to keep your junk. Near that was a new place under construction, Jeffrey, a drawing of a shoe on the outer wall of the construction site. First galleries, then restaurants and now a shoe store in the middle of the wholesale meat district, suddenly the hottest area of the city. Did Mel live here?

I'd crossed the street, and passed The Little Pie Shop, walking as far as Greenwich Street. Markt was open, hip-looking people sitting around drinking beer and eating moules frites. I'd looked for a bull terrier tied up outside, but there was no Bianca and no Mel. What was I doing, anyway? There was work to be done.

Walking slowly now, at Blanche's pace, I'd stopped at Florent, the little French bistro on Gansevoort Street that stayed open around the clock. I'd been seated at a small round table and after settling Blanche at my side and ordering a glass of wine, I'd asked the waiter if he remembered a veterinary office around the corner. He wore a necklace of painted wooden beads, the kind I used to string on long colored shoelaces when I was little. He shook his head, telling me no, he didn't know of any such place. And when I'd asked if he'd been here long, he bent closer so that he could whisper, "Oh, honey, you don't want to ask a question like that." His hand was flat on the table, his nails painted dark red.

On the way home, instead of lagging behind or wandering off to the side, Blanche had stayed close to my side. Every time I'd looked down at her, she'd looked back up at my face, her brow furrowed with concern, as if waiting for me to say something or do something that would allow her life to make sense again.

I'd stopped and knelt down. When she leaned against me, I'd put my arms around her and laid my face against her thick neck. I could hear the brakes of a bus somewhere in the direction we were heading, and people laughing. I'd told Blanche she was a good girl. I'd wanted to tell her more, that I'd take care of things, that everything would be okay, but I couldn't. I could lie to a human being when it was absolutely necessary, and be believed, but even if I was willing, there was no credible way to lie to a dog.

CHAPTER 9

I Took a Bite of My Sandwich

On my way uptown I called The School for the Deaf.

"It's Rachel Alexander," I said. "I'm so sorry, Ruth, but I have some bad news."

"We heard," she whispered.

I waited a moment. "I was wondering if we could talk, perhaps at lunchtime today."

"Okay," she said. "Meet me at noon, at Zeke's. It's not much, but it's close, right on the corner. You can't miss it."

"How will I know you?" It seemed a minute ago that I'd asked Sophie the same question. "Wait a minute," I said, "it's not a problem. I'll have a dog with me."

"Blanche?"

"No. My own dog. He's also white." I didn't tell her he was a pit bull. I didn't want to put her off.

I knew the school was on Twenty-Third Street and I knew I could get there with time to spare, too much time to spare, so I headed back to the meatpacking district, to the building I'd looked at last night. This time, I rang one of the first-floor bells, said my name when asked, and got buzzed in. The sign on the door told me this was a design firm, but it didn't say what sort of design. It turned out to be print design—stationery, business cards, advertising layouts. There was a young man at the desk, his eyebrows already raised when I opened the door.

"Ms. Alexander? What can we do for you?" he asked, his chair a half turn away from his computer now.

"I was actually looking for a veterinary practice I was told was in this building, on this floor. But I can't tell by the names on the bells."

"A veterinary practice, here? I don't think so." Now he turned his attention to Dashiell, perhaps wondering if he had a zoonotic illness, something he could catch merely by inhaling.

"Have you been here long?" I asked.

"Since the building was renovated. We were the third business to move in. We would have been the first, except for the tile man. It's still not right."

I nodded as if I cared.

"And you were with the firm then?"

"Well, no. I'm only here three months." His mouth looked as if he'd just tasted something surprisingly sour and he sat up straight in his chair, making himself appear at least a half inch taller.

"Is there someone I could talk to for just a minute, about the veterinary office? Perhaps someone who was here in the beginning might remember it. It might have been here for only a short while."

"I'll see if one of the partners will talk to you."

A moment later, he came back shaking his head.

"No."

"No they won't talk to me, or no they don't recall a vet's office here?"

"The latter," he said. He sat, swiveling his chair away so that he faced the computer. "Well, the former and the latter." Hands on the keyboard, he looked back at me once more, as if to ask why I was still standing there.

"Thanks," I told him on my way out.

"Anytime," he chirped back at me.

There were four offices on the first floor. Sophie had said the veterinary office was in the back. I tried the office on the right first. It was some sort of medical office, a lab, I thought, one of those places that tests bodily fluids and looks for conditions you don't want them to find, but I wasn't sure. It only said the doctor's name, P. Mellon, M.D. With two *l*'s, not like the fruit.

I didn't get to speak to P. Mellon. I spoke to a young woman who sat behind one of those off-putting Plexiglas partitions. She said she'd been with Dr. Mellon "forever" and didn't have any recollection of "a veterinary facility" in the building, neither in the office they occupied or in any other.

The back office next door was now occupied by a CPA, a J. Fleming, but no one answered the bell. It wasn't tax season. Maybe J. Fleming was in the south of France.

There was one more office on the ground floor, Ink, Inc. From the look of the waiting room, the walls covered with framed fabric samples, I thought the occupant might be a wholesale fabric dealer. But the business cards on the empty desk said Ink, Inc. was in book packaging. The pretty blond I expected back at the desk at any moment turned out to be a squatty senior citizen, short and wide, a cigarette dangling from her wound of a mouth, her bright red lipstick bleeding into the deep wrinkles on her upper lip.

"Help you?" She sounded like a bullfrog.

"I hope so. I'm looking for a veterinary office that used to be in this building. On this floor."

I smiled and waited.

She took the cigarette out of her mouth with two stained fingers and snubbed it out in her ashtray.

"A vet's office?"

"That's right."

"Not in my memory. Not in this building."

"And you've been here long?"

"Too long," she croaked. "One day I'm going to do something about that. But not today. Today I'm too busy to think about it. So, can I get back to work now or is there something else you want?"

Dash and I headed over to the east side.

Ruth was in a booth at the back and waved me over.

"I saw you through the window," she said, a woman of about forty whose pear-shaped body reflected her sedentary work. Her brown hair was short, in a boyish cut, and the round face was lost behind huge glasses with red frames.

"Ruth Stewart," she said. Her hand was cool.

"I hope I didn't keep you waiting," I said, sending Dash under the table and taking the seat across from her.

She waved her hand at me. "I just got here a moment ago myself, Rachel."

The booth was dark brown leatherette, with a couple of slits in the seat and one in the back. The menu had seen better days, too. She ordered tuna. I said, "Me, too." Ruth had only a half hour for lunch and I didn't want to waste my time mulling over the cuisine. I thanked her again for meeting me.

"I can't believe she's gone," she said. She wiped her eyes with her napkin.

I nodded.

"Her class is in an uproar. She was a very gifted teacher and had such a way with the kids. They knew about her disability, of course, and that helped some of the shyer kids relate to her and feel accepted."

"Had she ever had anything like this before, that you know of?"

"You mean, a seizure this serious?"

"Well, almost this serious."

"She had a few close calls, but most of them were before she got Blanche."

"That's one of the things I need to talk to you about."

"The dogs?"

I nodded. "One of the things I'm trying to find out is if Sophie has any family, someone who ought to be notified, someone, I'm hoping, who might be willing to provide a home for her pets."

"She never mentioned anyone."

"She never said she was going home for the holidays, nothing like that?"

"No. We always had Thanksgiving and Christmas dinner together. She never really traveled anywhere. She was always afraid she'd be away from her doctor when she got into trouble. She didn't want that to happen."

She took a bite of her sandwich and chewed carefully.

"What about a boyfriend? Was she involved with anyone?"

"You mean Herbie?" She didn't mean to, but she made a face.

"Right, Herbie." I took a bite of my sandwich. This time I made a face. You wouldn't think anyone could ruin canned tuna, it's not that terrific to begin with. "What was his last name?" I asked, as if it was on the tip of my tongue but I couldn't remember it.

"She never said. And I never thought to ask."

"Did you ever meet him, this Herbie? Did he ever come to the school to pick her up after work?"

"No, he never did. And anyway, that was a while ago. They hadn't been seeing each other recently."

"How long ago were they dating, Ruth?"

I wondered if Ruth had a sweetheart. I wondered if she and Sophie saw less of each other when Herbie was in the picture. I wondered if Ruth had been envious of Sophie, who had a beau when she didn't.

"She stopped talking about him a few months ago, maybe six months, I'm not sure. For a while, it was Herbie this and Herbie that. That's all she talked about. Then, nothing."

"No more Herbie?"

"Not a word."

"No explanation?"

"None."

"Did you ever ask?"

She looked at her plate for a while, the second half of her tuna on whole wheat toast sitting there untouched. Maybe she was thinking the chicken salad would have been a better choice. She reached for the sandwich, then changed her mind, picking up one of the pale, greasy French fries, dipping it into the pool of ketchup she'd poured onto her plate and putting it into her mouth.

"It was difficult for her to meet men," she said, reaching for another fry. "She hardly tried. She said the epilepsy always scared them off anyway, if not at first, then after they got to witness a seizure."

"It doesn't take much to scare people off."

"You can say that again." This time she picked up her Coke and drank about half of what was in her glass. "Even friends."

"What do you mean?"

Ruth shrugged.

"How come you weren't scared off?"

"We had a lot in common."

Her nose got red. Her eyes filled with tears again.

"Like what?"

I handed her a clean napkin and waited while she took off her glasses and dabbed her eyes.

"Well, work, for one thing. Our devotion to the kids."

Yeah, yeah, I thought, devotion to the kids.

"And we were both single."

"Go on."

I was still waiting for pay dirt.

"She got me this job." She was fighting off another onslaught of tears. "I'd been out of work for a while. I'd told her that when we met, and two weeks later, I was working at the school. It was serendipity, she said, that I needed a job just when the school needed a receptionist."

"Where did you meet?"

"The foundation."

"For epilepsy?"

Ruth nodded. "So I can tell you she was right. A lot of guys . . ."

I reached across the table and patted her hand.

"We were very close. We talked on the phone all the time."

"Ruth, did you talk to Sophie on Sunday, by any chance?"

She shook her head.

"I called her twice, but there was no answer and I didn't leave a message."

"Why not?"

She shrugged her shoulders and began to cry. I pulled another napkin from the dispenser and held it out for her.

"I thought . . ."

Ruth blew her nose.

"Sometimes it's hard for me to think someone really wants to talk to me." She tried to bury her face in the small napkin.

"But why?"

"Because of the epilepsy."

"But Sophie had the same—"

"It doesn't matter. Being different, it does terrible things to your self-esteem. Oh, I know Sophie loved me. And most of the time I was okay, at least with her. But I was having a bad weekend and when I'd talked to her the day before, on Saturday, she sort of blew me off. She was so preoccupied."

"Did she say what it was about?"

"Of course. She told me everything."

"Then you know why she hired me."

"I'm sorry about the mistake on the phone."

I waved my hand over my unfinished sandwich, to tell her not to give it a thought.

"It wasn't a mistake," she said.

"What do you mean?"

"Well, I didn't want to say, in case you weren't the PI."

"I see. Well, don't worry about it in either case."

"I don't know what she told you, Rachel," she said, not meeting my eyes, "but the real reason she hired you was to see if she could have me put on the list."

"The list?"

"For a Blanche clone."

"But—"

"Oh, I know what you're thinking, but you don't give up a good idea after trying only once, do you? And anyway, she said maybe the two other girls *are* alerting. That was one of the things she wanted to find out, once you put her in touch with Side by Side." She picked up her soda but didn't drink. "You *will* still do it, won't you?" she asked. "Because Sophie thought if the other girls were alerting, she'd let them clone Blanche again and that this time *I* would get the free puppy."

When I didn't answer her, she went on, leaning across the table and talking even faster.

"I don't have a lot of money. But I do have a steady job now, so I could borrow some. I don't know what you arranged with Sophie, but if it's a matter of money—"

"I don't understand something. Have you been looking for a seizure dog? Or did this just come up recently?"

"I've always been a little afraid of dogs." She started to tear little pieces off the damp napkin. "But I'm not afraid of Blanche."

Dashiell was using my left foot for a pillow. I wondered how she'd felt when I'd walked in with him.

"What about . . ." I indicated Dashiell's whereabouts with a tilt of my head.

"I saw you coming down the block and he seemed so . . ."

I raised my eyebrows.

"Sweet. It's the way he looks up at your face when you walk with him. He just didn't scare me. Anyway, Sophie worked on me. She convinced me that if I had a seizure-alert dog, it would help me to live a normal life."

A normal life, I thought, what the hell was that?

"And you feel you could overcome your fear," I asked her, "and that you wouldn't mind all the work?"

"No. I'm sure I could do it. Sophie said I'd love my dog to pieces and I wouldn't be at all afraid of her, that once I had her, I wouldn't be afraid of anything."

"Of anything?"

"Of living," she said. "And she told me the work of taking care of my dog would get easier and easier as I bonded with her. She said she'd never had a dog before and she came to love the work she did to take care of hers. It's part of it, when you have a dog, she told me, that you take good care of her and she takes good care of you." She took two fries this time. I waited for her to go on. "You give them the best food you can afford, she told me, and lots and lots of exercise. She met Herbie at the dog run, you know."

"I wonder if he still goes there."

"Why not? Unless he moved away or his dog died." She picked up another handful of fries.

"What kind did he have?" I asked, figuring it would be easier to identify him by a description of his dog than one of himself—brown hair, medium height, you know, average looking. Good luck on that, unless he had a prominent scar or was six foot seven.

"What kind of what?" she asked.

"Dog. Did Sophie ever say?"

She shrugged. "Oh, just a dog, I guess. Sophie usually talked about him, not the dog."

"Did she ever describe him to you?"

"Brown. No, maybe black. I don't remember."

"No, I mean Herbie. Did she ever show you a picture of him?"

Ruth's mouth was full. She shook her head.

"She never mentioned how blue his eyes were or—"

"He had blue eyes, Herbie? She never said."

I smiled. "I don't know if he had blue eyes. I was just asking that as an example of something Sophie might have said."

She nodded. "Oh. So you would be able to recognize him if you saw him at the dog run."

"Exactly. It's a slim chance, but a lot of what I do is. Sometimes you get lucky, despite the odds."

Ruth looked out the window for a moment, watching an

old woman make her way in front of the coffee shop, all bent over, balancing herself on one of those aluminum walkers. I wondered if I was getting enough calcium in my diet and thought about eating some of Blanche's Swiss chard when I got home.

"Will you continue to look for Side by Side?"

"I'm not sure. I want to see what I can find out when I get into Sophie's apartment. Without Sophie's help, this whole thing could come to a dead end in no time. But I'll be in touch. I'll let you know."

She nodded.

"Sophie told me something strange the day she hired me."

"Sunday?"

"Yes, on Sunday. She said that this woman who spoke to her about cloning Blanche, Lorna West, said she'd heard about Sophie from The School for the Deaf, that she'd called there looking for people with service dogs to interview for some sort of survey."

Ruth had her mouth full again, but she began to shake her head vigorously.

"Were you the receptionist then, two years ago?"

"Yes, but there was no such call."

"How can you be sure?" I asked her. "Like, for instance, now, while you're having lunch, isn't someone answering the phone?"

"Actually, no. We have voice mail. When I don't pick up, it's done electronically. If you know your party's extension, you can punch that right in and it'll ring through to their phone. The system also gives you the extension to dial for different departments. You can leave your name and number for information on the school. Then when I get back, I take care of the messages."

"And when you're out sick?"

"The same. They're not going to hire another receptionist. Basically, the school spends money on the kids. Everything else is no frills. As for the phone system, it works. It's efficient and most people use it."

"Meaning?"

"We don't get a lot of hang-ups."

"So one way or another, Lorna would have had to speak to you?"

"Me or the machine. And she didn't do either. I'd remember."

"Why are you so sure, with all the calls you must get? It's been two years, and—"

"There are only a few kinds of calls that come into the school. People call to speak with people they know, whether it's business or personal. Or they call because they have a deaf kid and they want information about the school to help them decide if it's the right place for them. Or they call to sell us stuff, anything from new phone systems to new devices for the kids, 'hearing gizmos' Sophie used to call them. No one calls about dogs, period. Only two of the kids use hearing dogs, and neither of them brings the dog to school. They don't need them there. They need them everywhere but there. And since they come and go by special bus, the dogs aren't needed for the trip. They can stay home. We signal with lights here. You don't need a dog to alert you that the bell is ringing. So how could I miss a call like that? Besides, the way Lorna told it, it involved my best friend. How would I forget something like that, or forget to tell Sophie about it if the call had come in?"

"I guess you wouldn't."

She took one last bite of her sandwich and wiped her lips while she was still chewing. I saw her look over at the clock behind the counter.

"Time to get back?" I asked.

"I still have five minutes."

"I only have one more question I can think of now. Do you think it would be possible for me to talk to the kids in Sophie's class? She may have told them things about herself, something that might help me locate family. Teachers do that, sometimes to get the kids to open up and talk."

"Oh, I doubt it. The school's very protective of the students. Especially now. Those poor things. They have a counselor talking to them. They're very upset to have lost their teacher."

"I understand."

"But, of course, if you were around after school, at three o'clock, let's say, no one would say anything if one or two of the children approached you, to pet your dog. I could meet you out front one day, to make sure you know which kids were hers."

"Thanks, Ruth. I'll give them another day or two and then try it. What age are her kids?"

"Third grade. Eight."

"And they all lip-read?"

"They do. You won't have any trouble talking to them."

I thanked her and paid for lunch. Then Dashiell and I walked home to wait for a message telling me that I could use the keys Mel had given me and move into Sophie's apartment for a day or two to see what I could learn.

CHAPTER 10

Find It, I Told Him

There were five messages waiting for me at home. The first was from Chip saying he'd be home around nine and would try to reach me then. He said to call his cell phone if I needed him. He left the number, as if I might have forgotten it. The third message was from Mel saying the police had released the apartment and told him he could take the animals back home. He said he and Bianca would be there about four-thirty, after his last walk. He left his cell phone number for me, too, just in case I needed to reach him before he got to Sophie's.

The other three messages were markedly less friendly. They were all from Sophie's number. They were all hang-ups. Except the last one. On that call, the machine had recorded someone breathing before the call had been disconnected.

I threw some clothes and my toothbrush into my back-pack, put the dogs' food into shopping bags, picked up the leashes, and headed for West Third Street, hoping I'd get the chance to surprise whoever it was who was leaving me those non-messages. That in itself made me walk as fast as Blanche would let me. But two blocks later, I discovered that the simple task of getting from one place to another by foot with a bull terrier was not as easy as it would have been with, say, a golden retriever. Whenever we passed a low wall, a bench, a compact grouping of trash bags, Blanche would choose the high road, climbing on top of things as if she were a mountain goat, Dashiell, a monkey-see, monkey-do kind of guy, following along behind her. I'd been a dog trainer. I could have asked them both to heel. But I didn't. I knew that it was a good thing that Blanche, at least for the moment, was acting like herself.

Even with the delays, we got to Sophie's in fifteen minutes. I unlocked the door and called out into the apartment.

"Is anyone here?"

I was answered only by silence. Whoever had been here was gone. Or they weren't speaking up.

I tried again.

"Is anyone home?"

I unleashed the dogs. If there was someone waiting inside, Dashiell and Blanche would find him. But Blanche just walked slowly around to the far side of the sofa and began to sniff the place where her mistress had fallen and died. As if she was following a chalk outline of her mistress's body, she began to slowly trace the area with her nose.

Dashiell ignored her, heading immediately to the closed door off to the right. He looked back at me and when I nodded, he hit the door with his front paws, shaking the wall. But the catch held. So he took the knob in his mouth and slowly turned his head to the left. I heard the latch retract and let go. This time when he hit the door with his front paws, it flew open and Dashiell disappeared into Sophie's bedroom.

Blanche was still inhaling the fading odor of her beloved mistress when I went after Dashiell to see what had so captured his attention in the next room, but standing in the doorway, all I could see was Dashiell's back. His front paws were up on Sophie's desk, his hind feet were leaving the ground as if he was dancing, his short tail wagging in complete circles. For a moment, I thought he'd found a defrosting steak.

The desk was against the wall, tucked under the sunny windowsill. I looked out the screened, open window into the garden, to see if anyone was there, if it was the anticipation of a chase that had gotten Dashiell so excited. But the garden was empty. And if someone had left suddenly by the window, they had taken the trouble to close the screen before hightailing it out of the yard. Unlikely.

That's when I spotted the cage, large enough to hold a baby gorilla.

I called Dashiell to my side so that I could see what was so interesting, and there, sprawled sideways on top of the combination telephone and answering machine, standing as tall as he could, his tail swishing back and forth, was a miniature prehistoric monster, horny and green, his head and back covered with a crest, making him look like a small but formidable dinosaur. His mouth was open, his dewlap enlarged, and he was hissing. Good move, I thought. If I were at the very bottom of the food chain and facing a large, strange carnivore, I'd do exactly the same thing.

Dashiell whined for the release word that would let him go back to where he'd been. Instead, I rudely shoved him into the living room and closed the door behind him.

The moment Dashiell was out of sight, the iguana

calmed down, turned toward the window, and resumed its sunbath. With the sun pouring in and the desk lamp on, the answering machine might just be the lizard's favorite spot. In fact, standing there, I was willing to bet he'd been there and back several times in the past few days, his face inches from the screen, eyes closed, basking in the sunshine. His front feet, long-toed but with his nails nicely groomed, hung partway over the top of the machine. His back legs kept moving as he adjusted himself on the bumpy surface, trying to get comfortable on all those buttons, his left leg over the one that said reset, the right on the button that said redial.

Sophie had called me once, on Sunday morning. Was it the iguana who'd called repeatedly throughout the night, and again this morning, never bothering to leave a message?

The iguana didn't seem to mind me at all. So I took a step closer and pressed the reset button. Then I pressed redial. Last I hit speakerphone. I heard the machine dialing. I heard the recording of Dashiell barking, then the beep.

So, fine. It was the iguana who had been trying to reach me.

Except for that last call. Because even when I held my breath and tried my damnedest to listen, I couldn't hear any heavy breathing coming from Mr. Lizard.

I took another step forward and rubbed the top of the iguana's head, which felt like small cobblestones, the stuff they paved the Village streets with a hundred or so years ago. He didn't hiss so I guessed he liked it. I rubbed his head some more, until he closed his eyes and wiggled his feet around, dialing my house yet again. Then I picked him up and carried him back to his cage.

There was hardly any water in his bowl and no food. I didn't know what the detectives thought when they found out they hadn't gotten all the pets out of the apartment. But it didn't seem they'd taken care of the pet who'd been left behind. If they had, they would surely have put him back in his cage and found a piece of lettuce for him. Or had they merely closed the bedroom door, thinking that that would be enough to keep the iguana out of trouble? Surely it had been open when Sophie was having the seizure or how else would Bianca have been able to fetch the medicine? But I couldn't remember one way or the other. I could only remember Sophie lying in front of the couch, the dogs lying there with her, one on each side.

I opened the bedroom door and, keeping Dashiell out, slid out into the living room and headed for Sophie's small kitchen, making a big circle around the place she'd fallen, just in front of the couch, got some greens, and, leaving the dogs where they were, slipped back into Sophie's room.

How did Sophie do this? If the iguana freaked when it saw a dog—and why wouldn't it?—how did Sophie juggle these animals? And why had she taken on such a high-maintenance pet when she already had two dogs that needed care?

That's when I remembered the cat she fed on six. Maybe the lizard was also one of those little jobs she took on to help pay Mel for walking Bianca.

As ironic as it seemed, taking care of someone else's animal so that she could pay someone to walk hers, it made sense. It took far less effort to feed an indoor pet than it did to exercise an adolescent bull terrier.

With the iguana fed and safe, I began my search for information by checking the nightstand, feeling both the excitement and the dread I always felt going into someone's home and poking through their things when they weren't there. There's a terrible feeling of trespassing, even when there isn't anyone around to mind.

But if no one was around, who had called me and kept the line open long enough for my answering machine to record the sound of their breathing?

And why?

There was some Tylenol in the nightstand, a small hairbrush with long red hairs tangled in the bristles, a copy of *My Dog Tulip* with a place mark two thirds of the way through. I picked it up, then put it down, reminding myself to pay attention to the job and not get lost in thought. There was a nail file, a small silver ring, a picture of Sophie as a little girl, smiling, a box of tissues.

Most of the snooping I would be doing would be about as interesting as getting stuck in rush-hour traffic. Still, there was some chance I'd get that question answered and all the others as well, a chance that by trying to decipher Sophie's life via the paperwork she'd left behind I'd make some telling discovery. I might find a notation in her calendar, a canceled check, a letter from a former lover, the address of a long-lost relative, something completely unpredictable that would afford me a startling insight, some trivial piece of information that would turn out to be important.

Despite past experience, I had the feeling that there'd be no great finds at Sophie's. The cops had already gone through the place with a fine-tooth comb, removing anything and everything that might have some meaning. They, too, needed to find relatives, though they were more interested in notifying next of kin than in finding a home for two bull terriers. And since the same information I needed would be valuable to them, there might not be a calendar or an address book for me to look at.

But there'd be something, I told myself. There was always something.

Standing on the desk chair, I pulled down shoe boxes

marked with the dates of the last three years from the top of her closet. If the cops had taken her current bank statements and checkbook, last year's tax receipts should give me some of the information I needed. I particularly wanted the name of Sophie's physician, thinking that he or she would be likely to have on record the names and whereabouts of any family members. At least I might be able to get that out of the way.

As I set the boxes on the desk, I thought about my earlier conversation with Ruth, and what she'd said about Sophie promising to get her on the list for a Blanche clone. Had Sophie lied to Ruth? Or had she been less than forthcoming with me about her reason for wanting to locate Side by Side? I wondered if she'd thought that helping her friend get a seizure-alert dog would seem less compelling than the story she'd told me, a tale of altruism, of concern for the greater good. Or if either reason was the truth.

There was a small photo album on the shelf in the closet. I took that down, too, placing it on the desk, next to Sophie's laptop. Working fast now, anxious to see what I'd discover, I opened the computer, turned it on, and listened to it whir. I opened the album and saw pictures of Blanche, Blanche at home, Blanche at school, Blanche at the dog run.

Then curious to see how the iguana would react to Blanche, I opened the bedroom door. I had the impression that iguanas were pretty solitary animals, but when Blanche went over to the cage, stuffed her nose partway between the bars and sneezed, there was no tail swishing, no big fat dewlap showing, and no hissing. The iguana turned to see who was there, then went right back to his salad.

Dashiell seemed happy for now to observe from a distance. He, too, had other things to do. In fact, I thought I ought to encourage that.

"Find it," I told him. "That's my boy."

I waited a moment, listening to the sound of his nose, then sat at the desk and began to open drawers, looking for Sophie's calendar. Next I checked her purse, which was still sitting on the coffee table. Had there been a calendar in it, it was no longer there. No way the police would have left it behind.

I had gone back to the desk to look for medical receipts in Sophie's most recent tax back up when Dashiell barked, signaling a find. I got up and went to see what he had, thinking it would be a pair of socks at the side of the bed or something else he deemed out of place and I'd deem meaningless. Still, we had to try.

It had probably been loose, perhaps a spare that had fallen off the desk and gotten kicked under the bed when the cops were checking out the apartment. It was certainly small enough to miss.

If not for the fact that Chip had one of these things, I probably would not have known what it was, this little dark-gray stick, not more than four inches long, a rounded point on one end, on the other end something that looked like a pen clip but wasn't. But I'd used it, and played with it, practicing the special graffiti you needed to keep your records in this very modern way. The little stick was the stylus of a PalmPilot, an electronic organizer. That meant, if Sophie was as efficient as her desk and her tax records made me think she was, there'd be a backup of everything on her computer.

I gave Dashiell a scratch behind his right ear, told him to continue looking, and turned my attention to Sophie's laptop.

CHAPTER 11

They Met at the Run

At four-thirty the dogs barked. A few moments later I heard a key in the lock.

"I thought you said the cops took your keys."

"They did. But I had another set at home." Ever the little Boy Scout.

"Is that a fact?"

He shrugged. "I didn't know for sure you'd still be here."

"And why didn't you bother to mention the iguana?"

I'm sure my hands were on my hips. Unless I was pointing at him.

"Leslie's here?"

I nodded. He took his jacket off and dropped it over the back of the couch, glancing at the place where Sophie had been the last time we had seen her.

"She belongs to a neighbor."

"He's a she?"

He nodded. "Sophie baby-sits her when Lydia goes down to Florida to visit her mother." He pointed at the ceiling. "One flight up."

One of the people who hadn't answered when I'd knocked.

The back door was open and the dogs were out in the garden, Blanche sitting on one haunch with her legs straight out in front of her watching Dashiell chase Bianca in as big a circle as the yard would allow.

"Was she out? Sophie kept her out a lot. The first time I saw her, she was on the back of the couch. She scared the hell out of me."

"She was on the desk. Dashiell discovered her. *He* wasn't one bit scared, but I sure was."

"I understand. Believe me."

"No. You don't. It was her phone calls."

Mel's forehead wrinkled like an attentive Boxer's.

"She called me about a dozen times, all after Sophie had died."

"What are you talking about?"

"This number kept showing up on my caller ID. It drove me nuts. Then when I came here, I found her on the phone."

"Talking?"

"Nah. And she never once left me a message either. She was resting on the phone. With her foot on the redial button."

He screwed up his face. "Like, wow."

"You can say that again," I told him. I didn't mention the last message.

He looked around and saw my backpack, on the floor and propped against the arm of the sofa.

"Is that yours? You staying over?"

"I am."

"Because of Leslie?"

I nodded.

"But she doesn't have to eat every day."

"Try telling her that. She ate like there was no tomorrow with two dogs in the room."

"Sophie said it was better for her to eat every other day. So if you were going to stay for her, you don't have to."

"Still."

"I can come in and make sure she has water and mist her. If you want me to. I don't care about the money or anything, Rachel. I'll take care of the pets as long as I have to."

"Thanks, but I need to look through Sophie's papers. It's easier to do if I stay over."

"There was this guy, used to wear his iguana, here," he said, tapping his shoulder, "take it to Washington Square Park. He'd sit on a bench and read, with this huge iguana draped around his neck, as if it were reading over his shoulder. Once in a while, if there weren't any dogs around, he'd put the thing down on the grass. He had this harness on it, so it couldn't run away. But it never tried to. It never moved an inch."

"Terrific. So what else did you forget to mention?"

His arms flew up, as if he were about to take off. "What do you mean?"

"Think, Mel. I'm hard up for facts here. In the past twelve months—"

"How did you—"

"I'm a detective."

He looked puzzled. News to him.

"In the past twelve months," I prodded, "you must have heard things, seen things, been told things. You must know things you haven't told me."

"I can't think of what. I mean, I'm sorry about the

iguana, but how was I supposed to know Lydia was away? Anyway, even if Sophie had mentioned it, I was pretty shook up. I've never seen a dead person before. Except in the movies. And they're not really dead, are they?"

"Not usually."

"Oh, I just thought of something. I once took Bianca to the vet."

"And?"

"Well, Sophie had to go to work. She tried never to miss it. The kids, she taught young ones, eight-year-olds, I think, she said they really missed her a lot if she didn't go in. Other teachers, she said, took mental health days. They'd go to the movies. Or Bloomingdale's. But she never did that. And Bianca was coughing. Sophie was afraid it was something serious and she asked me if I'd take Bianca in for a checkup. She offered to pay me extra," he said, "but I wouldn't take it."

"So where'd you take her?"

I'd already gone through the old check registers. There were checks to three different veterinary practices. On all the checks to one of the practices, she'd written "acupuncture." That was probably for Blanche's arthritis. But I didn't know which of the other two vets she'd taken the dogs to for the DNA test.

"Dr. Cohen. Sandra Cohen, on Bleecker Street."

"Was she Sophie's regular vet?"

"She didn't say. I mean, Sophie. Sophie didn't say. She just asked if I could take Bianca there instead of taking her to the run. But I did both. Dr. Cohen said it was no big deal, probably an allergy. So it wouldn't be contagious for the other dogs. So I took her from there to the dog run."

"That's it?"

He nodded. "Except that that was the first time Leslie was here and I wondered if maybe Bianca got sick from her. I heard you can, you know, get pretty sick from iguanas."

Something had been needling away at me ever since I'd seen Leslie sitting on the answering machine.

"Salmonella," I said. "From contact with their feces."

"But Sophie always washed her hands after touching Leslie."

I wiped mine down the sides of my jeans.

"Still," I said, "it wouldn't take much to pick up salmonella from an iguana, especially one that seems to have had the run of the house. She might even have picked it up from the phone. It would be so easy to forget, to grab the phone when it rang, then touch your mouth with that hand before you got to wash it."

"She used an antibacterial soap," Mel said. "I only know that because I cleaned the cage out for Sophie that time she was so sick. That's when she told me to use the soap. She kept it under the sink in the bathroom. But I didn't really need it. I'd used rubber gloves. Then I used the soap anyway. You can never be too careful."

"So what about Sophie's boyfriend? Was he ever here when you came? Or when you brought Bianca back home? Or did she ever mention him, you know, when she was home?"

"I'm the dog walker," he whined. "No one was ever here but Bianca."

"So nothing on the boyfriend? Zip? She never mentioned him? You never met him at the dog run?"

"The dog run?"

"His name is Herbie. They met at the run."

"Herbie?"

I nodded.

"Never met him. Never heard of him. Maybe some dog walkers, it's like they're Dear Abby or something. Me, I'm on a schedule. I always had a special soft spot for Sophie, because of her, you know, problem, and for Bianca, because she didn't have a father. But there were only a couple of times I talked to Sophie, and when someone's sick and scared, they're not going to tell you about their boyfriend."

"Got it."

"Who told you about him?"

"Someone at the school."

He nodded.

"And did they know about Bianca, too?"

"She did."

Mel's eyes fluttered. "I thought Sophie wasn't supposed to tell anyone about the cloning, that it was supposed to be some sort of big secret."

"That's the impression I got. She said this Lorna West person had said it was so top secret that she had to lie when she called The School for the Deaf instead of telling them what she really wanted."

Then I thought about what Ruth had told me, that the whole thing was a fabrication, that there had never been such a phone call. I looked at Mel, who was watching the dogs playing in the yard. He didn't ask anything about Lorna's story, so I didn't volunteer any details. Maybe he didn't need to ask. Sophie might have told him everything she told me. She didn't seem to be very good in the keeping-her-mouth-shut department. On the other hand, if she really spread it around, she'd only have people thinking she was nuts, laughing at her the way one of her veterinarians had.

"You okay here?" Mel asked. "I'd be too spooked to stay."

"I'm okay. There's nothing here to hurt me."

He nodded. But I could tell he didn't agree.

"If you're finished grilling me, I better get home and walk Margaret."

"Sorry," I said. "But I have to—"

He flapped his hand at me.

"I know you're only doing your job, Rachel. And that it's not fun. But you are a little intense. After all, it's not like you have a client anymore."

He slipped on his jacket and picked up Bianca's leash.

"You don't have to take her."

"I don't mind. Really I don't."

I shook my head. "And you don't have to walk her tomorrow. I have to take her somewhere with me."

"Where?"

"I'll call you tomorrow night, about Thursday's walk."

He stood there staring for a moment. "You're sure?"

I nodded.

"But, Mel . . ."

"Yeah?"

"Keep thinking. You might know more than you realize. Any detail, no matter how small, let me know."

He walked out into the yard and called Bianca over to him. Then he bent down and scratched behind her big ears. Bianca sat there, where she'd been with Mel, watching him leave.

I wondered if he'd take her permanently, if there was no one else. Then I looked over at Blanche, and suddenly, the core of sadness about Sophie's death became the fate of her animals, where they'd end up, whether or not they could stay together and if there would be someone to love them as much as Sophie had.

CHAPTER 12

I Went Quickly into the Garden

After calling Chip's pager and punching in Sophie's number, I decided to feed the dogs before settling down to do more work. I took out the list with Blanche's diet on it and stuck it onto the side of Sophie's fridge with a little magnet of a bull terrier she had there. Before getting started, I looked at the other stuff stuck onto the refrigerator, dog cartoons, photos of the dogs, a snapshot of a guy, late thirties, curly hair, nice eyes.

Was that the ex, Herbie?

I studied the photo but didn't take it down to take a closer look because there were three hungry dogs waiting to be fed. Instead, checking the list, I began to pull things out of the refrigerator, adding extra for Dashiell, then on second thought, for me. Of course, I wouldn't eat *everything* I was feeding the dogs. But the chopped raw vegetables would be a better dinner than my usual catch-as-catch-can way of eating. Going back to the gym, to strengthen the arm that had gotten broken on my last case, had made me reassess the poor way I took care of myself, almost always too busy to do it properly. But it wasn't only my trainer who got after me about the way I ate. Dr. Chen had some ideas on that, too, that I eat ginger to warm my insides, that I eat more yang and less yin. Or was it the other way around?

I began to scrub the carrots, twisting off the tops and washing them, too, to chop and add to the dogs' portion. I tried to remember if carrots were yin or yang. I'd have to ask Dr. Chen when I saw him the next week.

Bianca had come in and was sitting and watching me prepare her dinner, her head cocked to one side, her legs straight out in front of her, a comical way for a dog to sit. I looked beyond her and saw Blanche and Dashiell, sleeping side by side on the Persian rug, that little black smudge at the corner of Blanche's closed right eye. And then I looked back at Bianca again, at how sad she seemed, even watching me make her dinner, the black spot looking like a tear now, thinking that one day soon, both dogs would forget Sophie, but those little black tears would be there forever.

She was such a swell pup, healthy looking, full of beans, friendly. Why were people so freaked out by cloning? Why was I?

I shut off the Cuisinart and pulled out my cell phone, dialing a number I hadn't called in months.

"It's me, Rachel," I said, startled that he'd answered because he hardly ever did, thinking I'd have to leave a message and wait for him to call me back, a call that might not ever come. I told him about the case. He listened without interrupting.

"About the cloning," I started to say. But then I stopped. What exactly did I want to ask him? "Do you think any good will come of it?"

"Yes. And no."

"You mean it'll be good and bad? Oh, I see what you mean, that the cloning of animals, that's okay, or at least sometimes it's okay, depending upon the reason, the motive, for the cloning, right? That if the cloning is meant to provide medication, or more food, or organs for transplantation, that would be okay, a positive use of knowledge, but if someone was spending millions of dollars to get a duplicate of their pet, then that's just some ridiculous paean to narcissism."

"You think too much," he said.

"What do you mean?"

"No use spinning your wheels, Rachel. Good or bad, it's inevitable."

I waited for more, but there was no more.

I meant to tell him I'd try to get over and see him soon, an empty promise that made me hesitate, and as I did, I heard the click, and then the dial tone.

I looked up Ruth's home number and dialed it next.

"It's me, Rachel," I said. Again. "Can I meet you tomorrow, after school? I'd like to see if any of Sophie's students—"

"I thought you were going to wait a few days."

"I thought so, too," I told her. "I'm at the apartment now. At Sophie's. And I see her rent was paid on the twentieth of the month, not the first. So I don't have as much time as I thought I did. Unless I want to pay the rent, these animals, and all Sophie's stuff, are going to have to be out of here in a week. I don't know that I could do that legally even if I wanted to."

"Do what?"

"Pay her rent."

"How come?"

"I'm not a relative. And once this place becomes vacant,

the rent will go up. So why would they want to delay that? Anyway, can you meet me? I'm hoping that she talked to the kids about her family. So far, I haven't found anything here that would lead me in that direction."

"They get out at three. I can meet you out front."

"I'll be there. And Ruth, I'm bringing Bianca."

"Why Bianca and not Blanche?"

"Because I want to attract them over to us with a dog that looks like the one they saw every day, but I don't want to shock them. I think bringing Blanche might do that."

"I don't know. Whatever you think."

"And one more thing . . ."

"Yes?"

"There's a photograph on the refrigerator door, a picture of a nice-looking young man, thirtyish, curly hair, nice eyes." Holding the phone in place by hiking up one shoulder, I used both hands to slide the snapshot out from under the little magnetized bone that held it to the fridge.

"It must be Herbie."

I turned it over, then turned it back, waiting for Ruth to continue.

"We were talking on the phone one time while she was seeing him and she said she liked to look at him while she got the dogs' food ready. That's so sad, isn't it?"

"That she liked to look at his picture while she made the dogs' dinner?"

His name was printed neatly on the back of the snapshot Herbie. That's all. No last name.

"No. That she kept it there, even after they broke up. I guess you can't stay mad forever."

"Was Sophie mad at him?"

There was a long pause.

"I assumed so. She never actually said."

"Maybe she just forgot that the picture was there."

She didn't say anything.

"I don't believe that either," I said.

"I'll see you tomorrow, Rachel. Right out front." Getting off the phone before she started to cry.

I put the picture on the far end of the counter and started feeding vegetables into the Cuisinart, grinding them to a pulp, then doing the quiet work, mixing in the cod-liver oil and yogurt for the dogs, making salad dressing for myself, lost in thought about cloning until my cell phone rang, startling all of us. Dashiell woke up barking and the two bullies, unfamiliar with the sound, ran to the front door.

"Where were you?" he said.

"I'm at Sophie's."

"I figured that part out, but this is the third time I'm calling."

"I didn't hear the phone. The Cuisinart was on. Listen, Chip, can you tell me the names of the veterinarians who were making all those cloning jokes? I have Sophie's checks and it seems she used three practices. I'd like to know if any of her vets were at the convention, particularly if the one who did the DNA test for the bullies was there, and if he or she was the one who started the talk about cloning."

"It would be easier if you told me the three names you have. We had twelve at our table. I don't know that I could rattle off all the names, but if you hit one, I think I'd remember it."

"Sandra Cohen."

"Yes. Sandy Cohen. She was there. But she seemed much more interested in neutering than in cloning. Not much sense of humor either."

"Okay, hang on, I have my list on Sophie's desk." I could hear him talking to Betty as I went for the list. "How about Mark Murray?"

"Yes. Big guy. Not too talkative. Rather grumpy look-ing, but smart. When he spoke, it was worth listening. He came to my talk. Of course, that made me like him, too."

"What about Cohen?"

"Didn't come. More points against her."

"And Chad Finkelstein, if you believe that for a name."

"Hey, I went to grade school with a Montgomery Rosenberg. I'll believe anything. And yes, he was there, too. He's short, fat, bald, chatty, thinks he's funnier than he actually is, and he's got sweaty hands. But, boy, did he go for Betty. Said he had a Shepherd when he was a kid and he's loved them ever since."

"Did he ask if he could clone her?"

"Actually, no one would have asked that once the jokes got going. It's not a popular idea."

"So I hear."

"People are afraid of anything new. And with this, the consensus of opinion was that it was stepping on God's toes, which makes a strange assumption right there, in my humble opinion."

"Well, don't they always picture Him in sandals?"

"You got me there."

"So, you were at the New York Jewish table, or what?"

"Actually, Chad wasn't at the table. He came to the talk and stayed afterward, to commune with Betty. He got down on the floor with her, and pressed his head against hers. He called it mind melding. He said there's nothing like a German shepherd for it."

"Mind melding?"

"ESP. He said his Shepherd used to tell him things that way."

"And Betty let him do it?"

"To my total surprise, she did. In fact, she seemed to like it. Or maybe she just liked him. Their admiration was quite mutual. Before he left, he gave me his home number, in case, he said, I decided to breed Betty. He thinks she's aces and he'd like a pup."

"He said 'breed'? So he wasn't the one who started the cloning jokes?"

"I can't say. They apparently started when I was teaching at the shelter, before I ever got to the hotel."

"And he wasn't at your table when the jokes were being made?"

"No."

"What about the others, Cohen and Murray? Where were they on all this?"

"Let me think. After a lot of clone jokes, Cohen said she thought it was okay for farm animals, but that if pet owners ever tried it, they'd be disappointed."

"No news there."

"Murray just stuck with the jokes."

"The cops were telling them, too. Really b-a-a-ad ones."

"It makes people nervous, Rachel. Even veterinarians and the police."

"But Bianca is a perfectly lovely dog. She's not a monster."

"So have you found out what the deal was yet?"

"I've got a lot more to do. I'm staying here. I'll work as late as I can so that I only have to stay a night or two."

"Be careful, will you?"

"I've got an attack-trained pit bull with me."

"Seriously, Rachel."

"I am serious."

The line was open. He was waiting.

I sighed.

"I promise."

When I walked back to the kitchen, they were all waiting there with accusing looks on their faces. I finished the food, added all the supplements, and fed them. Then I took my salad out into the garden, passing my own reflection in the dark glass, thinking for just a moment that someone was out there.

Sophie had described the place to me, her paradise. Sitting on a stone bench that was set close to the side wall, I looked around. The ivy-covered brick wall extended from the house to my left to about the middle of the garden, where it abutted a small, stucco back cottage that served as the other half of the fence, separating Sophie's yard from the one beyond it, the one belonging to the house on West Fourth Street. The wall behind me was concrete.

The building next door had a two-story extension built behind it, so instead of a garden, there was an extra back room on the two lower floors. Because of that, this area of the yard would be shady much of the day. All around me, there was pachysandra, with a row of hosta along the path. The other side of the yard must have gotten sun in the afternoon because there Sophie had planted flowers—fairy roses, hydrangia, day lilies—though in a month or so, when the cold weather arrived, they'd be gone. At least the ivy and pachysandra would stay green.

But that would be for someone else's pleasure. Sophie wasn't here any longer and her pets would be lucky to have homes, even ones without yards.

The fence across from where I sat was wooden and old. I could see where slats had been broken and repaired in several places. In front of the fence, the flowers were planted in raised beds. It seems Sophie had pretty much taught the dogs to keep off that area, because very few of the flowers were trampled or broken. Perhaps they'd only gone up there occasionally to retrieve a ball that had bounced out of bounds.

That's when I heard the music, a piano concerto. Someone had just put on a CD or the radio, someone whose window was open. I looked around but couldn't tell where it was coming from. In New York, where buildings are so close and so tall, sound can bounce around the flat surfaces, seeming to come from one when in fact it's coming from the opposite direction. The music was so beautiful I felt swept away, closing my eyes and just listening.

When the music stopped, I finished eating and went back to the computer, checking Sophie's address book and calendar, looking for anyone with the same last name, looking to see when it was she'd been seeing Herbie and if I could find his last name and number in the backup of her addresses. The trouble with an electronic calendar, though, was that instead of crossing out a name, which often left it readable, on the PalmPilot you could delete anyone who was no longer in your life, an old boyfriend, even a relative you no longer got along with. And the next time you used the HotSync function, the name might be erased on your hard drive, too, unless you set up your system to archive the information you deleted on the PalmPilot itself. But since the police had that, this wasn't something I'd be able to check.

I decided to check Sophie's E-mail first, but there were no saved messages. Even more curious, there was no E-mail address book. There was a list of favorite web sites she'd saved for quick, repeated access, and there I found the site of the Epilepsy Foundation. Spending the next hour or so there, I noticed some interesting things. First, I discovered that I probably would not find a wine cellar in the apartment. Epileptics could not safely consume alcohol. Next I checked the long list of anticonvulsants and discovered they all had one side effect in common. They were all teratogenic, whatever the hell that meant. I made a note to drop in to a pharmacy and find out. There was, to my surprise, only a paragraph about seizure-alert dogs. It was a warning, actually. It said that this ability had only been reported anecdotally and that patients should exercise extreme caution in dealing with any school that offered to supply or train a dog who could predict the onset of a seizure. Someone was getting hives at the thought of something so profound working when it couldn't be scientifically tested.

There wasn't anyone in Sophie's backup address book with the last name of Gordon. Nor was there an Aunt Beth or an Uncle Craig. There wasn't anyone with the first name of Herbie, either, or anyone with the first initial *h*. She'd apparently expunged the bum. But kept his photo on the refrigerator.

While I was checking things out and making notes in my old-fashioned, paper notepad, I could hear dogs' nails clicking in the other room. I stopped and listened. For a moment, I thought Bianca and Dashiell might be wrestling again, or chasing each other. But it was only one dog walking around. When Dashiell barked, I thought someone might be at the door. But as soon as I walked out into the living room, I realized he'd gone back to his search.

He was sitting next to the couch, totally pleased with himself. When he saw I'd come, he barked once more. I pulled the coffee table back and knelt, close to where Sophie had fallen. There, under the sofa, was a pair of red slipper socks.

"Good boy," I told him, reaching under and taking them out. "Excellent boy. Go find."

Back at the computer, I sat still for a moment, just listening. When Dashiell crossed one of the rugs, there'd be silence. Then I'd hear the comforting click of his nails again. The sound changed when he was in the kitchen, on the terra-cotta tile. I heard him drinking from the water bowl, his tags clanging against the pan, then the tick-tick of his nails resumed, and trusting him to do his job, I went back to mine.

The bedroom blinds were open and, though I hadn't switched on the garden lights, they were on. Perhaps there was one of those sensors that turned on the lights automatically when it got dark. I left the blinds open, looking out every once in a while at the shadows of the bushes against the wall of the little cottage. The one small window, on the upper floor, was dark. I thought that perhaps whoever lived in the town house beyond used the cottage as a studio, an office, or even a guest house. Or else whoever lived there wasn't home.

Before I had the chance to do much more, Dashiell barked again, one woof, summoning me to hurry up and see what he'd found.

He had nosed open the hall closet and there on the floor, in between the snow boots and a pair of sneakers, was a set of keys.

I bent to scratch Dashiell's neck with one hand and scoop up the keys with my other. Turning the keys over in my hand, they looked familiar. I opened Sophie's door and tried the keys. Why would a set of keys to her apartment be on the floor of the closet?

When I turned, I had my answer. There was Bianca, her tail wagging furiously. I tossed the keys over to the rug, and she scrambled on the wooden hall floor to go and retrieve them, bringing them back, dropping them at my feet and waiting for another toss. Good for Sophie, I thought, playing with more than just a ball. But, still, using live keys seemed strange to me. It wasn't as if she couldn't pick them up if she dropped them, as if she'd been in a wheelchair. When she couldn't function, it seemed to me, the only thing she needed was her pills. Perhaps this was Herbie's set, returned to Sophie when they broke up. That made sense. That could explain why she'd given them to Bianca to use as a toy, why she'd turned something unhappy into something cheerful.

I gave Bianca one more toss, then put the keys on top of the bookshelf outside the small kitchen, stopping for a moment to look at Sophie's cookbooks, thinking how sad it was, all that organic food, all those healthy meals, and she had died so young anyway. It wasn't as simple as eat this, don't eat that, exercise, take your vitamins. There were genes involved, what you got along with the fiery red hair and the porcelain skin, what booby traps lay hidden, waiting for the right circumstances—inordinate stress, the deterioration of age, an inopportune infection, and God only knows what else. And there was luck involved as well, whether yours was good or not so good. Sophie's, apparently, had been not so good.

Reading some of the material posted on the epilepsy site, I'd learned that the disease was sometimes caused by trauma, not genetics—a deprivation of oxygen during birth, head injury, physical abuse, a car accident. But just as many cases were considered idiopathic, meaning no one knew what had caused them. Either way, lousy luck. I hadn't asked Sophie her history and she hadn't volunteered it. It wasn't the point of our first conversation, and, unfortunately, there wouldn't be future ones in which she could add to what she'd told me.

Back at the desk, looking at the screen, my eyes felt really tired. So, leaving the laptop on, I began to poke through the desk drawers, finding a folder for the dogs, with printouts from their veterinary visits. Bingo. I had in my sweaty little hand the receipt for the DNA test. It had been done at Mark Murray's office. Finkelstein, the vet with sweaty hands, was either an acupuncturist or had one at his office. That's where Blanche had gone off and on for the last eight months. Dr. Cohen must have been the dogs' regular vet, which made sense, since her office was the closest to where Sophie lived.

I looked through the rest of the file, photos of both dogs, apart and together. If not for the fact that Sophie had printed the name of the dog on the back of each picture, I wouldn't be sure who was who. Of course, in the full-body shots you could tell. Blanche was heftier. Bianca still had the narrow body of an adolescent. But in those Norma Desmond close-ups, Blanche and Bianca could not have looked more alike.

I went back into the living room. Dashiell had gone out and was searching the garden now, my little workaholic. But it was the bullies I'd come to see. They were asleep on the rug, leaning against each other. When I crouched down, Blanche opened her sleepy eyes, thumped her tail once, then went immediately back to sleep. Bianca's legs were twitching, her eyes moving rapidly under closed lids. I looked at the black smudge on each dog, the pink strip along the crest of their noses, the one dark freckle near the leather of their noses, slightly left of center, then their feet. Both dogs had clear toenails on their front paws, except for the left-outside toe. Those were black.

I wondered what the chances were of finding two dogs so identical in appearance.

Big deal, Chip would say, it wouldn't be difficult to find a dozen dogs whose nails looked just like that.

Still, I would have said.

Because I couldn't find anything on either dog that didn't match the other exactly.

And while I was looking, because I would have been as happy as anyone else to believe that Blanche had not been cloned, Dashiell barked again.

I went quickly into the garden, hoping to get to him before he woke the neighbors. It was late, and most of the windows I could see from the garden were dark now. He was at the wooden fence, standing in the flowers, standing right in the place where the flowers were bent. I called him back and went to investigate, seeing nothing on the ground, even parting the flowers with my hands to try to find what he had. When I turned and shrugged, he barked again, his front paws coming off the ground, his ears rising and, this time, only one folding down again.

"Come and show me," I said.

And he did.

He bounded up into the raised bed and hit the repaired slats behind me with his nose. I heard the wood creak as the new boards scraped against the older part of the fence, and suddenly, I could see into the garden next door.

"Good *boy.*"

I pushed the slats myself, seeing that the opening would be big enough for a person to come and go, assuming the person was crouched and duck-walked through the opening. Obviously, someone had done just that, because this was the only place where the flowers had been stepped on.

But what did it mean? If Sophie had died of a fatal seizure, what difference could it possibly make if there was an opening in the fence between her garden and the one next door?

CHAPTER 13

Stop Right Where You Are, I Said

I went back inside and was about to put away the dogs' file when I remembered something. So I took everything out of the folder, reading each item, then putting it back, one at a time. I found what I was looking for in the middle of a pile of notes, little slips of paper that looked like the ones I had in Dashiell's file, things jotted down in a hurry, sometimes abbreviated, while on the phone with the veterinarian. I held the slip of paper in my hand and looked at it. It was the list of Bianca's shots. I wondered if Lorna had copied them down from the puppies' file at Side by Side. Or if the vet who'd given the shots to Bianca and the other two clones had written it. With ragged edges, even the beginning of one of the words missing, it had obviously been torn from a larger piece of paper. When I held it under the light and looked more closely, I saw part of a line at the upper right and again in the lower right-hand corner, lines designating where to write the patient's name and where the doctor should sign his own. The list had been written on a prescription pad. Then the parts with pertinent information had been torn away.

I slipped the note into my wallet, which was in the pocket of my backpack, in the other room.

I hadn't brought my things into the bedroom because I didn't plan on sleeping in Sophie's bed. It was a double and the sheets looked clean. Maybe she'd changed them that last day. There was a light quilt on the bed, a patchwork design with lots of blue in it. The sheets were blue, too, a color my mother used to call "sailor blue." I was tired and the bed would have looked mighty inviting were the circumstances different. But they weren't.

Leslie was draped over a branch in her cage. I thought about taking her out; instead, I went into Sophie's bathroom to check out what was under the sink. Just as Mel had told me, there was antibacterial soap there. And a box of disposable rubber gloves right next to it. Still, I thought I'd call Marty Shapiro, my cop friend, and mention to him that there was a lizard in the house, and see if he wanted to mention that, and the issue of salmonella, to the detectives handling the case. I could have called Burns or Burke myself. But I wasn't in the mood for any more cloning jokes.

Is that ewe? they might have said.

Or, We were hoping you'd stop baaaa.

I looked at the rest of the dog file before putting it away, thinking that if Sophie had made any sort of arrangements for the dogs, there might be a note to that effect in this file. But nothing was there other than their medical records, some photos, and the original of the letter from the New York City Department of Health, registering Blanche as a service dog. Sophie probably carried a copy with her.

I looked at the shoe boxes with three years' worth of tax

backup. I was tired, and it was late, but I told myself I could manage one more hour. I carried all three boxes out to the coffee table, sat on the couch, and began to look through the envelopes. It wasn't as daunting as I'd thought it would be. I didn't have to open all of the envelopes. And since Sophie was salaried, not a freelancer, she didn't have nearly the number of receipts saved that I did.

I was able to find the name of her doctor, Tanya Maas. Her address and phone number would probably be in the PalmPilot backup on the computer. I found no canceled checks made out to Side by Side, or to Lorna West, or to the Horatio Street Veterinary Practice. So it seemed that most of what Sophie had told me had been true.

Had there been a check written to Herbie, I could have learned his last name. But there weren't any. All I could do was take his picture to the dog run and ask around. Beyond that, I was out of ideas.

I worked on the tax backup for about an hour and then I was really too tired to do any more. I made a list of what I had to do in the morning, found Dr. Maas's phone number, took the dogs out for a walk around the block, then got ready for bed. There was an extra blanket on the shelf in the bedroom closet and I took one of the pillows from Sophie's bed. When everything was ready, I noticed that there were no curtains in the living room, but I still didn't want to sleep in the bedroom. I can't really explain it. At first, it just felt intrusive. Then I thought it might be too confusing for her dogs. Finally, it was fear that kept me out of Sophie's bed, the fear that by sleeping there, I could somehow take on her fate.

Whatever it was, I couldn't talk myself into changing my mind. So I shut off the living room light and changed in the dark. Then I lifted the blanket and slipped underneath it, but not faster than Blanche. She burrowed down to the part of the couch where my feet would have gone had she not been there. Bianca lay on the floor, her back up against the couch. Dashiell waited until I was lying down. Then he lifted the blanket with his nose, squeezed onto the couch, and turned around so that I could lie against his warm back, both of us facing the garden, which mysteriously had gotten dark, too. Did that sensor shut off the lights when Sophie's lights went out?

But I didn't have the chance to come up with an answer. My eyes were suddenly attracted up to the single small window in the side of the back cottage that faced Sophie's apartment. Apparently, whoever lived there had just come home, because behind the curtain of the little window, which had been dark all evening, there was now light.

I felt Blanche slip out from under the blanket and a moment later heard the sound of her nails on the wooden floor. I could see her white form, moving slowly, like a ghost, as she walked toward Sophie's bedroom. The door had swung shut, but the lock hadn't clicked. She pushed the door with her great nose and disappeared behind it. I heard the bottom of the iguana cage creak, thinking Leslie must have turned around to see who was there. I heard the bed moan as Blanche went to sleep where she belonged, in her mistress's bed. I hugged Dashiell tighter, and fell immediately asleep.

It was the sound of the tumbler turning over that woke me. Or was it the dogs? Dashiell was missing and had pulled the cover half off me when he'd left. Bianca was gone, too.

I sat up, my eyes adjusting to the dark.

Dashiell barked, Bianca backing him up.

I crawled over to the foot of the couch, which gave me a view of the dark hallway, then a slice of light as the door to Sophie's apartment opened.

With only the dim light coming from the hall behind him, I couldn't see his face. But I could see that he was short and wide, nearly as wide as the doorway it seemed.

"Stop right where you are," I said.

"Who's here?"

"Who are you?"

He stayed where he was, neither dog moving away to let him in.

"It's Joe, the super."

"What the hell are you doing here in the middle of the night?"

"The lights was out," he said.

I squinted at my watch.

"It's three in the fucking morning. Of course the lights are out. I'm trying to sleep."

"Well, who the hell are you?"

"A friend. I'm a friend of Sophie's. I'm staying here to take care of her dogs."

"Why didn't you say so in the first place?"

But before I had the chance to answer, he'd slammed the door and locked it. I sat on the couch in the dark, a dog on either side of me, for a long time, the blanket wrapped around me like a cocoon. The window on the second floor of the back cottage was dark again, but the moon was shining into the garden. I hadn't noticed that earlier. There might have been cloud cover then.

Suddenly, Dash and Bianca were at the garden door, whining, hackles up, tails as stiff as if they'd been starched. I jumped up to see what it was this time.

He was standing up on his haunches, nearly as big as a cat, his dark, beady eyes looking straight at us, then he took off in the direction of that back brick wall and disappeared. The last thing I could see was his long, hairless tail.

I went back to the couch to wait for morning.

CHAPTER 14

Are You a Cop? She Asked

The doorbell woke me. Dashiell barked but the bullies merely wagged their tails, pushing him out of the way so that they could greet the visitor first.

"Is Sophie here?" she asked, a woman of about sixty with a long gray braid, a long Indian-style dress with a sweater over it, Birkenstocks with socks on her long narrow feet. "I've come for . . ." She stopped and stared. Perhaps it was the fact that I'd thrown Sophie's raincoat over my T-shirt and underpants before answering the door.

"For Leslie?"

"Yes. I promised Sophie I'd come early, before she had to leave for school."

She looked confused, and who could blame her. She didn't know who the hell I was or why I was standing there. She didn't know where Sophie was. Now I was going to have to tell her. I opened my mouth but she beat me to it.

"Something's wrong. Is it Leslie?"

"No," I said, "it's Sophie. You better come in."

I offered her tea, which she refused, but after I told her what had happened, she changed her mind.

"Green tea, please." She was pointing. "The second canister, the blue one."

I put on the kettle. She went to get Leslie. I could hear her talking to the iguana the moment the bedroom door was open.

"Thank you for taking care of her." She stood in the doorway of the kitchen with Leslie on her shoulder, her nails poking through the stitches of the sweater. "Let it steep," she said.

I looked up.

"The tea. And I take it with a spoon of honey in it."

We sat on the couch. Leslie walked onto the back pillows and stretched out. Looking into her eyes for the first time, I understood there was an intelligent being in there and I remembered the time I'd gotten past my fear and peered into the eyes of a snake and felt the same way. Lydia sipped her green tea, then reached into her pocket and pulled out a strawberry, biting off a little piece and offering it to Leslie from her hand.

"Sad thing."

I nodded.

"She was a nice girl. Very sweet. Hardworking. Independent." She shook her head. "The nicest ones always go."

"Lydia, did Sophie ever mention any family to you? I'm concerned about the dogs, about who might take them now that Sophie's gone."

"Family? Oh, I don't think so. 'Lydia,' she used to say, 'you make me happy I'm an orphan.' But she didn't mean that. She only said it because Mother is so difficult and she was thinking she was lucky she didn't have to fly down to Florida every three weeks to get berated by some old bat from the moment she got off the plane until the moment she got back on. 'Sure, run back to Leslie,' she shouted as I was leaving. 'You love that lizard more than you've ever loved me.' Mother still drives, though I doubt you'd want to be on the road when she's doing it, the stubborn old goat. She's ninety-three. Still strong enough to push me around, too. I said, 'Mother, there are wonderful facilities where you wouldn't have to lift a finger.' 'What am I, a cripple?' she said. 'All of a sudden I can't shop and cook?' "

Lydia bit off another piece of strawberry for Leslie.

"Oh, I'm sorry, Rachel, it's just that—"

"Please don't apologize. I understand. So there was no family that—"

"What should I do with the money?"

"The money?"

She reached into a pocket and took out some bills. "Sophie's. Yours. For taking care of Leslie."

I shook my head. "Just forget it, okay? But, Lydia, I could use your help. If you could take a minute or so to think back about conversations you had with Sophie over tea. Did she ever mention anyone who might take the animals if . . ."

She shook her head. "Not to me."

When it was time to go, Leslie walked onto Lydia's shoulder and got her footing, reminding me for just a second of the way my father used to ride me to bed when I was little. I asked Lydia if she needed any of the veggies from Sophie's refrigerator, but she waved a hand at me.

"We're fine. I have all her favorites," she said.

Following her, Leslie watching, I carried the cage upstairs.

"Lydia, the super came in last night—in the middle of the night. I was wondering . . ."

"He was always worrying about her, about Sophie, because, you know, her condition, it made people feel protective of her."

"But he had to know she was dead."

"Well, maybe he saw the light and didn't know who was there. Maybe he thought someone was messing with her stuff, or with the animals."

"Did she ever talk to you about the young man she was seeing?"

"Shame about that."

"What was?"

"The way it ended."

"And how was that?" I asked.

"Suddenly."

"Do you . . . ?"

She shook her head. "I was with Mother. When I came back to pick up my Leslie, she was crying. She said Herbie had left. He left. That's all she said."

"And you didn't ask?"

"I never pry."

"I understand. Unfortunately, I have to, otherwise these animals will be without a home."

"It's nice you're doing that. Are you from the school?"

"I'm a friend from the dog run," I said.

"So you knew him, Herbie?"

"No. We were never there at the same time. Did you?"

"Did I what?"

"Ever meet Herbie?"

"No, no, no. I don't go to the dog run."

"I meant here."

"Why would they want an old lady around when they had each other?"

"One more thing, Lydia. Was Sophie afraid of anything that you know of, something she might have mentioned to you?"

"Yeah."

"What was that?"

"Dying," She put the iguana on the table and put the rest of the strawberry in front of her. "Same as all of us."

I waited a moment, just standing there, then I gave her my card and asked her to call if she thought of anything else. "You will," I told her. "I'm sure of it."

I went back downstairs, got dressed, and headed for the dog run with all three dogs in tow; the moment we were settled, Bianca and Dash running in great circles and Blanche curled up next to me on the bench, I dialed the Bomb Squad's direct line.

My friend Marty worked with the bomb dogs, work most people found terrifying, work he claimed was much safer than being on the street in a uniform waiting for some fourteen-year-old with a gun to send you to your maker just to see what it felt like.

"Marty, it's Rachel. It's about the Gordon case. There's something I thought—"

"That was *you?*"

"What do you mean?"

"Burke and Burns have been, oh, never mind. I should have known. Rachel, don't tell me you actually believe the younger bully was cloned from the older one?"

"What do you think I think?"

The cloned bull terrier was on the other end of the run, being chased by Dashiell and three other lustful males.

"That's better. If I knew it was you they were talking about, I would have told them, 'Hey, guys, forget about it. She's just pulling your leg,' So, what's up?"

"The apartment was released yesterday, Marty, and I

took the dogs there. I wanted to look through her stuff, to see if she'd made any kind of arrangements for them."

"Find anything?"

"Not yet. But there was another pet in the apartment."

"The iguana?"

"You know about that?"

"You'd think, with what those guys see, well, what's the big deal, Godzilla's in the bedroom."

"Marty, she's only fifteen or sixteen inches long."

"It figures."

"Luckily, the neighbor who owns her came to pick her up this morning. I thought I was going to have to find a home for her, too, but Sophie was just baby-sitting the iguana to pick up a little extra money."

"Which neighbor?"

"One flight up. Look, Marty, the reason I called, you can get a pretty nasty case of salmonella from an iguana, sometimes even fatal. It probably wasn't that. I mean, I'd seen her earlier that day and she didn't look sick. Still, I thought maybe someone should mention this to the ME, but I didn't want to call Burns or Burke directly because—"

"Gotcha. I'll walk this in to them, let them take it from there."

"Thanks, Marty. Like I said, it's probably nothing, but I figured it's better to call than not."

I called Dr. Maas's number, got a machine, and left a message, though I doubted the doctor would call me back. I'd have to try again, and again.

There were eleven people in the run, not counting me. I had Herbie's picture in my pocket, but before showing it around, I wanted to see for myself if any of these people were a match. To be sitting here now, you'd have to be unemployed or have unconventional work hours, not a nine-to-five. Coming with Dashiell during the day, I'd met artists, writers, and would-be actors who had jobs waiting tables at local restaurants later on in the day. There were seven women sitting around the periphery of the run, and four men. But no Herbie.

One of the guys was Asian. I'd seen him come in right after me, with a little sesame Shiba Inu. One of the guys was black. He had been here when I arrived and I didn't know which dog was his. There was an old guy with his coat buttoned wrong, wearing a knit hat. He kept running over to his dog, a small, white mixed breed and telling her she was doing something wrong, like the nervous parents at the playground on the opposite side of the park. The fourth guy seemed a little overdressed for the run. He might have been a lawyer or a stockbroker, taking his dog for exercise before going in to the office. His hair was gray at the temples, neatly combed, and he'd had a shave before coming. Not so for the guy with the hat, gray stubble all over his face. He probably hadn't brushed his teeth either. And lucky me, I was about to find out.

He shook his head when I showed him the picture.

"Never seen him."

"You're sure?"

"What are you, deaf, lady? I said I never seen him. Not here. Not there," pointing toward the small brick buildings to the south of the run that housed the bathrooms, "not anywhere."

"You're here every day?"

"Twice a day," he said. Then he was off. "Phoebe, Phoebe, none of that now. You're making a scene."

There was a pregnant woman reading on the next bench.

"Are you a cop?" she asked when I showed her the picture.

I shook my head.

"Then what's it your business if I know him or not?"

You've got to love this city.

"Look," I said, "I'm a friend of his ex-girlfriend, who just died and—"

"Like I need to buy into this stress?"

The two older women talking to each other on the next bench both peered at the picture and shook their heads. They went back to their conversation while I was still there, the picture of Herbie extended toward them.

The Asian guy took his Shiba and left before I got to him. The black guy was hooking up his dog when I showed him the photo. He shrugged, then opened the gate to go, couldn't care less who the dude in the picture was or why I was so anxious to find him.

A boy of about ten, without a dog, came in as the black guy went out. One of the women got up and asked him what he wanted. For safety's sake, kids weren't supposed to be in the run without their parents. I saw her hand land on his shoulder as she steered him back toward the double gates.

"That's good," she said when he hung over the fence to watch from the outside. "Much safer there."

I walked over to the well-groomed man, looking down to see all the dust that now covered his polished shoes.

"I'm trying to find this guy," I said, showing him the picture, "and I was told he comes here with his dog."

He took the picture and studied it, even pulled a pair of reading glasses out of his inside jacket pocket so that he could get a better look. Then he smiled, shook his head, and handed back the photo.

At the next bench, I was forced to interrupt a young, pretty blond whose head was tilted back so that she could get some sun. New Yorkers, always trying to do at least two things at a time. I held the picture out, but her cell phone rang. She took the picture from me and slipped the phone out of her pocket.

"Do you know this man, by any chance?" I asked.

She answered the phone and almost immediately started laughing. "No, no, I'm not doing anything," she said. "Saturday? Sure. That sounds great. Me, too."

Then she covered the mouthpiece with the hand holding Herbie's picture. "Ex*cuse* me. This is important."

She turned her back to me and continued her conversation. I had to walk around her to get the photo back. She'd never looked at it, and I had no reason to think she ever would.

That was as close as I got. I went back to sit with Blanche, making sure that Dashiell and Bianca weren't getting into any trouble. Blanche was whining in her sleep and I picked up my jacket and bent to whisper in her ear. When I looked back up, the blond was gone. So was the saluki that had been playing near the water bowl.

But something was off. No one else had left. Four new people had come in. One more was coming in the gate while I was looking around. I counted the people again. Then I counted the dogs. That was odd. Not counting myself and the three dogs I'd brought with me, there were fourteen people in the run. And only thirteen dogs.

On the weekend, couples sometimes came together with their dog. They'd sit together on a bench and watch their offspring socialize. But during the week, that almost never happens. It's more common to have more dogs than owners. There was always someone here, like myself, who had come with more than one dog. In the afternoon, it was even more out of balance. Then the walkers would come, each with four, five, or even six dogs in tow.

I tried to figure out which dog was with which human, but it wasn't possible. The dogs were doing what they

came here for, running, digging, and wrestling, not going
back to check in with their owners.

On the way to the drugstore, I remembered two other
times the number of people and the number of dogs hadn't
added up properly. In the first instance, like today, there
seemed to be an extra person. Not that that's against the law
or anything. There was this weird guy who came every day
for a week or two and sat watching the dogs. Sometimes
he'd ask about one or the other, saying he wanted to get a
dog and was coming to the run to help figure out which
kind would be right for him. Once he brought biscuits and
none of us would let him feed our dogs. We thought he was
a creep and didn't know what he was really up to. In some
places, love is in the air. In New York, it's paranoia.

The second time the count was off was one of those
cold days where there were so few people brave enough to
go to the run that you could count the shivering souls in a
glance. There were six of us there, wrapped up so that we
were barely recognizable. And there were eight dogs. This
didn't have to mean trouble. Lots and lots of New Yorkers
have more than one dog. But after I was there for a while,
Dashiell running around and me sitting still and freezing, a
young woman came up to me and pointed to a little mutt.
She's been here all morning, she said. I don't think there's
an owner here.

People did that sometimes, dumped a dog they no
longer wanted at the run, figuring one of the dog lovers
there would simply take her home. We walked around together and sure enough, no one there owned the little girl.
Or knew who did. And just as we were discussing which of
us would take her home and see if we could find her a permanent place to stay, a young man opened the double
gates, went up to her, and hooked on the leash he pulled
out of his pocket.

The woman I'd been talking to flew at him, asking him how dare he leave his dog unattended for all these hours. Hey, he said, I had something to do. With that, he turned to leave, the little dog trotting along behind him.

I stopped at the drugstore on the corner of Tenth and Bleecker, asking all three dogs to sit in the corner near the pharmacist's counter. Then I asked him what "teratogenic" meant, the word that came up as a possible side effect of every single medication listed at the epilepsy site. The dictionary at Sophie's had said it meant "monster-making." The pharmacist said what that meant was that it could affect the fetus, if someone was taking one of these medications when pregnant. So unless Sophie could have survived nine months of seizures without medication, she hadn't had the choice about whether or not she would be a parent.

I asked him how anticonvulsive drugs worked, what happened when you took them, what they might interact with badly, and if they ever worked for a while and then suddenly stopped being effective.

Walking home, I wondered what difference any of that made now. Sophie was dead. It no longer mattered whether or not she'd pined for the child she couldn't have, or if she'd be alive if Bianca had gotten there a minute sooner, or if the pup had gotten there in time but the meds hadn't worked. I unlocked the gate and watched Dashiell run on ahead through the dark tunnel and into the sunlight of the garden, the bullies close behind him, thinking that even if it hadn't been a seizure that had killed her, but salmonella, so what. The only thing that counted now was finding a home for her dogs. And toward that end, I still had a lot of checking to do.

CHAPTER 15

I Sat There Holding the Phone

I could hear the house phone when I came out of the tunnel that led into my garden. I ran for the door and got it just as the machine was picking up.

"Don't go away. I'm here."

I waited for the machine to click off. Whoever was on the other end waited, too. "Rach?"

"Marty. Hey."

"Listen, I passed on the info you gave me about the iguana."

"Yeah?"

"Burke said he didn't know what he'd do without you."

"Oh, great. Now what? Iguana jokes? Look, Marty, I said it was a slim chance. I knew that. But I think it's better to have all the information—"

"You did the right thing, Rachel."

"Only?"

"Only it wasn't salmonella."

"You got the ME's report?"

"We did."

"And?"

"It wasn't a seizure either."

"What?"

"It was something she ingested."

"I don't get it. Like what?"

I wondered if it had been something she ate at dinner, if she'd gotten a really bad case of food poisoning.

"It was the pill she took, the capsule."

No more jokes. His voice serious now.

"You mean the dog brought her the wrong medication?"

"What the hell does the dog have to do with this?"

"She taught the dog to get her medication on command. The older one, Blanche, alerted her when a seizure was coming. Sometimes twenty minutes before, sometimes two minutes before. When she was out of the house, she carried the medication on her, in a little belt pouch or a fanny pack. So it was always available. But at home, shit, she could be in the bathtub or asleep when the dog gave her the word. So she taught the little one, Bianca, to get her the meds and bring them to her."

"The clone?"

I sighed audibly. "Yeah—the clone. So what are you saying, she should have taught her to read the prescription bottle more carefully?"

"Good thought, but it wouldn't have helped. It was the right container."

"I don't get it."

"What she ingested—Ms. Gordon—the particular pill she took, it wasn't her medication."

"What was it?" I asked, pressing the phone closer.

"Vacor."

"Which is?"

"Rat poison."

"Jesus."

"Where are you now?"

"Home. Why?"

"Because if you were at her place, I'd tell you to get the hell out. Now."

I waited.

"The medication found next to her, the stuff the dog was lying on, the clone." I could hear him lighting a cigarette, inhaling, blowing the smoke out before he continued. "It was the right stuff, her regular prescription. Burke called her doctor and checked it out."

"You're saying Bianca brought her the anticonvulsant?"

"To the best of her knowledge. At least it was the right container. And probably, in the right place, on her nightstand more than likely. Did she mention what she taught the dog to do, Rach, if it was by location? That would have made the most sense."

"I don't know how she did it, Marty. It was a friend of hers who told me about this, a woman who worked with her."

"Name?"

"Ruth Stewart. She's the receptionist."

I heard him talking to someone else. Then there was a pause, Marty writing down the name I'd given him.

"That would have been the easiest way," I said, "to teach her to retrieve the medicine from the nightstand by back-chaining, you know, start the dog where you want her to end up, where the vial with the pills was kept, and work backward, a few feet at a time until she'd get it and take it to wherever Sophie was, anywhere in the house or garden."

"I know what back-chaining is, Rachel."

"Right. But I didn't get the opportunity to discuss this with my client so I don't know exactly how she taught the dog . . ."

"Doesn't make much difference now."

"Anyway, if it were me, I'd check the container the dog brought me, just to make sure."

"Like I said, it was the right container. And when the victim opened it and removed a capsule, it looked the same as it always did, just the way it should have. But someone had emptied out one of the capsules, cleaned it out, and filled it with Vacor, someone knowing that eventually she'd get alerted that she was going to have a seizure and eventually she'd take the tainted pill."

"What do you mean, one of the capsules?"

"The rest of them, they were fine. They had the anti-convulsant in it that she took to ward off her seizures."

"Then how do you know the Vacor was in one of the capsules?"

"The ME recovered the outer material and no traces of the medication that should have been in it. And enough Vacor not to just make her wish she was dead, but to actually get the job done."

"But all the other pills—"

"Were as they came from the pharmacy. Whoever killed her—"

"Was willing to wait, let it happen when it happened."

"Precisely."

"Someone not in a rush."

"Gives me the creeps," he said, "someone can be that calculating."

"That's why you're with the Bomb Squad."

"No one likes a wise ass, Rachel."

I heard someone talking in the background, saying, "I told him, fifty bucks for a haircut? That's robbery."

Marty asked me to hold on.

"That's because you went to a stylist," another voice said, "instead of a barbershop."

And then Marty came back on the line, saying he had another call, he had to go. But he didn't hang up. "Someone else got it," he said.

For a moment, neither of us spoke.

"Marty, I wonder if whoever did this was counting on the fact that there'd be no autopsy because of the increased risk of death with epilepsy. Maybe he figured the cause of death would be assumed to be epilepsy related."

"No one makes detective by assuming, Rachel. Things aren't always what they seem to be. You know that."

"I do. But maybe whoever used the Vacor didn't know that. I did some research on epilepsy. There's a higher rate of suicide among epileptics. There are more accidental deaths, especially drowning, and there's something called 'unexplained death syndrome.' "

"And there's murder."

"That, too."

"Watch your back," he said. "You hear?"

I sat there holding the phone, thinking about what had happened a few hours earlier, the super coming in, using his key and walking into Sophie's apartment without knocking. Then I thought about what had happened right afterward, about the unwelcome visitor in the garden, the price you pay for outdoor space in Manhattan.

Joe, the super. He'd have rat poison in the basement. He'd have to.

But why would he want Sophie dead?

I called the dogs into the house, gave them each a biscuit, and headed back to Sophie's to have a talk with Joe in broad daylight.

CHAPTER 16

I'm Doing Some Work for the Landlord

Underneath the bells for all the apartments in Sophie's building, there was a small plaque that directed me to the building next door, Apartment B, for the super. I walked to that doorway, found the bell, and rang it, not knowing what I'd say if anyone answered.

Improvise, my former boss used to say when, in the beginning, I'd once asked him how to get where I had to go. You're a college graduate, he'd added, I shouldn't have to be telling *you* how to do the job.

The intercom crackled.

"Who's there?" The accent was Russian and so thick she sounded as if she had several golf balls in her mouth.

"I need to get into the cellar," I said. I'm quick, you have to give me that.

"Con Ed?"

She was doing my job for me, giving me the excuse I

needed to check around downstairs. But I was wearing jeans and a T-shirt. Con Ed? I didn't think so.

"I'm doing some work for the landlord and I have to check something in the cellar."

"I buzz you in."

I pushed open the door, followed the long hallway back, and opened the gray door on the left that led under the stairs and said Basement on it. I felt my way down in the dark.

She was waiting for me in the open doorway, someone who lived underground like a mole in this dank place, a woman of about fifty, or who appeared to be fifty because life hadn't been kind.

"What you need in cellar?"

"I have to check the tools. I'm doing some carpentry work for, well, over at the office, and I don't have the right saw."

Lame, I thought, wondering if she'd go for it.

She began to shake her head, making a sound in her throat that sounded as if something had gotten stuck there—my story, no doubt.

"No, no, no. Tools belong to Sergei. I can no let you take saw. You come back in one hour. Talk to him about saw."

"Sergei?"

"My husband. He super for this building and next-door building. He fixing toilet upstairs. You come back in one hour. He give you saw."

"I spoke to a man named Joe yesterday. He said he was the super here."

"No, no, no. Sergei. No Joe."

"What about . . . ?"

"No Joe here," she said, looking frightened and closing the door.

I made my way back up the dark, worn steps and headed for the dog run so that I could show Herbie's photo to a new group of dog owners; after sixteen more people told me they'd never seen the man in the picture, I went back to my cottage to pick up Bianca, to take her uptown to the school where Sophie taught in the hope that one of Sophie's students would have something worthwhile to tell me.

CHAPTER 17

We Were Her Family, She Said

I got to the school before three and positioned myself near the front of a group of mothers waiting to pick up their kids, Bianca at my side, so that the kids would see us when they came out the main door. When Ruth joined me at five to three, stopping to say hi to several of the parents, Bianca strained at the leash to get to her, becoming very excited and jumping up on her when she got close. To my surprise, Ruth knelt down and let Bianca kiss her face. And she stayed there, crouched down, while Bianca put her paws around her neck and leaned her big face against Ruth's, her tail wagging as if she'd just found a long-lost friend, which, apparently, she had.

The kids burst out from the double doors as if they'd been shot from a cannon, some heading right for the curb where buses were already waiting for them. I waited impatiently, but every time I looked at Ruth, she shook her head. Finally, two boys came out, heavy backpacks slung over their shoulders, one eating a cookie. Ruth touched my arm, but the boys were so involved in their conversation that, heading for their bus, I thought they'd see nothing but each other. Then one of them looked around, saw Bianca and began to pull on the other boy's arm.

"The tall one's Everett, the one with the hearing aid is Bob," Ruth whispered.

"Can I pet your dog, lady?" Everett said in the thick, uninflected way of people who can't hear their own voices.

"Sure thing."

He slipped off his purple backpack and knelt next to Bianca, letting her sniff the back of his hand, then slowly, as if he was concentrating very hard, he lifted the hand she'd smelled and placed it on the top of her head, and, as if gravity were doing the work for him, let it slide down the slope of her nose. Bianca closed her little pig eyes and wagged her short fat tail. It was one of the few times I'd seen her sit relatively still for more than a couple of seconds.

"She's the clone, isn't she?" he asked, wide eyes watching my face.

I nodded.

"Jeez, she's gorgeous. I knew it was true. I knew it."

Bob was still standing. He looked at Bianca, at me, at Everett, and then at Ruth. "It's her? It's Bianca, Ms. Gordon's other dog?"

Ruth nodded.

He shook his head slowly from side to side. This time he addressed me. "Can I touch her?" He was thin, with a long horsy face and wire-rimmed round glasses that made his eyes look too big. The hearing aid was in his left ear.

"Of course."

His backpack was forest green. He shrugged it off and knelt next to his friend, both of them petting Bianca so tenderly that my heart broke all over again, thinking of Sophie and what a wonderful teacher she must have been, how tender, trusting, and honest with her students.

And what a big mouth she had about what was supposed to be kept secret.

More kids were pouring out of the doorway, some signing, some talking. It wasn't nearly as loud as it would have been at a school for hearing kids. For some of them, I thought, going home wasn't as much fun as school. Going home, in fact, might be a lonely thing to do.

I crouched down and touched the two boys on their shoulders. A little girl wandered over, too big to be sucking her thumb but doing it anyway.

I smiled at her, then addressed the boys.

"Ms. Gordon told you all about Bianca?"

"She did," Everett said. "She told us someone had cloned Blanche so that other people with epilepsy could have seizure-alert dogs, but she never brought Bianca to school with her, only Blanche."

"Where is Blanche?" Bob asked.

"She's with me, at my house. I'm taking care of her until I can find out if Ms. Gordon arranged for anyone to take care of them when she no longer could."

"Which is now," Bob said.

"That's right," I told him.

Ruth took out a wad of tissues and blew her nose.

"She told us she was tested," Everett said. I watched him as intensely as he was watching me, both of us needing to lip-read to be sure we understood each other.

"That's right," I told him. "Both bullies had a DNA test recently."

"That's because Ms. Gordon didn't trust the first one."

"What do you mean?"

"She said Bianca was tested when she was a puppy, before Ms. Gordon got her, but that when you test a puppy, you sometimes get the mother's milk on the swab and then you might have the mother's DNA. Ms. Gordon wanted to be sure Bianca was really a clone. That's why she had her tested again."

"She told you everything?"

He nodded. "We were her family, she said."

"Just like family," Bob said.

"It's almost the same thing," Everett said. He was crying.

"Did Ms. Gordon ever mention her other family to you, in class, you know, her blood relatives?"

"Just her sister," Everett said.

I nodded. "Did she mention her name?"

"Rhoda," he told me. "That's hard to say. She made us all practice it."

"Rhoda," Bob said.

The little girl took her thumb out of her mouth and said, "Rhoda," making bubbles as she did, popping the thumb back in as soon as she'd said it. A woman carrying a bag of groceries tapped her on the shoulder. She smiled and reached for her hand.

Another boy joined us, blond and nearly as pale as an albino.

"Hi, Will," Ruth said.

"Hello, Ms. Stewart. Is it Blanche?" he asked. "She got skinny. She must be grieving, too."

"This one's Bianca," Ruth told him.

"The clone?"

We all nodded. Bianca had two more hands on her now, which was mighty fine with her.

"So, what else did Ms. Gordon tell you about her sister? If I can find her, then maybe she'll give the dogs a good home. That's why I'm asking."

"It's okay to tell her whatever you know," Ruth told Will. "Rachel is a good person and she's trying to help. She's been taking care of Blanche and Bianca."

"You won't find her," Everett said.

"Why not?"

"She's dead, too," he said.

"Yeah. She died when Ms. Gordon was real little. In a car accident," Bob said, "But Ms. Gordon didn't. She only got epilepsy."

I looked at Ruth. She shrugged her shoulders. "In all this time, she never once . . ."

"She wanted us to write about something sad," Will said. "So she said she'd tell us the saddest thing in her life to help us get started."

"Ms. Gordon said if you write down the things that bother you," Bob said, "they won't hurt your feelings as much as they used to. She said it helps to talk and write about things."

"She said it's different, writing and talking," Everett said. "She said they both help, but in different ways."

"And was that true for you? Did you write about something sad after she told you about her sister dying, and did it make you feel better?"

"I wrote about being deaf," Bob said. "But I still can't hear."

Everett punched him in the arm. Then Will signed something to both of them and they put their backpacks on.

"The bus is flashing its lights," Ruth said. "They have to go."

"There were no other relatives she mentioned?" I asked.

They shook their heads.

"Will you bring Bianca again?" Will asked. "I hardly had a chance to see her."

I looked at Ruth. She nodded.

"Okay."

"And Blanche, too?"

"And Blanche, too."

"We miss her. Ms. Gordon," Everett said. "She was the best teacher I ever had." Then all three boys headed for the bus.

I looked at Ruth.

"She never told you?"

"Not a word."

"Does that make you feel worse?"

"I'm not sure. She probably . . ."

She knelt and began to pet Bianca. I could barely hear her when she spoke.

"It was probably a kindness, the omission."

I watched her petting Bianca, not saying anything.

"I'm heading downtown," I said after she stood up. "Which way do you go?"

"Oh, I have to go back inside. I don't get off until four-thirty."

"Thank you for this, Ruth."

She nodded.

"I was wondering, how many kids were in her class?"

"Only twelve. And most of them stay for after-school programs."

"Will I be able to bring the bullies into her class one day before they're . . . placed?"

"I'm sure I can arrange that. Now that we've seen how three of the kids reacted to Bianca, I think it would be a very good idea."

"I'll be in touch."

Bianca and I headed off and I decided that, before going home, I'd give the dog run one more shot. With so little other information, I was obsessed with finding Herbie.

The run got crowded after three, and by the time I got

there, it was jammed. I let Bianca off leash and started at one end, showing the picture of Herbie to each and every person there, asking the same question, over and over. It was the third time I'd canvased the run, the third time I'd asked people to stop their conversations or stop watching their dogs and look at the snapshot I'd found on my client's refrigerator, held there with a little, white bone magnet, saved when it should have been torn up and pitched out, the third time I'd waited for a response, a what's-it-to-you or a shake of the head, and, finally, when I got to the far end of the run, just past the water bucket, someone said yes.

CHAPTER 18

The Driver Began to Shake His Head

Standing in the cavernous main room at Penn Station, waiting to be told which track my train would be on, I took the picture of Herbie out of my pocket again. I'd found him. In less than an hour, we'd be face-to-face.

"Sure, I know him," the dark young woman had said, her miniature schnauzer digging a hole under the bench.

"You do? Terrific."

"That's Herbie Sussman. But you won't see him here anymore. He and Murray moved to Metuchen."

"New Jersey?"

"Yeah. That's what I told him. 'What're you leaving *the city* and moving to New Jersey for?' It's crazy, don't you think?" She had what my mother used to call "dirty blond" hair, uncombed looking, as if she'd been in a rush, pulled back with a purple elastic. She was wearing gray sweatpants and an oversize top. She hadn't bothered to put on makeup. "The city," she said, "is where it's at. I don't get it. But he went, 'Murray and I are moving to New Jersey. Now do you want my address or not?' You know Herbie."

"Murray's his dog?" I asked.

"Oh," she said, squinting up at me. I took the seat next to her, glancing over at the dogs, then looking back at her, the picture of Herbie still in her hand. "Then you don't know him, Herbie?"

"Not actually, but I need to ask him something. It's really important. Do you have his address in Metuchen?"

She unzipped her small purse and pulled out her calendar, flipping to the part that held her addresses.

"Nice town," she said. "Lots of old houses. I only went once. I smuggled Parker onto the train with me. She and Murray were really tight. Best friends." She nodded. "I don't know," she said, closing her address book and squinting up at me, the sun in her eyes. "Where'd you get this?" She looked at the photo of Herbie, then back at me.

"From his ex-girlfriend," I said, thinking I was so close now, hoping I wouldn't blow it, hoping she'd open the book again and give me his address. Never mind, I thought, Metuchen, New Jersey, I could get it from the operator, tell her it's a new listing.

"Sophie?"

I nodded.

"I guess it's okay then," she said.

She didn't know.

She pulled a piece of paper out of the purse, fished around and found a pen, and wrote it all down for me: Herbie Sussman, 1132 Bellamy Road, Metuchen. "He had a problem with his phone number," she said, dropping the calendar into her purse. "It belonged to a cab company. Can you believe that? They're supposed to wait a year, I think. Or is it six months? Whatever. They must've waited a week. He'd come home, his voice mail was full. He'd missed God knows how many calls. He just E-mailed me about it. So that number's dead and he doesn't have the new one yet. You want his E-mail?"

"Sure."

She wrote that down.

"He was pissed," she said.

"About the phone number?"

"About his job moving him out to Jersey. But he didn't think it was a good idea to quit, not with all his credit-card debt; you know Herbie." She looked up at me again, covering her eyes with one hand, squinting anyway. "Oh, that's right," she said, "I forgot. You don't know him. Well, don't tell him I told you he's in debt. I have enough people pissed at me right now."

I thanked her, took the picture back, and continued around the run anyway. Who knows what else you can learn, asking around. Well, usually nothing. But you never know, I'd thought, the excitement growing.

I'd E-mailed Herbie the moment I'd gotten home, told him I was a friend of Sophie, his ex, asked if I could come out and see him, there was something important I needed to ask him. He must have been on-line because I'd gotten his answer right away: "Why not ask me via E-mail?" I wrote again, saying I was an old-fashioned girl and I'd rather talk face-to-face. He wrote back saying, "Sure, whatever, you want to schlep all the way out to Metuchen just to ask me a couple of questions, why not?" He'd said he'd be home all morning. Then he'd asked me to give his regards to Sophie.

He didn't know either.

I told him I'd be there in an hour and a half.

It was the same voice it had always been since I'd gone on the train with my mother when I was seven, to visit her cousin in Atlantic City: "The northeast corridor train to Trenton, ready on track three, all aboard."

And like sheep being herded through a small gate by a Border collie who had been bred to disregard the fact that he was outnumbered, the crowd turned around and headed for the escalator that led to tracks three and four, the music that filled the main room fading as we rode down to the tracks and moved, as one animal, onto the train.

As the swell narrowed and squeezed into the door to the closest car, I grabbed the first seat I could, across from a woman with big hair, taupe nail polish, rings on three fingers, including the pointer, too much perfume, and an ankle bracelet of a type I hadn't seen since I was a kid and Laura Weisbart got one from the only boy in ninth grade who didn't have zits. But he had full braces and so did Laura. You don't want to hear the comments.

The vista out the window wasn't any better. Though it was September, there was nothing green in sight. The sky hung thick and low, a sickly gray. Off in the distance gigantic smokestacks poured chemical waste into the Jersey air. The ground was brown, the trees leafless, the air visible. We passed a factory that was flying the flag. Old Glory, in the Garden State, was red, gray, and blue. It was not a comforting view.

But halfway there, everything greened up, and even close to the tracks there were rows of pretty little houses with neat front lawns and asters or mums along the front walk. There was a tricycle here, a friendly mailman there. The American dream was alive and well.

The taxi stand was across from the station. The driver told me Bellamy Road was only a few minutes away. "It only runs a block," he said. "Park across the street. You like ducks?" he asked.

"Love 'em," I told him.

I could see the ducks as we approached, only they were geese. On the side opposite the park there were little clapboard houses with small front yards. Except for my taxi, there was no traffic.

The driver began to shake his head.

"You sure you got that number right?" he asked. "These don't even go up to a hundred, looks like forty-two's the highest number."

I looked at the paper I'd been given.

"Can you wait?" I asked the driver.

"Meter keeps running, I can wait."

I told him that was as it should be. I rang some bells. There was no number 1132. There wasn't another Bellamy Road, or anything that sounded like it. There were no new neighbors either. No one had moved to or from this street for at least five years.

I stood outside the last house and looked up and down the block at the green lawns and the curtained windows. Then I walked back to the cab, told the driver to take me back to where he'd found me, and waited twenty-two minutes for the train that would take me back to New York.

Sitting near a window again, I took the picture of Herbie out of my pocket. He had a bland face and the sort of smile you'd see in high school yearbook pictures. But, of course, he wasn't a teenager.

And whoever he was, this pleasant-looking man with wavy hair, he hadn't been Sophie Gordon's boyfriend either.

Turning the photo over, I looked at where someone had written his name, to make sure I'd look for the man in the picture. To make sure I'd go on not just this one, but many wild goose chases.

I was sure now that if I looked carefully at the printing on the back of the photo and compared it to Sophie's writing, I'd see it was different. I knew just where to look, too, because she'd written the names of her dogs on the backs of their photos and those pictures were in a file in her desk. And if by some chance I couldn't tell if the handwriting was different or the same, I knew someone who could.

But why bother? I was sure now that neither the photo nor the handwriting was genuine. •

I'd been manipulated. Someone was orchestrating what I found. And, more important, what I didn't find.

Sophie had expunged all mention of Herbie from her calendar. She wouldn't have kept his picture on her refrigerator, not unless she expected him to come back. And in that case, she wouldn't have deleted his phone number. His birthday would still be noted on her PalmPilot. Their first date would have been in her calendar, perhaps some little notation there, too, indicating how special the night had been.

The train arrived at Penn Station and once again, I was swept along by the crowd, moved onto the escalator, and then I rose up into the music. I took a deep breath that smelled of soft-baked pretzels, Dunkin' Donuts, and coffee. I was back in New York. I was home.

But I didn't know anything more than I'd known before I'd left. Except that someone was playing games with me. Someone knew I was on the job.

Was he trying to scare me away?

Or did he have plans for me, like the plans he'd had for Sophie, plans that required great patience and included the thrill of the wait?

CHAPTER 19

One Thing Kept Coming Back

Standing in the rotunda of Penn Station, travelers all around me, numbers rolling over on the huge board that displayed departures, I pulled out my cell phone and dialed Chip's pager. But I couldn't get through. I was in a dead zone. When I got outside, I tried again. My phone rang as I was walking downtown on Ninth Avenue, passing the Italian specialty shops, the aroma of garlic coming at me like a sledgehammer. I couldn't remember the last time I'd eaten.

"Hey," I said.

"Hey, yourself."

"Where are you?" Now I was one of those people talking on the phone in the street. What was the world coming to?

"In the car, heading north on the Palisades, client in Sneden's Landing with a biting Chow. So where are you? I hear heavy traffic. Doesn't sound like the Village."

"I'm on Ninth Avenue, walking downtown from Penn Station and heading for the Village, but I have this awful feeling that when I get there, there's going to be a big gate with a sign that says, Abandon Hope, All Ye Who Enter Here."

"What happened?"

"Well, for starters, it seems that Bianca brought Sophie the medication, as she was trained to do, and that Sophie had time to take the pill she needed."

"But?"

"But someone had removed the medication from the capsule, swabbed it clean, and filled it with a rodenticide called Vacor."

"Not a fun way to go," he said.

"I've never been able to figure out a way that was."

I thought about my father closing the book he was reading and turning off the bedside lamp.

"She appeared . . ."

But I stopped, thinking that it wasn't really necessary to describe the grimace on her face or the convulsed state of her body. Chip didn't need my help figuring out what Sophie had gone through after ingesting rat poison.

"It seems the murderer is a very patient customer."

"How so?"

"All the rest of the pills were unadulterated."

"You mean whoever did this was willing to wait until Sophie took the tainted pill, no matter how long that took? He was willing to leave the timing to chance?"

"Apparently. Had she taken any one of the others, she'd still be alive. At least, for now."

"But eventually she would have taken that one."

"Yes. She would have. But the killer wasn't in any kind of rush." Nor was he with me, I thought. He'd prolong it, waiting until he was good and ready to strike. "Whoever did this," I said, "didn't act in the heat of the moment. This was entirely cold-blooded, something calculated. I bet that not knowing when was part of the thrill."

"Like Russian roulette."

"Except that in this case the other player didn't consent to play."

"That's a rather significant difference."

"It is."

"What were you doing at Penn Station, Rach?"

"I went out to Jersey to talk to her ex-boyfriend."

"Was he any help?"

"He wasn't. That is to say, he wasn't where I was told he'd be. Where *he* told me he'd be."

"You spoke?"

"E-mailed. I'd gone to the dog run with this picture I found on Sophie's refrigerator with the name of her boyfriend on the back of it, just in case I wasn't bright enough to make that assumption."

"What do you mean?"

"This woman said she recognized him, that they were friends, she and 'Herbie.' She told me he'd moved out to Metuchen for work. Then she gave me his E-mail and I wrote and he wrote right back. Anyway, he said I could come. Only when I got to where he was supposed to be, the address he'd given me didn't exist. I think someone's orchestrating this whole thing, Chip, the way they orchestrated Sophie's death, someone who gets a kick out of playing with people in the most elaborate way. Sophie didn't leave a picture of her ex on her refrigerator. The fact that it was there bothered me from the moment I found it, but I was so greedy to succeed, I ignored my better judgment and allowed myself to believe it was what it appeared to be even though it made no sense. After all, she didn't save his phone number, his birth date, love notes. There was nothing like that in the apartment. I think whoever killed her put that there for me to find."

"How do they know about you?"

"It seems that Sophie had trouble keeping secrets. Who knows who she told that she was going to hire a private investigator? She went around telling everyone in sight that Bianca was a clone, even though she'd been told that this was top-secret information. She told the dog walker, her friend at school, her students, her veterinarian. For all I know, there isn't a soul she ran into who doesn't know everything about her life. Some people are like that."

"It sounds as if she was very lonely."

"That could explain it. It's an isolating disease, epilepsy. And she'd had it for a long, long time. One of her students told me she told the class that she'd had a sister who was killed in a car accident and that she'd survived, but that's how it started, probably from a head injury."

"What a strange thing to tell her class."

"I think she meant it to be inspirational, a 'march on despite your disability' story. The kids said she told them they'd feel better if they talked and wrote about their own disabilities. That was the reason she'd talked about her sister, you know, teacher's doing it. You're next."

"It's still a heavy thing to hit them with. What are they, eight?"

"But profoundly disabled. That makes them a lot older than eight in some ways. This kid, the one who told me, I had the impression he handled it okay. When it comes to tragedy, these are not innocents. I get the feeling that Sophie was a terrific teacher and I'm willing to trust that she knew what the kids could and couldn't handle and what might help them open up. But she sure did talk a lot about personal things."

"Not someone I'd want to share a secret with."

"Too late for that anyway."

"Can I call you later, babe? I'm in my client's driveway. I'm late, the front door just opened, and, you'll never believe this, the biting Chow is out and she's off leash."

"Be careful."

"That's precisely what I was going to say to you. I'll call you later."

I was down in the teens already, just a block from the Chelsea Market. I got in line at Amy's Bread, ordered a rosemary round and three prosciutto twists, and began eating one of the twists on my way back out to Ninth Avenue.

Outside, I began mulling over the things I'd learned, trying to see if I could make sense out of the little I had. But one thing kept coming back: Vacor. So instead of going home, I headed for Third Street, one hand in my jacket pocket, holding Sophie's keys as if they were an amulet.

CHAPTER 20

I Could Hear the Patter of Little Feet

I didn't stop at the door to Sophie's building. I passed it and went to the next building, ringing the bell that said Supt. This time a man answered.

"Sergei?"

"Who is it?"

"I'm working for your boss. I need to talk to you," I said, glad I hadn't stopped to pick up the three dogs. Explaining them would have been a challenge.

"I come up," he said and the static disappeared.

The Minetta Garage was across the street, a few small, brick multi-tenant dwellings next to it, a pizza place on the corner. Alongside the building where I waited was a Japanese restaurant, dark blue flags with Japanese lettering flying out front. Then the door opened and Sergei was there, his hair unnaturally black looking, his skin too old for that hair. He was short and wide, like his wife, but not as frightened looking as she had been.

"Yes?"

"I'm doing some shelves for the office," I said, making it up as I went along, "and I was told I could use your tools. I'd like to see what you have?"

Sergei looked dumbfounded.

"What shelves? I make plenty shelves for office, do electrical work, fix plumbing, take care of all buildings." He swirled his big callused hand around as if he was mixing potato salad without a spoon. "I do all. Why he ask you—"

"It's a trade," I told him, as sincerely as I could. I sighed, letting him know that I, too, would rather he was building the damn shelves, but what's a person to do?

Sergei was unmoved. In fact, he was blocking the doorway with his short wide body, keeping me from where I needed to go. I had no choice but to try to be more convincing than I'd been thus far.

"Barter," I whispered, as if I was saying something I couldn't afford to allow that couple leaving the Japanese restaurant to hear. "I owe him some money. Back rent. I don't have it."

The frown changed to a look of concern. "From one of his other buildings?"

I nodded. "So I'm making the shelves, instead of paying him cash." I shrugged.

He finally got it, stepping back and extending one arm, his big hand open, to show me the way.

"Thanks. I really appreciate this," I told him, already planning my next move. He passed me and I followed him to the door I'd used the other day and down the dark, narrow stairway to the cellar where Sergei and Mrs. Sergei lived, free from the oppression of Communism. We passed the door to his apartment and continued down to the end of the dimly lit hallway. When he opened the door to the cellar, I felt less celebratory about having cleverly left my dog at home.

It was a dank room, low ceilinged and musty. When he stopped at his workbench, I stopped, too, but it wasn't quite as quiet as it should have been. For just a moment, I could hear the patter of little feet from behind some old furniture.

That aside, it was time for part two. I waited until my eyes adjusted better to the poor light. Sergei lifted a large tool box onto the workbench, opened it, and stepped back.

"Take what you need," he said. "Not having cash, this I understand."

I nodded but I didn't move.

"What happen to you, husband desert?"

I nodded again. I love it when other people do my work for me.

"Happens in Russia, too. Not enough money, too much love of vodka. Children?"

"A boy and a girl."

"Make shelves. Everything will be okay soon. You need help, you call Sergei."

I nodded and wiped my eyes with the heels of my hands.

"Do you think I might have a glass of water? I feel dizzy."

"Sit, sit," he said, pulling out a stool from under the lip of the workbench. "I get you water."

"And, if you have one, an aspirin. Please."

"Don't fall, hold table. I be right back."

The moment he was gone, I took the huge flashlight from the workbench and began to shine it around the cellar. Only once did something shine back at me, two small, very dark, very intelligent-looking eyes, here, perhaps, because what I was looking for wasn't. And, when I thought about it, I wondered why I'd bothered to look.

I could hear Sergei coming back, his work boots squeaking on the vinyl tiles of the short hallway. I sat on the stool and put my hands on the workbench, as if I was holding on for dear life.

He handed me two aspirins, folded into a tissue, and a glass of water so cold, the glass was sweating almost as profusely as he was, and so full, water had spilled down one leg of his trousers.

I took the aspirin, drank the water, and smiled weakly.

"Carla make tea. You come," he said, his English deteriorating as his concern increased. Perhaps I'd laid it on too thick. Sometimes when I should sprinkle, I use a trowel.

He held my elbow as we walked back down the hall to his apartment, and Carla, in an apron, the very image that took the romance out of marriage for me, was waiting just inside the door. There was a round table in the combination living and dining room and she had covered it with what appeared to be her finest tablecloth, thick cream-colored linen. The napkins were linen, too, the silverware in place, the cups sat on matching saucers, and in the middle of the table there was a teapot on a trivet, a plate of plain cookies, and a little dish of raspberry-colored jam. I was awash in guilt.

"This is beautiful, Carla. Thank you."

"Is nothing."

I handed her the bag with the rosemary bread and the last prosciutto roll, as if I'd known all along I'd be invited to tea and actually practiced the good manners my mother had tried so hard to instill in me. She looked inside.

"Oh, this is wonderful. This is too much, much too much. Look, Sergei." He did, probably expecting to see a standing rib roast from the fuss Carla was making. Then he smiled, showing me his missing teeth, and pulled out my chair.

"You didn't find right tools?" Carla poured the tea.

I looked at Sergei, who was looking back at me.

"I'll come back when I feel a little better."

"Goot. You come anytime. If I not here, Carla show you tools."

"Okay."

I took a sip of the tea, rich as baker's chocolate and nearly as bitter. Carla cut the bread, offering me the first slice.

"Do you live nearby?" Carla asked.

"Yes—I'm in one of the other buildings," I said, hoping she wouldn't ask me which one. "And a friend of mine lived next door in the garden apartment."

Carla's hands shot to her mouth. "Miss Gordon?"

I nodded.

"No wonder you don't feel well, to lose a friend, so young, such a fine person, a teacher."

I nodded again. "I've been staying at her place, taking care of the animals. In fact, I wanted to tell you, I got very scared the other night. The dogs started to bark and woke me and I saw a rat in the garden."

Sergei reached out and patted my hand. "I take care. Not to worry."

"Should I keep the dogs out of the garden?"

"No. I dig holes near fence and around trees and bury poison. I use in cellar, too, not where dogs go. Miss Gordon, she worried all the time about dogs. I never leave poison where dogs can get."

"So you'll do it today? Because I want to stay over again, tonight."

"Not today. Must call exterminator. I get poison for rodents from him."

"Okay, good. So I'll keep the door to the garden closed tonight."

"Nothing will come in when the dogs are there. Sergei takes care of problem, but you don't worry. It make you feel . . ." She twirled her hand in the air.

"Dizzy," I said.

"Dizzy. Thank you. My English is . . ." Again she twirled her hand. "I'm still nervous. Makes me dizzy like you. Police come here, ask questions, take Vacor from cellar. Now Sergei has to buy more. But I don't understand, all the questions, what it means."

"I guess they have to check out everything," I said, taking a bite of bread as an excuse to stop explaining the activities of the Sixth Precinct.

"Two tenants complain, they hear mice in walls. This building is so old."

"Shush, Carla. We have home. I have job. We have freedom."

At the north end of the apartment, there were two windows high up on the wall, like the kind you'd see in a dungeon. They were openings where the ground had been dug out and shored up in the garden so some light and air came from above to this subterranean paradise Sergei and Carla gratefully called home.

"What did the police ask?"

"Nothing, nothing," Sergei said. "Not for you to worry about. They check everything."

"Did they take anything else, besides the Vacor?"

"No, nothing else."

"Well, thank you for the tea." I put my napkin on the table and stood. "I feel much better."

"You take pager number," Sergei said. "When you need tools, you page me."

I took the slip of paper he'd written his pager number on and waited for him to open the door for me. Then I thanked them both and took the stairs back up to the entrance hall,

feeling surprised that it was still daytime, the way you are
when you come out of an afternoon movie.

It was getting late and there was still so much I needed
to do. I headed home to pick up the dogs and walk them
back to Sophie's. Unless the police insisted on keeping the
apartment intact for a while longer, there wasn't all that
much time left for me to look through her things. Once her
place was packed up, God knows what done with her stuff,
it would be all the more difficult to try to find any family
to take care of the animals or to find out who wanted Sophie dead, and why.

CHAPTER 21

Are You Staying Over, He Asked

I unlocked Sophie's door, stepped aside, and let the three dogs charge in ahead of me. The cool north light coming into the living room from the garden gave the room a solemn feeling, but it didn't seem to dampen canine enthusiasm one bit, at least not for Dashiell and Bianca. But instead of heading for the garden door, so that they could continue the wrestling they'd done at home to celebrate my arrival, they were at the door to Sophie's bedroom, whining and scratching, Dashiell turning back to look at me to see if he could open the door and see Leslie. Before I was able to remind him that the iguana had gone home, the door opened and there was Mel, looking almost as startled to see me as I was to see him.

"I didn't know if you'd remember to mist her." He had the spray bottle in his left hand. "Or if she was warm enough. They're more delicate than they look and I know you'd feel awful if anything happened to her, Rachel."

"What are you talking about?"

"Leslie. Where is she?"

"That was very thoughtful of you," I said, the dogs busily sniffing his shoes and pants, "but why didn't you just call? I would have told you that Lydia's back. She came for Leslie early this morning."

He shrugged. "I was in the neighborhood anyway."

I opened the door to the garden so that the dogs could go out if they so chose, then went into Sophie's small kitchen and began to take vegetables out of the refrigerator for their dinner. I didn't see Mel move and when I had everything ready and turned to look, he was still standing in front of the door to Sophie's bedroom.

"Can I help?"

"I can manage."

Bianca had lured Dashiell out. Blanche was sitting in the entrance to the kitchen, her big head tilted up, her small eyes focused on the counter, where the food was. I gave her a carrot to eat while she waited and she slid down right where she was, holding it between her front paws as if it were a bone.

"I only thought, you have so much to do and all."

He was still holding the spray bottle. He seemed to notice it then. He raised it up, gave me a lopsided grin, and disappeared into the bedroom, Blanche leaving her carrot and trailing after him. He closed the door behind him but I could still hear him talking to Blanche. Then there was silence. A few moments later, he was talking again, the words so muffled I couldn't make out what he was saying. Perhaps he was telling her that dinner would be ready soon. He seemed to talk to the dogs a lot, whispering his plans into their big ears. When he came out, Blanche was right behind him.

He was acting so strange, I wanted to go into the bedroom and check things out for myself. Instead, I kept chopping and grinding. I thought it would be better to act as if nothing was bothering me and wait until he was gone before I got to work.

He stood there watching. "Did you find out anything else?"

I shook my head. I didn't mention Herbie. Or Vacor. I thought it would be better to get information, not to give any. At this point, now that I knew Sophie had been murdered, I had to view everyone as a possible enemy. But even though Mel seemed more tense than he'd been previously, I couldn't imagine him as the killer. Even thinking creatively, it was hard to come up with a motive that would inspire him to kill his client.

He asked me if I'd found any relatives. I shook my head again. Then he said if I didn't, he'd take Bianca. He seemed enthusiastic about it. Almost anxious. He shuffled his feet around, looked out into the garden, then asked if he should come by the next day and take Bianca to the run. I told him no, I'd do it, no problem. He said he wouldn't mind and he didn't care about the money. I still declined, anxious for him to leave. But he didn't. He hung around, leaning against one wall, then moving to another, as if he needed something outside himself to prop him up. After a long silence, he thought of another reason to stay. He asked if I wanted pizza. I bet you're not eating, he said. He told me he thought I'd lost some weight and that he'd get the pizza if I wanted it. It was no trouble, he said, the pizza place across the street was terrific. He always got a couple of slices, he told me, after walking Bianca, sometimes even on the way to the run, even though you're not supposed to bring food in there because it's inflammatory for some dogs. I shook my head, no, I didn't want pizza, thank you very much. How about Japanese? he wanted to know. It's only two doors away. Or did I want a sandwich? He knew a good place for sandwiches he said, and he didn't mind going there. He'd take Bianca with him, he said. He said he missed walking her.

I told him I wasn't hungry, that what I wanted was the chance to look through Sophie's papers one more time, while I still had the chance. I told him I didn't think the apartment would be kept intact much longer. He asked me why. I just shrugged. When he asked a second time, I told him I thought the landlord would be anxious to rent it again. He nodded.

"Are you staying over?" he asked.

I hadn't decided what I'd do. I had my notes with me, and the tapes I'd made when I talked to Sophie, but I told him I was going home and wished he would, too, so that I could get to work.

He shrugged and shuffled his feet some more. I took his arm and walked him to the door. I thanked him for being so helpful. I said I couldn't possibly get through all this without him. At that, he gave me a big smile. I promised I'd let him know what was going on, looking as sincere as I could but not meaning what I said. Finally, though I was beginning to think he never would, he left. I waited until I thought he was out of the building, then went back to the kitchen to finish preparing the dogs' food.

While the dogs were eating, I went into Sophie's room. Everything looked the same. I wondered why Mel had been acting so peculiar, not that I'd ever seen him act any other way. But I didn't have time to worry about it. I pulled out my cell phone and tried the doctor's office again, surprised when I got a person instead of a machine.

I explained what had happened and asked for the name and address of Sophie's next of kin, trying to sound as official as I could. But the nurse told me that the doctor's policy forbade giving out personal information unless the patient had signed a release or if I was a relative.

"But that's the whole point," I said. "If I was a relative, I'd know the other relatives. I wouldn't need you at all. But since I'm not, I don't, and Sophie's dead, so she can't sign a release."

"You don't seem to understand," she said, much more patient than I had been. But then, she wasn't racing the clock.

"No," I said, "you don't seem to understand. I'm taking care of Sophie's dogs—"

"You have Blanche?"

"Yes. And the puppy, Bianca. I need to find Sophie's next of kin to see if they'll take—"

"Hold on."

I did. She was back in a minute.

"She did give us a name, just in case. Some people don't like to, but with epilepsy, doctor insists. It's Preston Wexford. He's a cousin."

She gave me two numbers with an area code I didn't recognize, and I thanked her profusely. Then I hit reset and dialed the first one, getting an answering machine. The message said I'd reached Wexford Realty and that my call was extremely important to them. I was urged to leave my name and number so that my call could be returned promptly. I did, leaving Sophie's number as well as my own. A machine picked up when I called the second number, too.

I began to pull files out of the desk drawer, the dog file first. I took my wallet out of my pocket and pulled out the picture of Herbie. Then I had half a dozen photos on the desk, all facedown. I knew exactly what to expect. The same person had not written all the names. Sophie's printing was small and neat. She had been a teacher, after all. There was a uniformity to her letters, no confusing a *t* and an *l*. The printing on the back of the photo of the young man was different. For instance, the first *e* and the second *e* were different. If a teacher did that, the kids would only get confused. And the *h* was capitalized, but so was the *b*. I'd been so happy to find the photo, I hadn't examined the writing. Instead, I'd wasted a morning and let whoever my opponent was think I was dumb as a brick.

Which might work to my advantage.

At least, that was the thought I chose to soothe myself with.

I looked through the dog file again, determined to be thorough this time because I had the feeling that, one way or another, I'd be losing access to the apartment soon. If Burke and Burns didn't decide to come back and have another look-see, surely the landlord would want to have the place emptied, painted, and ready to rent.

This time I looked at each page of the medical files, hoping to find something that would tell me where to go with this case. I stopped when I got to a pamphlet about the BAER test and that's when I realized that one of the notations on the slip of paper Sophie had gotten from Lorna West did not refer to an inoculation. I fished in my wallet for that paper and lay it down on the desk. Bianca had had a six-in-one shot to protect her against distemper, parvovirus, leptospirosis, hepatitis, adenovirus, and parainfluenza. The usual suspects. Next to that was the date the shot had been given and when the boosters were due. Bianca had been too young for a rabies shot, so that wasn't listed. But at the bottom of the page, it said "B test, normal." Side by Side had had Bianca's hearing tested. White dogs, like the bullies, have a higher percentage of deafness than the rest of the dog population. Someone wanted to be certain that they weren't giving a handicapped dog to a handicapped owner.

I held the piece of paper in my hand, thinking about that. I could see Bianca out in the garden, playing with Dashiell. She was bright and energetic, a really terrific dog. When I whistled softly, she and Dashiell both turned and looked at me. Bianca's hearing was perfect. Watching Bianca twirling around like a dervish, I couldn't find any fault with her. Sometimes when you fool around with Mother Nature, you end up with a specimen that can't reproduce. But so far, that didn't seem to be the case with cloning; Dolly the sheep had just given birth to three lambs.

Wherever we ended up, Dash and Bianca would sleep well. They'd been racing since dinner and showed no signs of quitting. Blanche was behind me, asleep on Sophie's bed, her head on the pillow, her feet twitching. She was sleeping most of the time now, especially when she was home.

I thought about taking her to see Sophie's class. I wondered if that would cheer her up or, since she'd only been to school with Sophie, if it would depress her all the more.

Thinking about what the boys had said, I turned on the laptop, went on-line, and, before doing a search, checked Sophie's list of favorite web sites, then clicked on exactly what I was looking for, VetGen, the lab that had tested Blanche and Bianca's DNA. There I found instructions for collecting DNA samples. There was nothing about contamination from mother's milk, but it did suggest that in order to avoid contamination from dog food, the samples should be collected at least two hours after the dog's last meal or snack. It said the dog could have access to water at any time, which reminded me of something I'd read elsewhere, suggesting the dog be given water before DNA collection to make sure there weren't "foreign" particles in the mouth. Sophie must have been told about the mother's milk contamination by someone else, Lorna or the vet she'd gone to.

VetGen only gave instructions for using their kit and collecting cheek swabs, but I also knew blood samples could be used for DNA testing. It had been all over the news for years.

As long as I had the computer on, I checked all the PalmPilot files one more time for any mention of Herbie, but found nothing. He'd been expunged. Then I looked for Rhoda references and also came up blank. I checked the desk drawers again to see if there was a file with old photos. Zip. So I went out into the living room to check the bookcase. On the second shelf, stuck between the cookbooks and the bull terrier books, there was a loose-leaf binder. I slipped it out and took it back to Sophie's desk. And there she was, Rhoda, standing next to Sophie, right on the second page. Only I couldn't tell which was which.

I closed the notebook and carried it out into the garden. The lights had come on already, but still the dogs were playing. They'd collapsed in the far corner of the garden, near the ivy-covered brick wall, and they were chewing earnestly on each other's faces. For a moment, I wondered how Dashiell would react when I found a home for Bianca.

I heard my cell phone ringing, looked over at Dashiell, then changed my mind and went for it myself, flipping it open as I walked back out to the garden.

"I saw you from my window," Lydia said. "I remembered something. Sophie had a cousin. I don't know how I could have forgotten except that . . ."

"Yes?"

"She never saw him. Not since they were kids. He's her mother's brother's kid. Well, he's not a kid anymore. Lives in upstate New York. She said they used to talk on the phone, you know, his birthday, her birthday, Christmas.

His name is Preston. She referred to him as Pres. Stupid name, don't you think?"

"Where did you say he lives?" I was already wondering how far I'd have to take the dogs.

"Cambridge. It's a little town not far from Albany. Sophie showed it to me on a map once. She said he was always asking her to come up, but she was afraid to travel, in case she got sick. She didn't want to be that far from her doctor. But she thought about it. He's in real estate and she used to say she wished she could ask him to find her a little place with some land for the dogs, but she never did."

"Because she loved her job?"

"Because she couldn't drive. How could you exist in a one-horse town like that without a car? It's not like there's a subway. And work, too. Where could she find a job in a place like that? Naw. It never would have worked. It was just a dream of hers. She had lots of dreams, that girl."

"Thank you, Lydia. Keep thinking."

Sitting on the backless stone bench, I opened the notebook again. There were pictures of Sophie's parents on the first page, first together, then one of her mom holding the twin baby girls. I looked at Rhoda and Sophie again, on the next page, dressed identically for some occasion in coats with matching leggings, holding hands, smiling. And then I began turning pages and found pictures of Sophie with someone else, not her parents but a grim-looking older woman, a grandmother or a great-aunt. As I turned the pages, Sophie the little girl, then Sophie the adolescent became sadder and sadder. Finally, there were only pictures of dogs—like the ones in the other album, Blanche, then Blanche and Bianca; no Herbie, no Sophie, nothing more. I went through the book twice, but there were no pictures of Preston Wexford either, unless he was the little boy in the family shot taken a year or two before the accident.

Sophie hadn't told her kids the whole story. No wonder. It was just too damn sad to tell, that her parents had died in the crash, too, that she had been the only survivor to be raised afterward by a sour-faced old woman, and as if that hadn't been enough, to grow up knowing that she faced a lifetime of epileptic seizures to make good and sure she never forgot the day that had so changed her life.

CHAPTER 22

Better Safe Than Sorry

It must have been close to two in the morning when I realized I couldn't do anymore. I turned on the shower and adjusted the water so that it was as hot as I could stand it, something to get the kinks out of my shoulders. My arm was hurting, too. Maybe it was going to rain. Or maybe it was because I'd ignored the advice of my doctor. I'd been chopping food, hauling three exuberant dogs around, not resting at all, and not elevating my arm, as I was told I should.

I put on the kettle before getting into the shower, thinking how nice it would be to sit on the couch for a few minutes, dogs all around me and a cup of tea warming my hands, then my insides. It was too late and I was too tired to take the dogs around the block. Instead, I shooed them out into the quiet garden and, remembering the visitor of the other night, I closed the door. With three dogs in the yard, I didn't think he'd show up again, but with city rats I couldn't be sure. They were as bold as politicians, and just as appealing. And if our friend did show, the dogs would chase him. They were terriers, after all. I just wanted to be sure they didn't chase him *in*. Better safe than sorry.

I must have had some energy left, maybe just the nervous kind, or maybe I sang show tunes while I let the hot water beat down on me because I had done all the thinking I could stand for one day. My head ached. My legs felt wooden. My eyelids were as heavy as anvils. I stood there singing my heart out, my voice echoing off the tile.

There was a blue terry robe hanging on the back of the bathroom door. I slipped it on, tied the belt, and opened the bathroom door.

I didn't see him immediately. I was towel drying my hair, heading for the kitchen, thinking about that cup of tea. But then I heard him, the same raspy voice I'd heard the other night.

"Turn around," he said. "Face the garden."

Heart pounding, I did, seeing the dogs I'd locked out all staring in, staring at the man who was behind me.

"So it's the super again," I said. "What is it this time? Here to fix the plumbing?"

"I've been asked to tell you it's time to go back to your own house and mind your own business."

"Yeah? By whom?"

"What?"

"Who the fuck asked you to remind me to mind my own business?"

"That's none of your business."

"But it *is* my business. It's what I get paid to do. But you and whoever sent you already know that, don't you?"

"We know everything we have to know," he said. "You'd be surprised by what we know."

"Perhaps I would," I said, taking a small step to the side

so that I could see his reflection in the glass, stopping when he began to shout.

"Don't turn around. If you see me, I'm not going to have a choice anymore. I'm going to have to kill you. I have a gun."

"A gun? You mean you're going to shoot me? I thought poison was your specialty."

Dashiell began to bark.

I could see Joe's right arm, hanging down at his side, the weapon in his hand. He wasn't brandishing it. He was subtle. You had to give him that.

He took a step toward me and that put him directly beneath the hall light, giving me a better look at him. And at what he was packing.

"Still deciding?" I asked. "Well, one way or the other, I wish you'd get on with it. I don't have time to waste with you. I have work to do here."

I could hear his breathing now, a familiar sound, one I'd heard on my answering machine a few days ago when he'd hit redial to find out who Sophie had called last, waiting a moment to see if I'd pick up.

Beyond the glass, Dashiell was hopping mad. At last there was work with his name on it, important work, and through no fault of his own, he couldn't do the only thing he knew he should. It was what I wanted, too, to dispatch this asshole so that I could get some rest.

"Get him," I shouted, lifting my aching arm and pointing toward Sophie's bedroom.

I saw Joe turn his head, confused. Then I saw his hand begin to rise.

I was already turning when I heard it, a metallic ripping sound, nails scrabbling across wood, the answering machine hitting the floor, and then Joe moved faster than I'd ever seen a human being go. He wheeled around and opened the apartment door, slamming it behind him. Dashiell hit the door a moment after that and when I opened it for him, both of us mad enough to kill, the hallway was empty. Except for a wrench lying at the side of the stairs. Clearly, the man had no scruples. He was not only a murderer, he was a liar, too.

I had to pull Dashiell back into the apartment. His back was up, his hackles electrified from his thick neck to the base of his tail. The bullies were barking now, too. Before opening the door to the garden for them, I looked into Sophie's room to check the damage. The answering machine was upside down on the floor, the receiver as far away as the cord had let it go, the screen was torn, the hole about the size of a leaping, angry pit bull, and there were deep scratches on the desk where Dashiell had kicked off after landing.

I let Blanche and Bianca in, and went into the kitchen to make that cup of tea, but I'd apparently forgotten to light the burner. Or had I? When I touched the kettle, it was hot. Then another strange thing happened. I could hear someone playing the piano. I looked around, but there weren't any lights on in the windows I could see. No surprise. It was five to four. I walked out and sat on the bench in the dark, listening carefully, trying to locate the source. But the way sound bounces off buildings in the city, it could have been coming from anywhere, even the other side of Third Street, in one of the apartments between the pizza place and the garage.

Sitting there in the dark, my feet pulled up onto the bench, Bianca up there next to me while Blanche slept at my feet and Dashiell, still hyper-alert, patrolled, I remembered that the first time Sophie had called me, I'd heard music. At the time, I'd thought she had her radio playing. But it wasn't that. She'd been out in her garden, talking about hiring a PI.

A chill went up my back and down my aching right arm.

Could someone have overheard her? Of course. That made lots of what had happened make sense.

Someone had been watching her all along.

And now that someone was watching me.

I got up and went inside, calling the dogs to follow, locking the door behind me. Then I shut off the living room lights. I walked down the little hall to Sophie's front door and slipped the chain lock on. Then, followed by all three dogs, I went into Sophie's room and closed the window over the desk, turning the lock and checking to make sure it held. I thought we'd all had quite enough activity for one night.

But I couldn't sleep. Nor did I want to. With all the lights off, I got dressed, and, leaving the bullies at home, Dashiell and I left the apartment, locked the door, and headed not out, but up the stairs.

CHAPTER 23

Someone Had Insomnia

Dashiell ran ahead, turning to wait for me at each landing. Normally, he would have thought this was a game. He might have run down to the landing below, then bumped me in the leg on his way past me, just to show me he was the faster animal, and the one with the wittier sense of humor. But after Joe's visit, Dash was all business, running ahead to make sure the way was safe for me, looking back to assure himself that I was on my way to join him, that nothing had stopped me or slowed me down.

All the way up, I prayed I'd find an unlocked door. When I finally got to six, my breath ragged but not enough to stop me, I looked for the door to the roof. Opening it and looking up the stairs, I could see the panic bar on the door and knew I could get out. It was a fire exit and had to be open.

We ran up the last flight and I hit the bar and let Dashiell out first. Then I slipped off my shoes, propping the door open with them. A door with panic hardware would definitely be locked from the outside and I didn't want to be locked out on the roof of Sophie's building with no way to get back in.

I walked to the back edge of the roof and knelt so that I could look over and still feel relatively safe. The parapet was only three feet high and had I stood there looking down, my stomach would have done the loop de loop until ten minutes after I was back downstairs at Sophie's.

It was nearly dawn and all the windows but one were dark. Someone had insomnia. Or a baby who'd cried for attention. No matter. I could still see what I wanted to—which windows overlooked Sophie's garden.

Someone could see her. Someone could listen to her phone calls when she took the cordless phone out into the garden and called a private investigator. Someone had seen something, or heard something, that made them want Sophie dead.

Looking over the edge I could see into the next garden, the one behind the brick wall, and the back of the town house to which it belonged, a house on West Fourth Street. All the tall windows were dark. Except one. Perhaps someone was reading late into the night. Or had eaten something that didn't sit well.

From the roof, I could see the entrance to the back cottage that abutted Sophie's yard. It was on the side of the building, at the end of a flagstone path from the back door of the main house. Perhaps a guest house. Or an office. But dark now. No one in it. Or no one awake.

The houses to the left and right of Sophie's building had oblique visual access to the garden, too, and anyone who cared to could have heard any or all of Sophie's conversations. But they wouldn't be able to see her when she was inside. Only the houses on Fourth Street had that view, the one directly behind this one, and the ones to the left and right of it. From the upper floors, you'd be able to see most of the garden and all of the apartment.

The house on the right was dark. As I watched, a light came on in one of the upper rooms in the house on the left.

Kneeling on the roof, Dashiell pressing against my side, I remembered an incident that had happened right after I'd split up with Jack. I'd just moved into the cottage, thinking I was the luckiest person in the world, the way Sophie felt when she finally got her garden. The Siegals were leaving for France and I had the whole place to myself, no one looking into my garden from the main house. Then the calls started, always late at night, always after I'd turned off the light and gone to sleep.

When I finally walked over to the precinct, the cops confirmed what I'd been thinking, that whoever was calling hadn't picked my name at random from the telephone book. Whoever it was could see into the garden. Whoever it was, the detective told me, could see me and liked what he saw.

But for what purpose? I'd asked.

Ma'am? he'd said.

You said he liked what he saw. But for what? He's not asking me on a date. He's trying to scare the hell out of me. And you know something, he's succeeding.

He'd nodded.

I'd waited.

That's correct, he'd told me. What he's after is to scare you, to dominate you in this way so that he can feel in control, because this person, in his day-to-day life, he's a loser, he's impotent, he can't control a thing. But when he hears fear in your voice, it makes him feel like a man. And he likes that feeling.

And you can do what about this? I'd asked.

You can make a date with him. We can try to be there.

Only try, Detective? I'd asked. I'd told him no thanks, I'd take care of it myself.

That night, I'd lay awake in the dark, waiting. I wanted to be alert when the call came, not sleepy and vulnerable.

Do you know who this is? he'd asked. After the first time, he'd always started out that way.

Yeah, asshole, I'd said, I do. And hung up on him.

He'd never called back, but I'd never found out where he was that he could see into my garden, where he could see the windows of the cottage and know when I'd shut off the lights. I never found out where he was, waiting an hour after the lights were off, until he was sure I was asleep, making sure that the jarring sound of the telephone would begin the work his voice would continue.

After a few weeks, I was able to stop leaving the light on in my office when I went to bed, end of story.

Whoever was watching Sophie had been far more persistent. And continued to be so. More important, he wasn't just a pathetic creep trying to feel like a big man by scaring strange women in the middle of the night from the safety of his own home and his anonymity. He was a murderer. And he was still out there stalking.

I waited until all the lights were out, all the windows dark, then duck-walked back a foot before standing up. Sitting on the top step, my back against the door, I put on my shoes and followed Dashiell back down to Sophie's.

CHAPTER 24

I Bent My Head to Listen

Dashiell knew something needed his attention before I did. When we got to the third-floor landing, he stopped, sneezed, and tested the air. Then he ran on ahead, not stopping and turning to see if I was following.

I ran, too. Going down the last flight, I could see the light spilling into the hallway. Sophie's door was wide open and Dashiell was nowhere in sight.

Was it Joe, back with a more effective weapon? Why had I thought he'd just go home and go to bed? Why had I been so careless?

Holding my breath, I listened for a moment, but it was another voice I heard.

I walked into Sophie's apartment and found him standing in the middle of the living room, all three dogs vying for his attention.

"What are you doing here at this hour?"

"I couldn't reach you. I tried you at the cottage, then

here. I got so worried I couldn't sleep. I kept thinking maybe something terrible had happened to you, too."

"But it's four-thirty in the morning." I checked my watch. "No, it's five-ten. Why were you trying to call me in the middle of the night? What on earth is wrong?"

"That's what I wanted to know. I didn't start calling you now. I've been calling since last evening. I got so scared, I couldn't stand it anymore."

"I don't understand. I was here."

We both turned to look at the telephone at the same time.

I picked up the wire and gave it a tug.

"Did it come out of the wall?"

"Not exactly."

I held up the end of the wire so that he could see it had been cut.

"The bedroom, too?"

"I'll go check," I said, knowing what I would find. Had the bedroom phone been functioning, I would have heard it ring when Mel called.

I took off my jacket and tossed it onto the bed, right next to where Mel had left his, then pulled out the desk and saw the phone wire dangling behind it, no big surprise there.

"Is that one cut, too?"

I nodded. "Time to blow this joint."

"Do you want me to take Bianca again?"

I stood there looking at them, all three dogs sitting and looking from Mel to me and back again, as if they were watching a tennis match.

"No," I said. "I want to keep the dogs together."

He screwed up his face, then surprised me by nodding.

"If that's what you want," he said. "But Judy wouldn't mind. She likes Bianca."

He must have realized his mistake instantly, at the same moment I did. His pale face turned red and when he opened his mouth to speak, he began to sputter.

"Take a deep breath," I told him. He did. "Good boy," I said. "Now, you want to explain that?"

He nodded.

"When I play with Bianca," he said, "like, when I throw a ball for her to catch, you know?"

Why was he telling me this stupid story? I headed for the kitchen and began to pack up food and supplements while he was talking. If he wasn't going to address the fact that he'd just called his dog by a different name, the hell with him. I was taking the dogs and going home.

Mel began to follow me, tripping on the edge of the carpet. He stopped and stood there, long skinny arms at his side, his face a tangle of concern.

"When she catches it," he continued from where he stood, "you know, in her mouth?" He nodded. "I always tell her, 'Good hands.' I don't want her thinking she has two left feet."

I stopped what I was doing and stared. Mel just smiled his lopsided smile and continued. "I do," he said. "And two left hands. I've never done anything right in my whole life. Including this."

"And what's this?" I walked back to where he was standing, close enough to make him back up. He looked around Sophie's apartment and made a choking sound in his throat. Then he lifted his hands and reached for me. This time I took a step back and he nearly fell, grabbing for me, then draping his long skinny arms around my shoulders and dipping his funny-looking face into the crook of my neck.

"You can tell me everything when we're on safer ground," I said, trying to pull away. "Let's just get out of here."

He nodded, but he didn't let go. He only held on tighter. "You're right. Let's get out of here. Forget about the food," he said into my neck. "It's just fruit and vegetables. We can buy more as soon as it's light out."

But we were already too late. When he stepped back, I saw Dashiell and Blanche heading for the open door, I saw the reflection in the garden window, one arm raised, and this time Joe wasn't packing a wrench. Mel screamed, "No, don't hurt her."

The hand with the gun swung down and hit Blanche, who was trying to block the way into the apartment not only with her own girth, but with her considerable grit as well, and who, in doing so, had so far kept Dashiell from the object of his disaffection. There was a dull thud and the sound of nails scrabbling as Blanche slid to the floor. Then time seemed to slow down as it does in a dream, and to my astonishment, I began to move without any effort on my part. Mel changed places with me, whipping me around behind his back, and immediately afterward, though it all seemed to happen at once, there was the shot, and a sound from Mel like air escaping from a tire. Joe screamed, Dashiell yelped, I heard the apartment door slam, and Mel slumped against me as if someone had suddenly removed the bones from his body. I held on while he, too, slid to the floor. Dashiell was in the hallway shaking his head. Behind him, Blanche made an amazingly small heap just inside the door to Sophie's apartment. When I looked back at Mel's face, which was already as gray as the sky above the garden just behind me, his blood spilling down his chest, hot and sticky on my hand, there was Bianca, licking his hands and whining.

"Phone, Dashiell," I told him, forgetting the wires had been cut.

I bunched up Mel's shirt and pressed it against the

wound, watching helplessly as the blood continued to ooze out around it.

Bianca was in near hysterics, licking Mel's face now, but it wasn't until after Dash came with my cell phone in his mouth and I had dialed nine-one-one that I realized what she was doing.

Mel opened his eyes and looked at me. "I told him he'd already gone too far," he said, barely audible. Then his eyes rolled up and he began to shake, legs kicking, arms jerking, saliva coming out of one side of his mouth, in the middle of it all making a honking noise, like a goose. I held on tight, keeping his head on my lap, trying to prevent further injury, thinking all along that if he didn't get emergency care soon, if he didn't get a transfusion, he'd be gone no matter what I did.

When Mel stopped shaking, I saw that Bianca was lying pressed against his side. I looked down the hall at Blanche and could see her torso moving up and down, her breathing as shallow as Mel's was now, both of them slipping away as I sat there waiting for help.

Mel opened his eyes once more, looking confused for a moment. When he opened his mouth, I bent my head to listen.

"I'm sorry," was all he said.

"Help is on the way," I whispered.

"It's okay," he said. "I feel better now."

I held him tight, one arm under his neck and around his shoulder, one hand still pressed against the wound, rocking him back and forth in my arms as if he were my baby, feeling his life running out between my fingers.

CHAPTER 25

Someone Has to Get the Dog

"There's a dog at his house," I'd told one of the officers who responded to the 911 call. "Someone will have to get her."

He nodded and wrote it down.

"Do you want me to . . . ?"

"No, ma'am. Thank you. We'll take care of checking out the victim's residence."

I winced.

"Sorry, ma'am. Were you close?"

I didn't know how to answer him. I hardly knew Mel Sugarman, but less than an hour earlier, he'd saved my life and lost his own in the process.

"We'll take care of the dog. It looks like you got enough on your hands as it is."

I looked down at my hands, soaked in blood, and for an odd moment thought that's what he meant.

But he must have meant the animals that were already

in my care, because he was looking at Dashiell, who was sitting next to the couch, pressed against my leg.

"Maybe Marty would take care of her for now," I said.

His eyebrows went up. "Ma'am?"

"The dog. Maybe Marty Shapiro could take her temporarily."

He still looked puzzled.

"He's with the Bomb Squad. At the Sixth."

He made a note of that, too.

An army had responded to my call. There was blue everywhere, paramedics, too. They'd put pressure pants on Mel, started an IV, but it was too little and too late. Much too late. Now they were waiting for the Crime Scene Unit, the detectives in dark-colored suits and cheap ties standing around and talking to each other, three of them out in the garden, two more in the short hallway, Bianca lying at Mel's side, not moving even when the paramedics tried to shoo her away. One look at that little black teardrop and they let her stay, working around her.

One of the officers had carried Blanche out into the garden and a paramedic seemed to be taking her vital signs. I couldn't see if she was still breathing. I could hardly breathe myself at that point.

"Ms. Alexander?"

I must have closed my eyes. When I looked up, the uniform was gone. A familiar-looking man in a suit was there in his place.

"Detective Agoudian," he said.

I started to get up but he put his hands on my shoulders, stopping me, crouching down so that I could see him without having to move. At least that's what I thought, and that he was a really nice man, sensitive, bending down like that so that I wouldn't have to crane my neck, but then he moved his hands and took my hands in his, standing and pulling me up, putting a hand on my back and leading me into Sophie's bedroom, backing me up to the bed, gently, insistently, the way a lover might, me thinking, Great, now I'll get blood on the bedspread, the way I'd gotten it on the couch, and while he pulled over the desk chair, so that he could sit in front of me, I began to wonder if we were here so that he could ask me how the screen had gotten torn. But he didn't. At first, he didn't say much at all and I wished he would, that he'd say something, anything that would take my mind off Mel lying dead on the rug in the next room.

"How well did you know the gentleman in the next room?" Agoudian asked, looking right at me, not taking notes.

"Not so well," I told him, trembling so hard I thought I'd bite my tongue.

"But he was here at four in the morning. Did you meet him at a party or a bar earlier in the evening?" He stood and reached behind me for a jacket, putting it over my shoulders.

"It was nothing like that," I said. "He was the dog walker. He walked Bianca, the smaller one."

He sat again. "And did he usually come to walk her at that hour?"

"No. Of course not. I don't know why he was here. What he said was that he'd tried to call me and got worried when I didn't answer. He said he tried me at home, then here, that he'd been calling since last night."

When I turned to look at the torn screen, the room spun. I put my arms into the sleeves of Mel's jacket, my hands into the pockets, finding his key ring and one other key, a smallish one that wasn't on the ring.

"It didn't make sense. Not until we discovered that the phone wires had been cut. But right then, all I wanted was out of here, because someone had been able to watch her, Sophie, and listen to her, especially when she was out in the garden, and that whoever it was had killed her, and that now they were watching me, and Mel said he'd help me get the animals out, so I didn't care about his story sounding fishy. Not then. Do you understand? Of course, before we got the chance to leave, he came, the man who called himself Joe, who said he was the super, but who wasn't. The super's name is Sergei."

I didn't think I was making any sense, but Agoudian was nodding, encouraging me to continue, to tell him more.

"You met Sergei. Well, I don't know if it was *you* personally. He said the police had come and taken the Vacor he kept on hand to kill the rats. One was there," I said, pointing toward the garden, toward the broken screen.

"How'd that happen? Is that how Joe got in here?"

"No. He has the keys. Dashiell did that. Joe was threatening me and the dogs were out in the garden because if the rat showed up, I didn't want them to chase it in."

"You mean last night?"

"No. He was here before. Twice before. He threatened me, told me to mind my own business. I didn't listen to him and now—"

"It's not your fault," he said. "You didn't shoot Mr. Sugarman."

"I know, but—"

"Listen to me, Rachel. You didn't do this."

I tried to speak, but my mouth seemed so dry, I couldn't form words.

"He has no ID on him. You said his name was Mel Sugarman, is that correct?"

"Yes."

Agoudian was waiting.

"I mean, that's what he told me. And you, well, some-one from the Sixth spoke to him before. When Sophie, Ms. Gordon, died."

He nodded.

"But maybe he didn't have any ID then either. No one asked me for mine at that time. They just made a lot of cloning jokes."

He nodded again, his expression patient and kind, as if to say *he* would never have done anything so adolescent at a crime scene. Or anywhere else.

"I don't know where he lives, but there's a dog there, at his apartment. Someone has to get the dog. She can't be left there with no food and water, without someone to walk her."

Agoudian got up and left the room. I wondered if I should mention anything else about the dog, like the fact that Mel had referred to her by the wrong name shortly be-fore he'd been shot. But when Agoudian returned, he had one of the paramedics with him, so I let that part go while the kid pulled down my lower eyelid, then put his moist, warm fingers on my wrist. When he'd finished, he gave Agoudian a look pregnant with meaning, only I didn't know what the meaning was.

"I'm fine," I told Agoudian. "Really. Just tired." Then I turned to the paramedic, a young kid, short and wide, his dark hair slicked down with something that made it look wet. Or maybe he was sweating. Maybe this was his first dead body, his first injured dog, his first babbling private eye. "The dog, Blanche, is she okay?" I asked him. "Can I see her?"

They looked at each other again.

"How old is she?" the kid asked.

"Nearly twelve," I told him.

He didn't look much more than twelve himself.

"That's old for a dog, isn't it?" He was looking at his shoes, brown Mephistos, not back at where Blanche was and not at me. My stomach tilted portside.

"Is she dead?" I asked him.

"Not yet."

I didn't remember when I'd eaten last, nor what I'd had, but whatever it was, it was suddenly in my throat.

"Can I take her to her vet?" I asked Agoudian. "If she has a chance . . ."

Agoudian didn't answer me. He turned to the kid instead. "Can you start a line on her?"

The kid nodded.

Agoudian nodded. "Do it."

The kid disappeared, but Agoudian didn't.

It was hours before he let me call Chip and allowed us to take the animals out of Sophie's apartment. But before that he did let me go outside and see Blanche as soon as she was getting fluids. When I walked out into the garden, the three detectives went in, huddling near the kitchen with Agoudian, deep in conversation. Or maybe they were telling cloning jokes. It's hard to say.

The kid crouched near Blanche and so did I. For a moment, we didn't speak. I heard some woman yelling at her kid, telling him he was late, he'd miss the bus. A dog was barking in another yard. And some kid was practicing the piano, making a lot of mistakes, starting and stopping, going back over what had just been played. The young paramedic asked if I'd stay with Blanche while he went to get an ice pack, and while he did, while I was alone in the garden with her, I turned my back to the apartment and pulled out my cell phone. When I started dialing, a phone rang somewhere near the garden, the sound echoing off the building so that I couldn't tell where it was coming from and the music stopped. Maybe they were coming from the same place.

I waited for my machine to pick up; I said I was off the case, that Bianca had alerted a seizure so I no longer had any need to locate Side by Side, and besides, I said, it had gotten too damn dangerous. I waited. Then I said, no, I wasn't disappointed. I was happy to turn the case over to the cops. That's their job, I told the tape. Why should I bust my ass doing their work for them when I'm not even on the payroll anymore, hoping as I spoke that Agoudian wasn't listening.

Me, too, I said, flipping the phone closed and putting it back in my pocket just as the kid showed up with the ice pack, handing it to me.

Blanche opened one eye when I put the ice pack against the side of her head where Joe had slammed her with his gun. She sighed and in a moment she was out again.

"That's a good sign, isn't it?" I asked the kid.

But he didn't answer me. He probably didn't know. Then all I could hear was that piano again, and Blanche breathing, the hollow noise you get when you press a seashell tight to your ear. Sitting back on his heels, one hand on Blanche's side, the kid just watched her stomach inflate and deflate, her rib cage move up and down, maybe hoping she'd make it, that he wouldn't be seeing his second dead body so soon after the first.

Agoudian was standing in the doorway. I took the kid's hand, moved it to the ice pack, and went back inside.

CHAPTER 26

I Took a Big Breath and Let It Out

"Will she be all right?" I asked.

Sandra Cohen was still holding the stethoscope against Blanche's side and didn't answer my question.

After what seemed to be a very long time, she took the instrument away from Blanche and out of her own ears, carefully laying it down on the counter behind her.

"There's just so much heartache an animal can handle," she said.

"You mean she's going to die?"

"I can't say for sure. But there's not much we can do for her. If you like, I'll keep her here. I can continue giving her fluids and keep an eye on her. We just have to wait and see if she has it in her to rally."

"The injury?"

She shook her head. "It's not that. The ice pack took the swelling down. But she's an old dog and she's had a lot of hard knocks, some more painful than a blow with a gun.

I'm sorry to have to ask you this, but will you be responsible for the bill?"

"Yes, but I'm not leaving her."

"I understand. I'm here in case you need me."

Chip was waiting for me in the car. When he saw me carrying Blanche, he got out and opened the door for me. I slid into the backseat, Blanche on my lap, not saying a word.

When we got home, he helped me get Blanche and the other dogs inside, then went to park the car. I lay Blanche on a folded quilt on the living room floor and gave Dash and Bianca fresh water outside. Then I began to prepare the raw food for all the pets, putting Blanche's portion in the blender until it had the consistency of baby food. When it was ready, I took a small portion of it and sat next to Blanche, talking to her and stroking her until she opened one whale eye and looked up at me, then I fed her what I could from my finger, offering small enough amounts so that she could swallow without lifting her head.

When she had eaten as much as she wanted, I lay down on the quilt along the line of her back, putting an arm across her side, my hand curled under her front leg and against her chest, feeling her breathe, whispering in her ear as she did. I heard Chip come in and take the food outside for Dash and Bianca and walk back in to where I lay on the floor with Blanche.

"Do you know what she said as I was leaving?"

He knelt, resting one hand on the top of Blanche's head.

"She said, 'At least you have the clone. It's not like losing her altogether.' "

"You told her?"

"Everything."

He closed his eyes and shook his head. "I knew there

was something wrong with that woman when she didn't attend my talk."

"Is that what people really think, that a clone *is* the original? That would make twins interchangeable, wouldn't it? It doesn't account at all for the development of character, of soul. You can't duplicate those things."

"There's some more bad news, Rach."

I slid my hand out from under Blanche's leg and sat up. "What?"

"I don't imagine you saw today's paper yet."

"No, of course not."

"They did some tests on Dolly and found that her telomeres were shorter than they should be."

"In English please."

"The telomeres are attached to the chromosomes and they get shorter each time a cell divides until eventually the cell dies. Dolly's shortened telomeres might reflect the age of the cell from which she was cloned."

"You really can't fool Mother Nature."

"It looks that way. At least for now. But this technology is moving faster than we can absorb it. They may, one day, find a way around this problem, too."

"But meanwhile, Bianca was cloned from a nine-and-a-half-year-old dog."

"That's right, Rachel. But so far, she's fine. She seems healthy and acts appropriately for her chronological age, exactly the way an adolescent should act."

I looked back down at Blanche, sleeping again.

"No matter how many ways we try to play God . . ."

"Only God can make a tree?"

"Correct."

He put his hand on the back of my head, leaned forward, and kissed my forehead.

"You should get some rest, Rachel. You had some night."

"He saved my life," I said.

He nodded.

"He did it deliberately, pulling me around behind him when he saw Joe, or whatever his name turns out to be, with the gun. And he said something so strange, Chip. He said, 'I told him he'd already gone too far.' Him who?"

"Are you going to . . . ?"

"I was hired to contact Side by Side, to tell them the talent they were cloning for did not translate, that the cloned dog wasn't alerting. But Bianca wasn't alerting because the job was taken. She wasn't needed. Blanche was doing the job for her. But when Blanche was incapacitated, and Mel . . ." I stopped and took a few breaths, thinking of Mel lying in my arms, bleeding to death, thinking how easily that could have been me. "When Mel was about to seizure from loss of blood, Bianca alerted him. She knew."

"So there's no need for you to find Side by Side."

"I think what Sophie would want—God, I hate it when people say that, but, still. I think Sophie would want me to take care of Blanche. And for now, that's what I intend to do."

"The police will find Joe."

I nodded.

"When they do, I guess they'll want you to ID him, and eventually testify against him."

"I suppose."

"You'll be able to?"

"No problem."

"And until then . . ."

Blanche's feet were moving. When she began to yelp in her sleep, we both reached out to stroke her.

"Do you think she'll make it?"

"If she's got a chance, Rachel, your taking care of her will give it to her. If you'd left her there . . ." He shook his head. "I don't think she would have lasted a day."

"I don't know if she'll last a day here."

"We have to wait and see."

After Chip left for work, promising he'd be back as early in the evening as he could, I called in the dogs and we all stayed with Blanche. I thought I'd sleep, lying against her back, the way I do with Dashiell. But as tired as I was, sleep did not come. I kept thinking about cloning, what it meant, where it would lead, if it would turn out to be another disastrous act of human hubris, like the atom bomb.

I sent Dash for the phone and dialed a familiar number, one I hadn't called in ages.

"Ida?" I said when she picked up.

"Rachel."

"I need a minute or two."

"Of course."

"Have you been following the news about cloning," I asked, "about Dolly, the sheep?"

"Cloning?"

"Yes."

"Well, yes, of course I've read about it. But what . . . ?"

"I have a client whose dog was cloned. She, the client, was an epileptic and someone approached her about cloning her seizure-alert dog."

"You said she *was* an epileptic?"

"She was murdered."

"How awful. And you're trying to find out who killed her?"

"I'm trying to find out how I feel about cloning right now. I feel really confused."

"Tell me about it."

"A lot of people think that procreation should be left to God."

"The Joyce Kilmer school of thinking?"

"Yes," I said.

"And you think?"

"Well, the thing is, yes, I'd agree with that. Or I would have. But this cloned dog, she's wonderful. There's nothing wrong with her."

"That you can see."

"That I can see."

"But perhaps . . ."

"What I can't see might be screwed up. Like this age thing, the shortened telomere. Or something else. Something worse."

"So what do you think about it, given that?"

"If I knew what I thought, I wouldn't have called."

"Ah. I was wondering about that. Why did you call?"

"I told you."

"What's really going on?" she asked, the way she always had. "I can hear that something's bothering you and I can't help wondering if it isn't something more personal."

I took a big breath and let it out. Blanche, in her sleep, did the same. Dashiell sat up and cocked his head. Bianca was running in her sleep this time. Outside, some birds were squabbling over a branch. And I could hear some crazy person yelling, from way over on Tenth Street. How was I supposed to think in this crowd?

But I did, suddenly seeing how stress and exhaustion had made me lose track of who I was and what I did. A moment later, the answer to her question came in the form of a picture, the image of Mel bleeding and dying in my arms. I looked down at myself, realizing I was still wearing the bloody shirt and jeans.

"You're right, as always," I said into the phone. "It *is* more personal. Thank you." Then I hung up without waiting for a response, my head clear again. I knew exactly what it was I had to do. I even knew why.

CHAPTER 27

I Rotated the Knob and Gave a Push

I put the phone down, lay my head on the carpet, right behind Blanche's, and with the comforting smell of dog filling my senses, finally fell asleep. At two-thirty, the afternoon sun coming in the open door, the damn birds, their recent conflict a thing of the past, singing so loud they could wake the dead, I woke up, my heart pounding until I could feel that Blanche was still breathing. I didn't realize until it rang again that it was the phone that had awakened me. Blanche opened her eyes as I eased my arm out from under her head. Her tail thumped against the rug and then she got up, taking her time, and walked slowly over to the open door.

The phone rang again.

"Alexander."

"Ms. Alexander? This is Preston Wexford, returning your call. You're calling at a great time, a perfect time, the ideal time to buy in upstate New York. The real estate boom hasn't hit us yet, but it will—"

"Hello," I said, wondering if I was hearing a person or a computer-generated message.

"It's still possible to buy property here very reasonably and I can almost guarantee you that your investment will—"

I spoke a little louder this time.

"MR. WEXFORD?"

Okay, I shouted. But it worked.

"Ma'am?"

"That's not why I called you."

"Oh. I apologize, but since you called my business number—"

"I'm calling about your cousin Sophie."

"Sophie? She's still alive?"

"Actually, she's not. She was killed a few days ago. That's why I'm calling . . ."

"I don't understand. How did you get this number?"

"From Sophie's doctor. She had you down as next of kin."

I could hear a dog barking on his end, a siren passing on mine. I waited, but nothing happened for a while.

"Mr. Wexford?"

"I haven't seen Sophie since we were kids, since a year or so after . . ."

"You weren't in touch recently, birthdays, Christmas?"

"I thought she was dead. I thought she died. My mother said she wrote her and the letter came back, oh, *years* ago. We assumed . . ."

I got up and walked over to the open door, stood next to Blanche, saw Dashiell and Bianca asleep on the warm flagstones that led to the tunnel.

"You know, because of her condition."

"I'm sorry to—"

"Yeah," he said. "And she had my number in her book?"

"Yes, but I got it from her doctor. She had you down as—"

"Right," he said. "Next of kin. You're sure there's no one else?"

"She didn't seem to think so."

"I don't know how to feel about this."

"That might take some time," I said.

Blanche walked down the stairs, squatted right on the flagstones, then came back inside, lying down on the floor near where I stood.

"Well, Mr. Wexford, as far as I can tell, you are next of kin. I'm sorry to be the one to give you this bad news, and to be so abrupt about everything, but, you see, I'm running out of time here. I'm trying to clean up Sophie's affairs before her apartment . . . the thing is, Mr. Wexford, Preston, I was wondering if you'd be willing to make arrangements for her."

I moved the phone away from my ear and swiped at my eyes. I didn't think Preston Wexford was going to be in any rush to respond.

"I could give you the number of the precinct."

"The precinct?"

"She was murdered, Preston."

"Murdered? You mean, like in a mugging?"

This time I took my time.

"Ask for Detective Burke," I said, giving him the number of the Sixth. "It's probably better if he explains it, gives you the official, uh, details."

"Okay," he said, overwhelmed.

"And that way, you can take some time. You can think about what you want to do, about your cousin. Look, it doesn't have to be real complicated. Something simple would—"

"I thought she died a long time ago," he said.

This wasn't going as well as I'd hoped. I was beginning to think I shouldn't bother to ask about the dogs. But if he was next of kin, I didn't really have a choice.

"She has two dogs that are going to need homes really soon," I said. "Although I'm pretty sure I can place the younger one with Sophie's best friend. If that's okay with you."

"Yes. Yes, of course. That would help," he said.

I heard a dog bark again.

"Do you have a—"

"Three of them. It's the country up here, you know. What kind is it, the other dog?"

"A bull terrier. She's old, Preston. It'd be swell for her to live in the country, have someone in the family to—"

"I don't know," he said. "Like I told you, I already have three. The last one, Roberta, she just found me. I woke up one morning, she was on the porch, no intention of leaving. So what could I do? I put out a bowl of food, then I took her to the vet and we went on from there."

He was starting to sound like a very nice man, startled by what I'd dropped on him, but very nice. Kind, too.

"Perhaps I should tell you that Blanche, the old dog, was a seizure-alert dog. She wasn't just a pet, Preston. She was a service dog and she made a radical, positive change in your cousin's . . ."

And then I just stopped, because Blanche had rolled over and put her head on my foot. I crouched down and stroked her cheek.

"If you don't mind, I'll keep her here. She's on a special diet. It takes about half an hour to get her food ready and it costs an arm and a leg. Anyway, we're used to each other."

"Were you and Sophie close?"

I watched as two tears landed on Blanche, leaving small gray spots on her fur.

"Yes," I said. "Very."

"Well, that would be fine," he said.

"What would?"

"What you said about her dogs."

"And her things?"

"Her things?"

"You see, this is New York City real estate we're dealing with here, Preston, so the landlord will want this place ASAP, so that he can raise the rent and get himself a brand-new tenant. But you talk this over with Detective Burke, okay? He'll help you figure it all out."

"Okay," he said, sounding seven.

"She was a wonderful woman, your cousin. It's sad she never called you. I know she thought about it, about calling you," I said, thinking about the white lies she'd told Lydia, something to make herself feel less alone. "You would have liked each other a whole lot."

I dropped the phone on the marble table and got some raw, chopped turkey for Blanche. She ate it from my hand, but before I had the chance to offer her a medley of vegetables and yogurt, she was back asleep. I showered and changed, then sat upstairs in my office and made a list of what I knew. And more important, what I didn't know.

When I was still training dogs and I had a tough problem, one in which the solution wasn't immediately obvious to me, I would let everything I thought I knew go, as if what I believed about the dog and what I'd been told were so many leaves I was tossing into the wind. Then I'd start from scratch, looking at the dog as if for the first time, making room for him and what he knew and what, if I paid careful attention, he would tell me about himself, about the world, and about me. And that, I knew, was exactly what I had to do now.

I took out the list of inoculations that Bianca had been

given, wondering who had written it. Then, with the list in my pocket, Dash and I headed over to Hudson Street to find Mel's mailbox. I tried several places that had mailboxes for rent, including the post office, and fifteen minutes later found a box that had the same number as Mel's key. Then I headed for Horatio Street with his spare key ring in my pocket, hoping the pocket could hold all that weight without tearing.

It was one of those perfect September days, the sky a bright middle blue, the clouds puffy, like the ones you see on picture postcards. It was cool enough that we could walk quickly, and the air seemed charged with energy. Or perhaps that was just me, my determination and anger propelling me forward. Dashiell stayed at my side, looking up at me every so often. Whatever it was, he felt it, too. We didn't know where we were going, but we were heading there at top speed.

I stopped outside the building on the corner of Horatio and Washington, the place where cells and blood had been taken from Blanche, someone not taking any chances, someone who wanted to make doubly sure he had what he needed. But I didn't go in this time, to look for an office I'd never find, one, I now thought, that had been set up for that one use, like a movie set. Instead, I stopped outside the building and read the plaque that was there, taking out a small pad and pen and writing down all the information. Perhaps someone at JSB Properties would be able to tell me who had rented an office on the ground floor for so short a time that no one could remember their ever being there.

Of course no one would remember them. It had been a Sunday. There wouldn't have been anyone else in the building.

Next we headed a block north, to Gansevoort Street, to

the place where Mel had seemed to vanish the night I met him back where the vet's office was supposed to be. Unless he'd started to run, the only way he could have disappeared was if he lived right there, in one of the lofts above street level. Standing on the corner, I looked at the other side of the street, a meat market on the corner, the little French bistro Florent a quarter of the way up the block, then an architect's office, and farther down the street, a bar named Hell. On the second story, on those buildings where there was one, there were apartments, and even more on the south side of the street, where Dash and I stood.

I went into the little deli on the corner first, describing Mel in great detail, the hair that looked as if he'd touched a live wire, the gangly, dangling arms, the too long legs, the smile that worked on one side of his face but not the other, saying he had a dog, maybe they remembered her, a mixed breed named Margaret. Or perhaps Judy.

But the guy shook his head and pointed at the door I'd just come in through.

"We don't allow dogs in the store," he said. "It's against the law. If you want to shop here, you'll have to tie him up outside."

"Oh, this one's okay," I told him, but not explaining, picking up some gum, a candy bar, and a small packet of Kleenex instead, thinking that spending a little money might make him friendlier. "Maybe you saw the guy without the dog."

But all he could think about was that I was spending less than two bucks and if someone from the Department of Health waltzed in to check the premises, he'd be the proud possessor of a three-hundred-dollar fine.

So once again, he shook his head and pointed. "I tol' you, lady. I never seen no one like that. Now"—he pointed to Dashiell—"you get me in trouble, lady, I lose my job."

So I paid for the tissues, candy, and gum and left, turning right onto Gansevoort, trying the gallery where I'd gone to meet another client, some weeks back, describing Mel again, mentioning that he had a dog, waiting and hoping. I tried the new restaurant on the corner, Le Gans, though I couldn't picture Mel sitting in such an upscale restaurant, white tablecloths, flowers on the tables. So I crossed the street and tried Florent, because anyone might show up at Florent, a movie star, or a skinny guy whose arms and legs flailed around like a marionette's. But no one knew a Mel Sugarman and no one remembered a dog named Margaret or Judy, a dog who might be waiting for her master even now, thirsty, hungry, and in need of a walk.

I even stopped a couple of people on the street, a young girl carrying a painting wrapped in brown paper and a short heavyset man in a bloody white apron heading back to one of the wholesale markets with his take-out coffee. A lot of people shook their heads when I asked about Mel. Maybe he hadn't lived here. Maybe there was more time than I remembered between when he left me on the corner of Horatio and when he seemed to disappear on Gansevoort. The truth was, I still didn't know anything. He could have lived anywhere.

I went back into Florent and checked the phone book, but somehow I didn't expect to find a Mel Sugarman and I didn't. Why would anything in this peculiar case be that easy?

But I wasn't giving up yet. I stuck my hand into my jacket pocket and pulled out that enormous key ring. A man who'd worried he'd leave someone else's dog without a walk if he lost his keys might also worry about his own dog. You lose your work keys, you might lose your house keys as well. Was that why he'd kept the key to his rented box separate from the rest of his keys?

I started at the east end of the block I was on, figuring I'd check the names on the bells, then try every key on the ring on the downstairs door, see if any of them worked. But halfway around the ring, I noticed something odd. A mail key. That meant that the set of keys on either side of that key could be Mel's, and if so, that I'd been right about one thing, that he'd left a duplicate of his own house keys at the mailbox, just in case.

I tried the keys to the left and to the right of the mail key, but they didn't work. And neither did any of the names—McSweeney, Zeichner, Polsky. Someone was coming out. I watched him check his mailbox. It was Zeichner. He stopped there, in the tiny hallway, eyeing me while he snipped off the end of a cigar and lit it. The smell of smoke filled the small area. Dashiell sneezed.

"Can I help you?"

"Maybe. I know this is going to sound stupid, but I'm supposed to walk a dog who lives on this block." I lifted the set of keys, to prove I wasn't lying. "But it's my first time here, and I'm not exactly sure of the address."

"You don't know the address?"

"The owner's name is Sugarman. I know it's not here, on the bells, but if he lives with someone else, I thought maybe the key would fit . . ."

He took another puff on that cigar and smoothed his scalp.

"Her name's Judy, the dog. She's a mix. Or Margaret," I added, feeling like a fool.

"You don't know the dog's name?"

I lifted the key ring again. "I have a lot of clients. And she's new."

Zeichner was shaking his head.

"No dogs in this building. Cats. We have three. My neighbors," he gestured with the cigar, "have one each. Maybe another building?"

I opened the door to the street and let Dash out, then turned back. Zeichner locked his mailbox and walked out past Dashiell. I followed him, describing what Mel looked like.

Zeichner shook his head. "I'd like to help you, but I don't know," he said.

"Well, thanks anyway." I headed for the next building.

"Wait a minute," he called after me. "There's a skinny guy I see a lot across the street." He pointed with the cigar. "But his dog doesn't look like a mix. I mean, not that I'm any expert. Are they usually solid colors, mixed breeds?"

"Some are, sure."

"Well, then maybe this one I saw is Margaret. Or Judy."

"Where did he come from?"

"The guy?"

"Yeah."

"There." He gestured with his head this time. "Only I still think the dog is a purebred."

"A bull terrier?" I asked, thinking he might have seen Mel with Bianca.

But he just shrugged. "Ask me if it's an Abyssinian or a Burmese, I can help you out. More than that—" He shrugged again.

I started to cross the street.

"What do they look like?" he asked. "Bull terriers."

"Medium size, white, Roman nose, shortish tail." I left out the part about the tear.

He shook his head, took a puff of his cigar. "Medium size? I don't think so. This one looked *much* bigger than medium size."

I thanked him and Dashiell and I crossed the street, but when I checked the name on the upper bell, it wasn't Sugarman. It was Madison. I turned to leave, but then turned back. The plaque on this building said it was managed by

JSB Properties, just like the building where some vet had taken cells from Blanche. For half a second, I wondered about that. But then I'd always been told that half the buildings in the West Village were owned by Bill Gottlieb. Maybe JSB Properties owned and managed a sizeable chunk of the other half. Because the brass plate on Zeichner's building had the same name on it, too, as building manager. The third key I tried unlocked the outer door. Then I stood in front of Madison's mailbox and hesitated. But not for long. A moment later, I was holding his phone bill in my hand.

Still, I reminded myself, Mel could easily have been taking care of cats, plants, and mail for someone who was away on vacation. Maybe this was where he'd gone the night I'd lost him, not because he lived here, but because he had an Egyptian hairless to feed, a litter box to clean, a coleus to water, and some bills to drop on Madison's desk. On C. Madison III's desk.

Hoo-hah, my grandmother Sonya would have said.

I had to agree. It didn't look like the kind of place a III would live. Still, you never know.

I looked down at Dashiell, who was looking back at me, his tail wagging, well, boss, are we going to see some action or not? written all over his face.

So I rang the bell. And heard barking.

The key to the left of the mailbox key opened the door to the stairway. Then mightn't the next one unlock Madison's door?

The stairs were worn down to almost nothing, uneven enough that I had to watch where I put my feet. I held on to the railing, listening to the sound of barking getting louder as I neared the apartment.

Dash was stuck behind me on the narrow stairway, but when I was halfway up, he couldn't contain himself any longer. He squeezed by me and scrambled on ahead, dipping his nose to the saddle of the door as soon as we got there, then turning back to see what was taking me so long.

The key in my hand was a Medico. So was the lock.

The barking had stopped. Now the dog on the other side of the door was sniffing at the saddle, trying to figure out who was there, friend or foe.

I slipped the key into the lock and gave it half a turn, then hesitated. If it wasn't Mel's apartment, I was trespassing. But that wasn't my concern. What I did care about was that if it wasn't Mel's place, then that wasn't Judy on the other side of the door. Whoever it was had a mighty big bark. Maybe it was something huge, something hugely unfriendly.

No matter what was in there, I had to get inside. I had to get to the bottom of this, and I had to do it now.

Dashiell was pressed against my side, his forehead wrinkled, his hackles up, his tail straight out behind him, stiff as a rudder. A low growl came from somewhere in the vicinity of his stomach. I turned the key until the tumbler turned over. The dog inside barked again. I rotated the knob and gave a push.

CHAPTER 28

I Said Her Name

Head down, legs wide, tail straight out behind her, she seemed to fill the doorway, a good trick for a forty-pound dog. She was wide and white, a ski slope for a nose, tiny no-frill whale eyes set in that massive head.

"Margaret?"

The dog didn't move a muscle.

"Judy?"

Nothing.

That's when I noticed the collar, one of those from R. C. Steele with the dog's name and phone number sewn on in contrasting colors. My stomach did a quick handstand.

I said her name. She took her eyes off Dashiell, looked up, and wagged her short thick tail.

And that's when I got a good look at her face, the pink strip abutting the leather of her nose, the little mustache underneath, the goofy smile and the little black teardrop at the outside corner of her right eye.

Not Judy, I thought.

Not Margaret.

And not Mel Sugarman.

C. Fucking Madison the Third. And Sugar. Clever, I thought. I couldn't help smiling. Then I remembered. Whatever his name was, he was dead, having intentionally taken a bullet that was meant for me.

I bent and scratched Sugar on the head. She turned back to Dashiell and bowed. Despite all the noise, she was still a puppy. I told Dash okay and he followed the clone down the length of the loft, one large room about twenty-five by eighty, sunlight pouring in from the huge back windows and down from the three skylights.

The bed was at this end of the apartment, covered with a leopard spread and strewn with dog toys. The open kitchen was in the middle of the apartment, under one of the skylights, a round marble table ringed by leather chairs across from it. Down at the far end, where the dogs were wrestling prior to heading back my way, there was a huge leather couch, a couple of comfortable-looking modern chairs, an Oriental rug that looked as if it had been in the family for generations but, like my aunt Ceil, had kept its glow, and a grand piano.

I let the door close and walked slowly down to the far end of the apartment thinking that no way on earth could someone live like this by walking other people's dogs for a living, rain or shine, like the postal service. It's not that dog walkers did so badly. But this was old money I was looking at, not cash earned by wearing out shoe leather.

Of course, he could have been an eccentric. Hell, as far as I could tell, he *had* been an eccentric. Sometimes people with tons of money do whatever it is they want to anyway, as if they didn't have all that dough, as if they had to work for a living. Dog walking? I didn't think so. I'd see the walkers schlepping dogs around when it was over ninety, faces red, T-shirts soaked with sweat, still a dozen more walks to do. And in the rain, the dog's tail tucked, ears back—even *he* didn't want to be out in all that slop.

I sat down on the leather couch and took the key ring out of my pocket, placing it on the cushion next to the one I sat on, looking hard at the keys, something I hadn't thought to do before. But now that I did, I could see that most of them were identical. Actually, there were keys for three different brands of locks and all the keys for each lock were copies. Clones. Apparently Mel had walked only one dog, aside from his own.

I wondered which dog I had seen that night on Horatio Street.

And how and why Mel was really there. Because what he'd told me, I now knew, was just another lie in a pack of lies.

I tried to picture Blanche that night, to remember how she'd acted. At first, she'd pulled toward Bianca, sniffing and checking her out. Bianca, or Sugar, had licked Blanche's mouth, typical behavior of a younger dog toward an older one. But then on the way home, Blanche was upset and clingy. I remembered that I'd stopped to comfort her, never thinking I had to look for a reason beyond the obvious, that she'd been upset because her mistress had just died. But she might have been upset because she thought she saw Bianca, then it turned out the dog was a stranger, only a look-alike and not the real thing. I couldn't know for sure, not with Mel, or C. Madison the Third, dead. But it was very possible Mel had had his own clone out, not Sophie's.

What I did know was that dogs were able to tell the difference between identical twins, by smell. And wasn't that what clones were, identical to the original and, in this case, each other?

If Mel had had Sugar with him the night I'd run into him on Horatio Street, that would explain why she had gotten friendly once the door was open. I wasn't a stranger. We'd met before.

I glanced around the apartment again. There were no photographs anywhere, not on the walls, none on the dresser or the nightstand.

If Mel lived here, around the corner from where I ran into him, might I have just met him by accident?

No way. There were far too many "accidents" in this case already. I had to assume that the meeting was intentional, which meant that one way or another someone knew where I was headed, someone who'd called Mel and told him to show up there, too, see what the hell I was up to, find out what I knew.

I wondered if he'd thought it was funny, bringing Sugar along, knowing I'd think she was Bianca, one more clone joke to add to the ana, but not one for the next veterinary conference, a very private joke this time.

I got up and walked back the way I'd come in, locking the door. Then I went straight for Mel's bathroom, opening the mirrored cabinet and checking out the medications, looking for anticonvulsants in particular. After that, while the dogs continued to play, I began to look for papers, anything that would tell me who this man was and how and why he had gotten connected to Sophie. And to me.

CHAPTER 29

I Probably Shouldn't Have Let Him Do That

I knew I shouldn't take Sugar with me when I left. I had no right to do that. Hell, I had no right to be in Mel's apartment, and worse, to go pawing through his things, make a list of the numbers he posted by his kitchen phone, write down the addresses that went with those names and numbers from the address book I found in his nightstand.

But I felt awful about leaving her alone, even after walking and feeding her. I stayed while she ate her food, wolfing it in great gulps as if she was starving, as if she didn't know where her next meal would be coming from. Watching her eat, I wondered when she'd eaten last. Unless Mel had hired the services of a dog walker, it couldn't have been today. I checked my watch. She'd be fine for eight hours, even nine. I'd just have to make sure I got back here before going to bed and give her another walk.

I was wondering if I should give her some more food

before I left when I heard it. Sugar and Dash heard it, too, someone coming up those creaky, worn-out stairs. I couldn't leave. There was no place to go. I grabbed Dashiell as he headed for the door, pulling him by his collar. I headed for the bathroom, yanking him backward until he was inside and closing the door. Then, because I had no idea who was coming or what they were after, I signaled him to jump into the tub, followed him in, and pulled the shower curtain closed around us. Then, trying to slow my breathing, I waited.

I heard Sugar barking. Once, and once again. That meant it was someone she knew. Sure enough, I heard a key in the lock, then the doorknob turning. Then I heard his voice, talking to her. Or perhaps to himself, asking where the damn leash was, sounding annoyed that he couldn't find it. Or perhaps it was something else. Perhaps he was still annoyed that his bullet had hit the wrong target, that he'd failed to kill me but had killed Mel instead, and that before getting the chance to try again, Dashiell had chased him out of Sophie's apartment.

There was a rumble coming from Dash's throat. Still holding his collar, I hoped I was feeling it, not hearing it. Joe probably still had his gun with him and I didn't have mine. No matter how he felt, Dashiell had to shut up, and fast. I pulled his chin up so that he had no choice, he'd be looking me right in the eye. Then, with my other hand, because if I could hear Joe, he could surely hear me, I put my hand up like a stop sign and moved it from side to side, our version of that'll do, the command that calls the Border collie off the sheep. I used it mostly when we were playing and he was being obsessive, to let him know I was quitting and he had to, too. His brow wrinkled, but he obeyed. Keeping my hand in his collar, I could feel that the rumbling had stopped.

I could hear Sugar's nails as she padded around the loft, following Joe.

"Here's the damn thing," he said: "I thought I was going to have to use a rope."

He must have put the leash on her and then dropped the handle because I heard her tick-ticking along the floor now, the leash dragging behind her.

Then the bathroom door opened. Dash looked up at me and saw the panic in my eyes. I felt something move under my hand and pulled up on his collar, taking his toes off the ground, then immediately setting them—soundlessly—back onto the porcelain, telling him in the only way I could not to growl. Our lives depended on his silence.

We stayed absolutely quiet while Joe peed, so quiet that I thought I could hear the drops of urine he shook off his penis hitting the water in the toilet. I tried hard to hold my breath, praying Dashiell wouldn't choose now to sneeze, waiting for the sound of Joe's zipper and the rush of water when he flushed. I heard the first sound, not the second, heard his shoes squeak as he turned and left, heard Sugar dancing around at the front door to go out, even though she'd just been walked. Fortunately, she seemed totally taken with the next project and had forgotten all about us.

I waited after the door slammed to hear the tumbler turn over, then I waited some more, for Joe and Sugar to get down those rickety stairs and out onto the street. I took a deep breath—it felt like hours since I'd done that—and told Dashiell, "*Good* boy. Okay."

I followed him out of the bathtub and stopped to flush the toilet. He'd left the seat up, too. What a guy. I looked around for Dashiell's leash. It wasn't where I'd left it. Joe had taken it, thinking it was Sugar's. It took me a couple of minutes to find hers, hanging on a hook in the closet. He was neat, Mel. You had to give him that. I took one last look around the loft, felt sadness wash over me like the waves did when I was little and visited my aunt Ceil in Sea Gate, then let Dashiell out, locking Mel's door behind me, not bothering to wipe the knob clean. I had no intention of making believe I hadn't been here. I'd just have to add the issue of why I hadn't called the precinct immediately to the rest of the uncomfortable questions I'd be asked one day soon.

I had a lot on my mind, but I no longer wondered what I'd do if the cops didn't locate Mel's apartment pretty soon. I was pretty sure Sugar wouldn't be coming back here so I no longer had to be concerned about running back to take care of her, or about taking a chance by taking her home with me. I was as sure as I could be that she was back with the people who were responsible for creating her in the first place and that when I tracked her down, to one of several addresses that were already in my pocket, I'd find out what was behind the murder of my client and the clumsy attempt on my own life.

Before Joe had shown up, I was thinking that maybe I should call Agoudian, tell him I'd run into Mel a block from where he lived, and so I'd come back this way and stumbled across his apartment, sort of by accident. I could have made sure he found Mel's place sooner rather than later. But now that the dog was taken care of, I thought about the other side of that call, explaining to him how I'd stumbled across Mel's apartment after finding his rental box key loose in his jacket pocket, palming it and stealing it at the crime scene, how I'd taken the keys he'd kept stashed there and tried them out on Gansevoort Street on a hunch rather than turning them in. That would go over big.

One way or another, the detectives would get here eventually. At least now I didn't have to worry about them dropping Sugar off at the ASPCA. Walking home with Dashiell

I thought about the dogs I'd seen there, dogs who were there because their owners had died and there was no relative willing or able to take them, old dogs, young dogs, all of them sad dogs. And in no time at all, if the right person didn't come along, they were dead dogs. No one had volunteered to do anything about Sophie's pets, no one besides Mel and myself.

What would have happened to Blanche and Bianca had we not been around? Would they have ended up in the shelter, dogs who could change the course of a disabled person's life?

I was so worried about the animals, I was forgetting to watch my own back. I had no way of knowing if the message I'd been trying to send by talking on the phone in the garden had been overheard, and if it had, if I had fooled anyone. I didn't know how long I'd be safe. Well, perhaps I did. It would be worse than foolish to assume that whoever had failed to silence me early this morning would give up for any reason. Whatever they were trying to gain, or hide, they were in too deep to stop now.

I hadn't pretended to look into a store window, see if anyone was following me. I hadn't stopped off anywhere, to be able to check the street when I came back out. I hadn't pulled out a mirror, pretended to check my hair, gotten a view of the street behind me. Anyway, even if I'd wanted to do that, I didn't have a mirror, so I couldn't. And if I did, what would I have looked for, Joe, going on ahead and then waiting to see if someone would be coming up behind him? If he knew I was there, he would have killed me in the shower, right after killing Dashiell.

So there were two clones. Maybe a third somewhere. Was Mel Sugarman, or whatever his name was, an epileptic, too? He'd had a seizure, but that could have been from loss of blood. And whatever was in his medicine cabinet and nightstand, or rather whatever wasn't there, hadn't made me think otherwise.

But if he wasn't an epileptic, why did he have one of the Blanche clones? And why did he lie and tell Sophie he was a dog walker? What on earth could have made him walk Sophie's dog five days a week, rain or shine, for a solid year when he wasn't a dog walker and didn't seem to need the money?

Sophie had been watched and listened to. Was Mel the spy? Fine. Mel was the spy. But for whom? Himself? And why? What was he after? What was he hiding? Who was Joe? And why did he have Mel's keys?

I'd detoured out of my way going home to check out an address on Barrow Street between Hudson and Greenwich. Unless this was another plant, a made-up list by the phone, a fake address book, an apartment set up just to fool me, I was in luck. It turned out to be a private house, a little red-brick Federal, about a century and a half old, and next door, a similar house with a similar stoop, a place for me to sit and listen, close enough to see and hear, if what I now hoped for was so. I climbed the stoop to the pilaster-framed doorway and checked the names on the bells. There was no name, but only one bell. Perfect.

Heading home, I was lost in thought, figuring out what to do. I barely noticed where I was walking, going on automatic pilot toward Tenth Street. But as soon as I'd turned onto my block, Dashiell snapped me back to reality. As he approached where he lived, he had things on his mind, too, and until I was brought up short by his leash, I hadn't noticed that he'd stopped to leave his own news item on a tied-up pile of newspapers. I probably shouldn't have let him do that, but in a city setting, there just aren't enough upright things for male dogs to mark without making *someone* unhappy. I thought of all the times I'd been yelled at for letting him lift his leg on the tire of a car, a tree, someone's stoop, the garbage bags some super was moving out to the curb. Mail storage boxes, no-no. Think about the poor mailman who had to go in there for his next sack of mail. Lampposts? Half of them had those front plates missing, exposed wires on the bottom. Someone at the run had said some dog got electrocuted, peeing on an open lamppost. No wonder there were people who didn't believe in keeping dogs in the city.

Standing there while Dashiell sniffed, then hiked his leg again, I began to read the headlines on the tied-up papers, reminding myself that I hadn't done anything normal for days now, hadn't read a paper, eaten a decent meal, paid my bills, spent time with my sweetheart.

Some cops were on trial for brutalizing a citizen. Who could you trust nowadays? Then I thought about Mel again, about the way he'd pulled me around behind him.

He knew Joe. He knew what Joe had gone there to do. He'd been in it, whatever it was, up to his skinny neck. Then why save me?

I unlocked the gate, let Dashiell off leash, and walked slowly to the cottage door, listening to the sound of only one dog barking. When I opened the door, Bianca jumped on me, then ran past me to be with Dashiell. I stepped inside.

Except for the ticking of the kitchen clock, the cottage was silent. There was no bull terrier in the living room. I ran upstairs, thinking she'd gone up to lie on the bed, the way she'd gone to lie on Sophie's bed, to wallow in the smells of her caretaker. But the unmade bed was empty. I checked the office. Then I ran back downstairs. And down the flight to the basement. Blanche wasn't there either. When I headed back up, there she was, standing at the top of the staircase, her tail wagging slowly from side to side.

She was warm, the way dogs are when they first wake up. She must have been curled up on the other side of the couch, so deep in sleep she hadn't heard me come in. Unless there was another problem, unless Blanche was losing her hearing. Or found it too difficult to get up unless she absolutely had to. I bent to hug her. When she started to squirm, I knew I'd held on too tight and too long.

I went into the kitchen and got food ready for the dogs. Then I went back upstairs to change, putting on Chip's denim shirt, a pair of jeans, an old, black jacket with a tear in the sleeve, and black sneakers, pinning up my hair and covering it with a black baseball cap, grabbing an oversize pair of dark glasses, too, so that I would blend in with the night. I did one more thing before leaving, something that would pretty much guarantee that no one would look in my direction. I took out the shopping cart and piled it full of newspapers, magazines, and the empty water and soda bottles I hadn't yet put in the recycling bin outside. I added a broom, stuffing it in upside down. I checked myself out in the mirror, holding on to the shopping cart. Unless someone tried to smell me, I'd pass.

I left the dogs at home, Dashiell giving me that puzzled look he gets when I go out without him, and headed for the nearest florist, giving them the address of the house I'd just seen on Barrow Street and the name I'd found in Mel's address book as well as some explicit instructions and a generous tip for the deliveryman who would carry them out. The owner kept his distance, kept shaking his head, having every reason not to want to do business with me, at least until I took out a wad of cash to pay for the flowers I'd ordered, adding an extra twenty for him. Then I headed back to Barrow Street myself to take my place on the stoop next door and wait.

I sat on the hard step for nearly an hour, hoping I wasn't waiting because the florist had called before sending his deliveryman and found out that no one was home. There were lights on in the house, but that didn't mean anything. People left lights on when they weren't home, too, to fool the burglar, a trick that probably wouldn't fool an observant ten-year-old.

I saw him coming up the block, a little guy with bandy legs, holding the bouquet by the stems until he saw me. I shook my head and he passed without a word, climbing the stairs next door and ringing the bell.

I heard the voice over the intercom, a woman's voice.

"Who is it?"

"Delivery," he said. He turned to look at me and once again, I shook my head.

"Who's it for?" she asked.

Good one. That's why people don't put their names on the bells of private houses in New York. Anyone can ring and say it's UPS or Fed Ex. God knows who'd be standing there when you opened your door.

The list at the phone had said only "Lizzie." There was only one Elizabeth in Mel's address book.

"Elizabeth Madison." He was holding the flowers upright now. No, he was holding them up to the intercom. Who did I expect would be delivering flowers, Einstein?

"Who did you say you were?"

I could see the little white envelope stapled to the flowered wrapping paper at the top end of the cone.

"Florist, miss." He waited for a response, but none came. "I was by twice earlier, but no one was home."

"*Flo*rist?"

"Yes, miss."

"Who would be sending me flowers?"

He shrugged.

"Who are they from?" She spoke louder this time, and spaced out her words.

He still didn't answer her.

"Who are the flowers from?" Shouting now. Losing her temper.

Better than I'd hoped for.

"Oh, I wouldn't know that, miss. I only delivers them."

"Hold on. I'll be down." As annoyed as if he'd gotten her out of the bathtub.

Sitting on the far end of the stoop next door, the cart parked in front of me, my head down as if I was napping, I wondered what the hell this would accomplish, a quick glance at someone whose number was next to Mel's phone? Someone with the same last name. But for now, it was all I could do, just take a look, let the deliveryman do what I'd tipped him to do, figure out the rest later. I sat there for longer than it would take to walk down from the top of the building, waiting for the door to open. And then it did.

She looked cold, the way she was hunched into her navy cardigan, a scowl on the oval face, a half-smoked cigarette sticking out of the side of her mouth, the eye on that side closed to keep smoke out of it. Her hair was blond now, hunched hack with a barrette, pieces sticking up like rabbit ears. But all that took was a trip to the drugstore and a pair of rubber gloves. I couldn't see if her nails were bitten. Still, I had no doubt about it, I had found Lorna West.

My man handed her the posies. She began to close the door.

"I need you to sign the receipt," he said.

"Yeah, sure." The cigarette bobbing with each word.

He fished in his jacket pockets. Then his pants pockets.

"I'm going to be in a heap of trouble."

She sighed. "Left it at the shop?"

"Looks that way, miss."

He looked at her, his face so screwed up I believed him

myself. This time I had a mirror because it would have been dangerous to appear to be paying attention to what shouldn't seem to be any of my business. I tilted it, so that I could see her face.

"How about if I write something on the envelope?"

"That would be fine, miss. I thank you from the bottom of my—"

"Yeah, yeah. Don't get all emotional about it. It's just a receipt." She took the cigarette out of her mouth and flipped it past him, into the street. I saw the coal break up, bits and pieces flying in all directions, then going out. She stood there waiting.

"A pen? No, don't bother. You forgot that, too, right?"

She handed him the flowers and went back inside, letting the door close in his face. But he put his foot out, clever man, and when the door hit his toes, it remained ajar. I listened to the sounds of her house, a television on somewhere in the back, nothing else, no dog barking from the yard or tick-ticking along the wooden floor after her mistress as she went to fetch the pen.

A moment later she appeared with a ballpoint pen, clicking it open and snapping the envelope with the card inside it off the bouquet.

"More trouble than it's worth."

"Write the date, miss, and the time, then received from deliveryman, one nice bouquet."

She looked at him, the scowl deepening. I palmed the mirror, afraid a reflection from the lighted doorway would catch her eye and make her look my way.

"You sure you don't want *War and Peace?*"

"Miss?"

I heard her strike a match and smelled the sulfur.

I heard nothing for a moment but kept my head down on my folded arms.

"Here."

"Don't forget the note."

I turned over the hand holding the mirror.

He pulled the note I'd had the florist write out of the little envelope and handed it to her.

I saw her take it in her fingers and turn it over. She inhaled hard, then slammed the door. I heard the lock turn over. I heard the chain go on. I listened, wondering if she'd move a bureau in front of the door next.

The little man stood there, the flowers in the crook of his arm, not exactly Miss America, but grinning as if he were.

He walked down the steps and, before he got to where I was, I got up and started down the block. I heard his feet shuffling along behind me. He caught up near the corner.

"Did I do it right?"

"You were perfect."

I handed him another ten. Hell, she'd screwed him out of a tip, it was the least I could do.

He handed me the flowers.

I shook my head. "You done for the day?"

He nodded.

"Take them home," I said. "I bet you never buy flowers for yourself."

When he smiled, I saw that he never went to the dentist either.

He left, carrying the posies. Halfway past the St. Luke's gardens, he started to whistle.

I leaned against a lamppost, fussing with the junk I'd piled into my shopping cart. After a few minutes, I saw a rectangle of light down the block as Elizabeth Madison opened her front door and stepped out. I waited for her to lock it and pass where I was standing, never looking in my direction though she was close enough at one point for me to smell the stale smell of smoke on her sweater. I waited for her to cross Hudson Street before ditching the shopping cart next to the nearest trash can, keeping only one of the empty soda cans, and heading east, walking quickly in the direction Lizzie had gone. But no matter if I lost her. I knew exactly where she was headed.

CHAPTER 30

He Hadn't Shaved

When Elizabeth Madison turned right onto West Fourth Street, I kept going, following her from behind a row of parked cars on the other side of the street. I stopped when she did, watched her ring the bell at the house behind Sophie's, and waited as the door opened and she disappeared inside. Then I waited another five minutes before crossing the street again, going up the same stoop she had and checking the name on the bell. This time there was one. Charles Madison. Why wasn't I surprised?

I leaned hard on the bell, heard a dog bark, and quickly went back to where I'd been, crouching behind a green Toyota that had a little handwritten sign in the window saying No Radio, the window next to it broken, the ground covered with tiny shards of green glass, as pale and shiny as jellyfish.

The door opened and there was Joe again, a white bull terrier at his side, her nose tilted high, her nostrils moving.

He hadn't shaved, poor thing. He looked a mess. It must be very stressful, killing the wrong person.

He looked left and right, then pulled the dog back inside and closed the door. I walked to the corner, checked out the drug dealers lined across all the paths in Washington Square Park, then headed around the block.

There were no cops standing around outside the building where Sophie had lived. The little brass plaque with the name and address of the building manager was tucked under the bells. I had to crouch to read it: WAM Realty. Three initials again. Or perhaps it was a name this time. I remembered seeing it on Sophie's rent check, wondering if it was Chinese, elevating my arm for five minutes so that I could tell my Chinese doctor I'd followed his instructions.

I unlocked the outside door. There were no cops inside either. The yellow tape made a big X over Sophie's door, but that didn't present a moral issue for me since that's not where I was headed.

I took the stairs, climbing slowly. I didn't expect to meet anyone, or find anyone when I got to where I was going. I didn't think anyone had followed me from Charles Madison's house. There was no reason to rush.

I could hear television sets playing and snippets of conversation as I approached each floor. When I got to the top, I pushed on the bar that opened the door, carefully letting it close on the Schweppes ginger ale can, and stepped out onto the tar-covered roof. For a moment, I stood still, my eyes adjusting to the light, listening to the sounds, smelling the honeysuckle that climbed a trellis on one of the back balconies of the building next door. Then I walked toward the edge, crouching when I neared the parapet and looking over at what was below. Looking straight down, which I did first, made my knees feel as if they'd turned to liquid. There was no light on in Sophie's garden, nor in the little cottage that backed up to it. The town house behind it, the one where Joe was, and Elizabeth Madison, was all lit up. No one had bothered to close the curtains either, and lucky me, I had my binoculars hanging around my neck under my jacket. I unzipped and held them up to my eyes.

I could see into the living room, an open loftlike space that ran undivided through to Fourth Street. The grand piano was near one of the garden windows, on the side opposite the tall, glass French doors. Beyond that, huddled together at a round table, were Joe, Elizabeth Madison, and Charles Madison, sitting with his back to me. Still, he looked familiar.

I backed up and looked around the roof for a rock, but found only tiny pebbles. I scooped up as many as I could hold and, keeping my foot in the doorway, filled the soda can with them. Then I slipped off my shoe, left it in the doorway, and went back to the edge of the roof. Standing, but not looking down, I hurled the can as far as I could. I heard barking, then I saw them, two white bull terriers, as game as they were meant to be, barking at the back door.

Madison got up and let them out. For a moment, he stood in the doorway. I peered through the binoculars trying to figure out where I knew him from. Then he turned and went back to the table, hunching over and leaning forward, Joe and Elizabeth leaning closer, whatever they were saying, neither of them wanting to miss a word.

I watched the bullies in the garden. They'd found the can. At first, they tried to play tug of war with it, pulling it in pieces, the pebbles spilling onto the flagstone walk. Then one, followed by the other, carried the treasure to the back door, put paws up, and pushed the doors in and open, vying to see who could get to the table first and drop the half can at Madison's feet.

He looked down, then slowly got to his feet and came

toward the back door, standing in the doorway again, this time looking all around the dark garden, then up at the buildings surrounding it. For a moment, I ducked even lower.

Elizabeth was smoking, her face crunched into a scowl. Joe got up and went to stand next to Madison. He whispered something to him. Madison nodded. Then they locked the doors and went back to where Elizabeth was sitting. I could no longer see the dogs.

I backed up, retrieved my shoe, and went quickly this time, and quietly, down the stairs, thankful that no one in the building had a pet that would bark and let people know I was there. At the bottom of the stairs I turned left, down the short hall that led back to Sophie's apartment. I took out my keys, unlocked the door, and pushed it in carefully, tearing the yellow tape where it had gone across the door and onto the frame. Then I slipped inside and locked the door behind me, leaving the lights off.

I went straight back to the dark garden, opening the sliding glass door, then quickly closing it behind me. Grateful I'd kept practicing the t'ai chi I'd learned while working on another case, I crouched as low as I could, then, hearing the voice of my old teacher, I sank even lower and skittered across the garden to the loose slats in the fence, pushing them open and squeezing into the garden next door.

There was a single lamp lit in the apartment next to Sophie's. I stayed where I was until my legs were burning, waiting to see if there was any movement, if anyone was at home. Then, staying low, I crossed the garden, slid up the bedroom screen, and when no alarm went off, no slathering Great Dane threatened to eat me, no gun was shoved in my face, did the same with the unlocked window and climbed in. I was nervous about the light, but when I looked back the way I'd come, I could see only the very top windows of the house on Fourth Street. If people stayed where they were, on the parlor floor, no one would be able to see into this apartment.

Of course, I had no idea whose apartment it was, or when whoever lived here would return. I suspected that whoever it was had something to do with my case, but I wasn't sure of that and didn't know what that connection was. I wasn't sure what I expected to find either, a signed confession, a checkbook or tax return pregnant with pertinent information, even some ID that would tell me the name of the tenant who occupied this apartment so that I could get the hell out before he or she occupied it again.

But what I found surprised me completely. Except for the lamp, the apartment was empty, as in unoccupied, and from the looks of things, had been this way for ages.

Leaving nothing, taking nothing, though the Crime Scene Unit would laugh themselves silly over that notion, I went out the way I'd come in, closing the window, then the screen, duck-walking back to the loose slat in the fence and quickly slipping into Sophie's apartment where, halfway in, I changed my mind. I turned and there was the little back cottage, just begging to be explored.

Staying low, I crossed the garden to the brick wall, pulling apart the thick ivy, hoping Mr. Rat wasn't close by and checking out the wall. Mortar had been chipped away and pulled loose by the ivy. There were bricks missing as well. I could see enough footholds to encourage me to try to scale the eight-foot wall. In fact, I thought if I took enough of it, like Rapunzel's hair, the ivy would serve as a rope to help me to the top.

Only once did the ivy start to pull away quickly and that time, I was close enough to the top to grab on and pull myself up and over. There was a stone bench near the wall, under where I was flattened on top, like a bug. I shinnied over a few feet to avoid it, and, taking one deep breath, dropped to the garden floor, falling forward onto my hands but not hurting myself. From where I was I checked out the cottage—a wooden door, painted a bright blue, two locks on it, probably both locked, and a window, open eight or nine inches at the bottom.

The sudden sound startled me and I went belly down in the pachysandra bed in which I'd landed. Madison and Elizabeth were still in the town house, at the table, talking loudly. She moved her hands a lot. He sat very still, unnaturally so, making my neck itch, making me sure I'd seen him before, but I couldn't for the life of me remember where. Joe was nowhere to be seen, maybe in the bathroom or out to purchase a new supply of Vacor.

I stayed low, watching the house as I closed in on the cottage, deciding not to even try the door because, open, it would be visible from their living room. Instead, I slid the window up just enough so that I could climb in headfirst, wiggling the rest of me through the narrow opening and closing the window partway once I was inside. Waiting for my eyes to adjust to the dark didn't take long because whatever light was coming in through the windows was shining on the stainless steel cabinets, playing on the microscopes and the tall shiny doors of the oversize refrigerator. I heard a floorboard creaking upstairs and ducked behind a lab table in the middle of the room, not much protection if someone came downstairs and turned on the lights, but the best I could find on short notice.

It was an old building, like the back cottage I lived in. The main floor had been gutted and made into a laboratory. Since the little back window had been dark, I guessed whoever I could hear now crossing the wooden floor lived there, and had been asleep. Had I awakened him? I thought

I'd been silent. That seemed a joke now. I heard the floor creak again. Then someone sneezed. I held my breath.

Would he come down or go back to bed? I decided not to find out. Backing up to the window, I nearly tripped over a pile of magazines and newspapers tied with a cord and waiting to be set curbside for recycling. I couldn't help looking, to see if whoever lived here read the *Wall Street Journal* or *Playboy*. But neither was on top of the pile. It was *Clone Magazine*. Clever me, I'd found Side by Side.

I tore off the cover and stuffed it into my back pocket, looking up at the ceiling and willing whoever was up there to go back to bed. But instead of hearing a door close, or the springs creak, I heard someone coming down the stairs.

I slid the window all the way open, not bothering to close it behind me this time, getting out of the cottage as fast as I could. I never stopped moving, using the bench to give a boost up the brick wall, tossing myself over the top and landing with a thud in the ivy on the other side.

Catching my breath, I saw him again. He'd been eating something in the center of the garden. The noise had made him stop and turn. For a moment, we stayed the way we were, two animals sizing each other up. Then he dropped to all fours and disappeared into the pachysandra.

I ran across the garden, into Sophie's apartment and straight out her front door, stopping only when I saw another rat. This one was looking down at what he was doing, unlocking the glass door from the street.

CHAPTER 31

It Was Probably His Eye Glasses Case

I had only two choices—back to Sophie's apartment, or up the stairs. I chose the stairs, taking them two at a time, moving as quietly as I could on the chance he hadn't seen me. But as I headed up to three, I heard him behind me, not moving quietly, his big feet slapping hard against the stairs, making them moan and creak despite the carpeting.

I thought about banging on someone's door, but if I waited and no one was home, he'd have me. So I kept going, straight up to the roof. I pushed the door open and stepped out into the dark, feeling wind coming from the west, seeing the top of the house on West Fourth Street, the windows dark, everyone downstairs, everyone waiting for Joe to come back, say he'd gotten the job done properly this time.

I had no soda can. I decided not to leave my shoe in the door either. I went to the edge and looked over, checking for a fire escape or a terrace I could jump down to. I thought I could hear him breathing behind me, but the door hadn't opened yet. I wondered if he had the gun this time, hoping he had only the wrench. I was full of hope, and so scared I sounded as if I was having an asthma attack.

The door opened and for a moment he stood there, the dim stair light behind him making him look even bigger and bulkier than he was. I looked at his hands, then for a bulge in his belt. Then I checked out his size again, comparing it to my own. I would have swallowed but my mouth was too dry.

He took a step forward. I stood where I was, the uncomfortably low parapet right behind me.

"Bitch," he said, still not moving out of the doorway. "You're more trouble than you're worth."

"Whatja bring this time, Joey? Let's see, we've done the Vacor, the wrench, the gun. How about a rope and a chandelier?"

He laughed, a man who once again was in no rush. "Rope and a chandelier? Not exactly, but close enough. Want to write a little note before you jump? Or shall we leave it a mystery, private eye, distraught over the death of her client, leaps to death from roof of West Village apartment building. It's got a nice ring to it, don't you think?"

This time I had enough saliva to swallow.

"You're right," I said. "I am depressed. I should have protected her. It's all my fault."

I bowed my head, clasped my hands, and mumbled to myself. Out of respect, Joe stayed put. He wasn't a complete boor, you had to give him that. Head still low, I turned, looked all the way down into Sophie's garden, my knees turning to water, anything I'd eaten since I was nine fighting to come back up and out. Then I glanced to the right and took off running, going over the low parapet, to the next building, and then the one after it, which was about as far as I could go on this block since the next building was two stories taller.

I didn't have to look, I could hear him behind me, his shoes on the tarry surface of the roof, his heavy breathing. I was sure he was getting angrier with every step. I went to the north parapet again and turned to face him. He was almost on top of me. I opened my mouth as if to speak, then closed it. He came at me fast now, his meaty hands straight out in front of him, aiming at my chest.

I waited as long as I could, and then a second longer. As he came at me, giving it all he had, I leaned to the side. Instead of hitting me dead center with both hands, his right hand hit my right shoulder, spinning me around and knocking me off balance. His left hand hit air. Joe, too, lost his balance, listing a little to his left, lurching forward, flipping headfirst over the low wall. Facing the way he went, I continued moving, too, over the parapet, still spinning from the impact, so that as I went over, I was facing the building. Reaching for what I had seen from the roof of Sophie's building, I grabbed with both hands, hoping that one of them would make sufficient contact with the ladder of the fire escape to stop my fall. But it didn't. Feeling one hand scrape along the rusty metal, I fell for what seemed like forever, landing with a loud clang and a double shot of pain on my hands and knees on the top level of the fire escape, the one below a window of the sixth-floor apartment. Eyes closed, mentally checking to make sure I was in one piece, I took a breath, staying exactly where I was, crouched like a dog.

Because of where I had positioned myself for the push that was supposed to unite me with my client and her dog walker, Joe had gone straight down. Well, maybe not straight down. With the fire escape that close, he may have banged his shoulder against it on the way, sending him a little farther to the left.

Steeling myself for the return of nausea, I opened my eyes and looked between the rusty metal slats beneath me. Everything spun. I took a deep breath and let it out. Joe lay still, five stories below me. He'd apparently hit the birdbath in the center of the garden with his head, as if the fall wouldn't have been enough to kill him. The birdbath was lying next to his body, the basin cracked in half, the spilled water making his dark hair even darker, pasting it down to his skull, making his round pale face shine, as if he were in the middle of a bad dream, sweating profusely from the fear. There was water all around him, too, dark and glistening. But maybe not. It was probably blood.

I reached for my cell phone, but it wasn't there. Looking down again, I saw it in the garden, close enough to Joe's hand that, were he able, he could make the call we needed himself. But maybe not. It was probably his eyeglass case or his wallet. A fall like that, things are bound to get out of place.

The curtain was pulled back. There, at the bottom of the window, was a small face, the large blue eyes fixed on mine. A moment later, a man opened the window.

"What in the hell . . . ," he said, the little boy now hiding behind him.

"Sorry to bother you," I said, still on my hands and knees, "but could you call nine-one-one? There's a dead man in the garden."

CHAPTER 32

He Pulled Down the Shade

Whoever lived in the apartment whose fire escape I'd landed on didn't offer to let me in through the window. Instead, he checked to make sure it was locked, and that the lock was holding. Then he pulled down the shade. "No," the little boy said. I could hear him whining as he was being dragged to the safety of another room.

I didn't stay there on the fire escape to wait for the cops. I had other things to do. I stood carefully, did a quick check of body parts—my own—and when I found I was more or less intact, climbed up the ladder I'd missed on the way down. My cell phone was next to the parapet between this building and the next. I picked it up, shoved it back into my pocket, and tried the door to the stairs, finding it locked.

Ignoring my scraped hands and bleeding knees, I went quickly over the low wall to the next building, the one abutting Sophie's. The fire door was locked there, too, but this building also had a fire escape. I climbed down the ladder, trying to think about anything but how much it was shaking and pulling away from the brick wall of the building, bits of mortar falling to the garden below as I descended as quickly as I could, trying my best not to make noise, which was, of course, a hopeless endeavor.

The second-floor fire escape was the last one. From that one you could lower a ladder to the garden next to Sophie's, if you had the tools to get it free. Apparently there hadn't been a fire in this building for fifty or a hundred years. No way was I going to get this ladder to slide down. So I climbed over the edge and hung by my torn hands, dropping gracelessly onto the brick patio outside the living room of the vacant apartment, spun around, pulled open the window, and, in no time, was out on Third Street and heading home.

I called Chip when I got to Bleecker Street, told him I was alive, skipped a few of the details, like the stuff that had happened on the roof and my escape through the empty apartment next door to Sophie's. But I did tell him I'd found the lab where the cloning had been done and that I had the name of the geneticist who'd done the astonishing work sub rosa. He asked if I wanted him to come over. I told him no, I had to do some research, find out all I could about Ruprecht Philips before morning.

"What then?"

"Depends on what I find."

No one said anything for a minute. I thought about changing my mind, asking him to come over, bring his laptop, help me with the research. Then I thought about him seeing my hands and knees all bloody and raw and decided it wasn't a good idea to risk clicking on the "Me Tarzan, You Jane" thing, making him feel he'd failed to protect me from the charging rhino.

"Not to worry," I said, wincing as my jeans pulled against one knee where the fabric had stuck to the wound, thinking if I wasn't in jail by morning, I might do something the good doctor and all his colleagues no longer did. I might make a house call.

There were no cops waiting for me on Tenth Street, only dogs, three of them, all acting as if I were Santa Claus with a bag full of liver treats. Dashiell spent a lot of time sniffing at my bloody knees. The bullies licked my hands. I fed them, let them out, and got to work.

At a quarter to four, the excitement of the hunt keeping me wide awake, I found what I was after, an article about Ruprecht Philips, whose name I'd gotten from the mailing label on the cover of *Clone Magazine*. He'd been doing research on cloning for a small lab that was hoping to corner the market on human body parts, hoping that instead of waiting for a new kidney, patients would be able to buy one. The lab had lost funding when Clinton called the ban on human cloning and my guess was that Charles Madison had seen that same article and had snagged him for Side by Side.

I wondered if it was Philips who had taken the DNA samples from Blanche, though it could just as easily have been Lorna, going into the back room and taking cheek swabs. Sophie said she never saw the vet. I'd read the instructions at VetGen's web site and it didn't seem to me you'd have to be a rocket scientist to follow them.

Okay, I thought, making notes as I did, let's say Madison set up a lab for Philips in the cottage, paid him a fat salary, had him there cloning dogs.

But why? What the hell was he doing there that made it worth killing Sophie?

And Mel?

Then I thought about the loft on Gansevoort Street,

about the name on the bell. Didn't that mean that Mel was Madison's son?

Impossible. No one would . . .

But he hadn't sent Joe to kill Mel. He'd sent him to kill me. Twice. Maybe three times, the klutz. All his money, Madison couldn't find a better goon?

And what now? Send someone else? Do it himself? He was in too deep to stop. Whatever it was he was after, nothing was going to stand in his way—no loss, no law, no anything.

I made a grilled cheese sandwich, putting a mug on top of it to make sure the cheese melted. Sitting at the table, I looked at my notes, trying to figure out what this was all about, how the different parts connected, and when I thought I had most of it, I locked the door, took a hot shower, and waited for morning.

CHAPTER 33

He Took a Step Toward the Gate

I called the house on West Fourth Street, and when he answered, told him where I'd be in an hour. He agreed to meet me so that we could talk. Then I showered, dressed, ate, and fed the dogs, taking the bullies for a walk, then leaving them home and taking Dashiell to the dog run.

He'd gotten there before me, taking the same seat he'd had the first time I'd met him, looking pretty much the same as he had then, overdressed for where he was. This time, perhaps to keep the sun out of his eyes, or maybe for some other reason, he was wearing dark glasses.

I kept Dashiell on leash and sat down next to him. He dipped his chin, but didn't speak.

"Why?" I asked him.

"You couldn't possibly understand."

"Try me."

He looked me over and exhaled through his nose, like a horse. Clearly, I wasn't up to his high standards.

"I'm your best shot," I said.

"It seemed an incredible opportunity for me, a dream come true. Except—"

"Except that you'd never be able to publish it, never be able to announce it, never get to take credit for it."

He shook his head. "No. That was part of the deal. Though I thought that one day he might change his mind. I hoped that, at least."

"If you were successful."

He smiled. "Yes, that big if."

"And you were. There were how many Blanche clones?"

"Just the three. Once we had those, we didn't try for more."

"Still, it's an astonishing accomplishment."

"Still," he said, staring straight ahead, across the run, focusing on God knows what.

"And fantastic as that was, something that would have assured your place in history, it was just the warm-up."

"Yes." No surprise showing on his face. Still staring straight ahead, as if he was talking to himself, not to me. And maybe, in a way, he was.

"The real work, how did that go?"

He shrugged. "It hardly matters now. The project ended last night."

"So I heard."

Now he turned his head and looked at me, at least I assumed he was looking at me. All I could see in those dark, dark glasses was a miniature reflection of myself, something akin to what Charles Madison had so longed to see.

"He wanted this enough to kill for it."

"I had no idea. I knew he wanted it enough to spend millions on it. The rest, when it happened . . ."

"But you didn't stop then. You didn't leave. You—"

"I was in so deep. I was so involved in the project. The thought of abandoning it, well, I just couldn't, I couldn't. I told myself—"

"That it wasn't your fault, what happened, it was his fault. He'd done it. You were just a scientist doing what you'd been trained to do, using your extraordinary talent, following along from question to question."

He turned back toward the other side of the run and nodded. "Yes. Something like that."

"Did you know, when Sophie died, what had been done?"

"Not at first. But then I heard talk."

"He was on the phone?"

"No. He was talking to his son. Arguing, actually. I was coming in from the lab, crossing the garden. I could hear them through the French doors."

"His son," I said.

"Adopted."

"Ah."

"And the daughter also?"

"Yes."

"So neither of them—"

"No. That was the gist of what he told me, that he was not able to father children but that more than anything in the world, he wanted one who would inherit his ability."

"Who would play the piano."

"Compose and play, yes."

"But the son and daughter?"

He shook his head. "I suppose it's a form of megalomania, not so different from his. But when he approached me, all I could see, all I allowed myself to look at was the opportunity to work with unlimited funds, with fewer restraints than I'd have anywhere else."

"Something you were unable to turn down."

"I expect I could have turned it down, Ms. Alexander. I don't want you to think I take no responsibility for my decision. I am not without backbone. But the temptation . . ."

"Nearly impossible to resist, a chance like that."

He nodded.

"And you had no idea how obsessive—"

"Obsessive? Oh, believe me. That, yes, I did see. But not how violent he was. Perhaps I was naive."

I didn't respond. I wondered, instead, how many of us could resist an offer like that, the dream of a lifetime on a silver platter.

"Did you live there, too?"

He nodded again.

"At the cottage, over the lab?"

"No. The main house, top floor."

"Then who lives at the cottage?"

"No one."

"What's upstairs? More lab space?"

He looked at me again. "You are something, aren't you? You were there, too?"

"Everywhere."

He smiled that cold smile of his. "No, not quite, Ms. Alexander."

"I sit corrected."

He nodded. "There are some things you still don't know. Isn't that why we're here rather than you being wherever it is you spend your time and me being in jail?"

"You didn't mind, living at the office, no escape from it?"

"Not for a long, long time. Work is pretty much my life," he said. He looked at his hands, the long slim fingers a pianist's hands.

Only he hadn't been the musician. Charles Madison had, Charles Madison whose sausage fingers had come toward me on the roof hours before, ready to send me flying into a cold, hard death so that his secret could remain so.

"Elizabeth?" I asked.

"She had nothing to do with any of it."

"Is that a fact?" I said. Blondes, apparently, do have more fun, assuming this broomstick of a man could be considered fun. "How about when she was performing her play in three acts as the lovely, dark-haired Lorna? Did she have nothing to do with any of it then?"

"She was only trying to . . ."

"To?"

"Please her father. He wasn't easy to . . ."

"Please?"

"She . . ." He swallowed hard. Something, it seemed, was stuck in his craw, whatever that means. "He was difficult to . . . Look, she only wanted to feel loved, the same as any kid does."

"Touching," I said.

He gave me a hard look. "There's no need to be sarcastic."

"Dr. Philips, it may have escaped your notice, but because of your employer's massive ego, and your own, three people are dead, including Elizabeth's father and brother. How did she handle that news?"

"How do you think?"

"Were they close?"

He turned the other way. In fact, he turned around, scanning the park, as if he had to see who might be listening before he could continue.

"Close? I wouldn't say they were, no, not especially."

"And the mother? Where was she?"

"No mother. He'd never married."

"Raised by wolves?"

I got that look again.

"By a nanny. A loving—"

"Yeah, yeah," I said. "You can tell by how secure and relaxed they both are, were, as adults."

For a moment, he screwed up his face. Something was troubling him, finally, after all this time, after all he'd let pass.

"But she—"

"Yup. You can see it all around you, women in the park with children not their own, talking to other nannies instead of to the kid. Loving, you said? I don't think so. Especially not with a prick like Charles Madison for an employer."

He examined his hands again.

"So, you say other than her role as the seducer of my client, other than delivering her to the faux veterinary practice, other than that, and delivering the cloned puppy to Sophie, Elizabeth had nothing to do with any of this? By the way, was it you who harvested Blanche's DNA, or was that Elizabeth?"

He shook his head dismissing my last question. "She knew what I was doing, of course. But she didn't know anything about Sophie's accident."

"Good one."

"She thought it was a seizure, a terrible mishap."

"A mishap? But not you. You didn't think it was a mishap."

"Well, yes. I mean, no. I had no idea he planned to kill her."

"With rat poison?"

"No idea. I never would have allowed him—"

"And how would you have stopped him, Dr. Philips?"

This time he turned slowly. I saw those long fingers

gripping his thighs so hard his nails were white, trying to regain the control he felt he was losing.

"Well, I could have threatened to leave. He wouldn't have liked that."

"But you didn't."

"It was all after the fact, when I found out what he'd done, that he'd killed her."

"He knew the amount to use? Clever, for a piano player, wouldn't you say?"

He stood.

"I wouldn't," I said.

"You wouldn't what?"

"Know the amount of Vacor to use, if I wanted to kill someone that way. But you would, Doctor. And I wouldn't be standing if I were you."

"What are you talking about?"

"Of course," I said, as much to myself as to him, "you wrote a prescription for the anticonvulsant Sophie used, emptied out all the capsules, filled them with Vacor, then left that vial near her bed, and after she was dead, you put her own undoctored pills next to her, so that it would seem the dog brought the pills too late to do any good."

"Have you lost your mind. I never—"

"It wasn't a matter of patience after all. Sophie was talking too much, way too much. She was going to blow your big secret if she kept it up. In fact, she already had, when she had the bullies' DNA tested. No, you weren't patient. Far from it. You wanted her dead *yesterday,* especially after you heard her call to me. You were so damn arrogant, all of you, assuming the police would be fooled, seeing an epileptic dead with her medicine vial at her side. You figured they might check out the pills, but you never thought they'd autopsy, did you?"

"You're being ridiculous. I was never in that woman's apartment."

"Of course not. It was a joint effort. You're a cooperative group, I have to give you that."

He exhaled through his nose, turned, and took a step toward the gate.

"Uh, uh, uh. You're upsetting me. You don't want to do that."

"Aren't you being a bit foolish now, Ms. Alexander? Why would I care that I was upsetting you? You're a stranger to me. And I have much on my mind at this time."

"I bet you do. Now, sit down. I'm not finished."

I pointed my left hand at him and nodded, not to him, to Dashiell.

Dashiell stood. But Dr. Philips only smiled that ice-cold smile of his.

That's when I felt it, cold and hard against the back of my neck.

"Don't turn around." I smelled the stale tobacco on her clothing and in her blond hair. I didn't have to turn to know who was there.

"Is that your father's gun?" I asked. "Or did you have one of your own, perhaps a Christmas or birthday present from the old man?"

"Shut up," she said. "I've had quite enough from you."

"Well, I haven't had enough from you, Lizzie. You never even thanked me for the flowers."

I looked around the run. No one was paying the least bit of attention to us, Dr. Philips, who had cloned a dog, standing in front of me, Elizabeth Madison on the outside of the run, standing behind the bench I sat on holding a gun against the back of my neck. I wondered what she had over her arm. Surely, even here in Greenwich Village, someone would have noticed the gun if she hadn't pulled it into the sleeve of her droopy sweater or tossed a jacket over her arm. After all, this wasn't the Wild West.

"Tell him it's okay," she said, "and then get up slowly, and hand Rudy the leash. We're getting out of here and you're coming with us."

"Hey, this is really interesting. You know the whole nature/nurture thing. For a while there, it seemed the nature people were way ahead, all those studies on twins who had been raised apart, ending up so similar anyway. But look at you, Elizabeth, a fucking paean to your adopted father, a walking advertisement for the power of nurturing to influence character."

She jammed the gun into my neck. I had the feeling she would have done more if there hadn't been so many people around. And if Dashiell hadn't been standing there.

"Tell him it's okay," she said between her teeth.

"I beg your pardon?"

"Your dog. Tell him it's okay. Call him off. You think I'm stupid. I saw you sic him on Rudy."

"Oh, yes. I nearly forgot."

"Do it now. And don't try anything funny."

"Oh, I would never," I told her. I looked hard at Dashiell. His eyes were on Elizabeth now. Whatever was hiding the gun didn't fool him. He could smell the gunpowder, taste it on his big tongue.

"Okay," I told him in no uncertain terms. I'm nothing if not obedient.

I let go of the leash and threw myself to the side, hitting the bench with my shoulder as Dashiell sailed over me, clearing the bench and the fence behind it, hitting Elizabeth square in the chest. I heard the rumble in his throat, muffled by her black sweater as he took the hand that had been holding the gun in his mouth and held tight. That was going to be one sore hand when he let go.

A dozen dogs had stopped what they were doing and run up to the fence; two stood next to me on the bench, all were barking wildly. One of them, an Irish terrier, cleared the fence the way Dashiell had and was pulling on Elizabeth's pants leg. The people had gathered, too, some of them shouting, some of them frightened, hanging back, trying to see what all the commotion was about.

"Hey," someone called out.

The gun was lying in the grass, near Elizabeth Madison's hip.

"It's under control," I said.

No one believed me.

"What now, Ms. Alexander?" Philips said. "A citizen's arrest for cloning?" He had that smirk on his face again. He was nearly gloating, not giving a rat's ass about what was happening to Elizabeth just a few feet away.

I checked my watch, then looked over at the path that led to the dog run. Agoudian was right on time, towering head and shoulders above Burke and Burns, all of them coming our way fast.

"No, Doctor, it's not a citizen's arrest. It's the old-fashioned kind. And the charge won't be cloning. It'll be murder."

The gate opened. Philips's mouth opened. Burke hadn't come into the run. He'd headed for Elizabeth. I knelt on the bench and told Dashiell out. He let go of her hand and backed up, still watching to make sure she didn't move a muscle. The terrier was another story. It took Burke to get him to let go. When I heard Burke scream and curse, I knew exactly what the dog had done afterward.

"In case it ever comes up again," I said, looking down at Elizabeth, who was now holding her hand against her chest, "when you tell a dog 'okay,' it means he can do whatever he wants to." I shook my head. "You tangled with the wrong dog, Ms. Madison. This particular dog, he doesn't like it when someone points a gun at me. As a point of interest, 'out' is the command you need when you want to call a dog off. But unless there's one of those outreach programs to teach dog training to women prisoners, you won't need that information where you're going."

She didn't thank me. In fact, she may have been in shock. Her eyes seemed dilated and looked a bit glassy, but hey, what do I know? I'm a detective, not a doctor.

She still hadn't thanked me for the flowers, either. Possibly she hadn't liked the note. What wasn't to like? I wondered. It was short and sweet. Love and kisses, it had said. It had been signed "Mel."

CHAPTER 34

I Climbed the Stairs

I called The School for the Deaf on my way over to Sophie's apartment. When Ruth answered, I told her I had some good news for her.

"Did you find Side by Side?" she asked.

"I did."

"And am I on the list?"

"That won't be necessary."

"But I was hoping . . ."

"I was hoping you'd agree to take Bianca, Ruth."

"Bianca? But I thought Bianca doesn't alert."

"She didn't for Sophie because she had no need to. The job was taken. Blanche always beat her to the punch."

"Oh. But then how do you know she'll work for me?"

"She will. I've seen her do it."

"I don't understand."

"Her walker was shot. He seizured from loss of blood and just before he did, Bianca knew it was coming. She alerted him, but in this case, there was nothing we could do."

"He was shot?" she whispered. "He's dead?"

"He is, Ruth."

I didn't tell her he wasn't really a dog walker, that he'd been there to please his father, to keep him in the loop. I didn't tell her who'd killed him, either, or what Mel had done for me, not on the phone anyway. "Everything that happened, it's not what we thought it was. I'll tell you all about it when I bring Bianca. I could come by tonight if you like. I have your address from Sophie's book."

"Yes, yes. That would be wonderful. Oh, oh, I'm so excited, I, I don't know what to say. It's not just that I'll have a seizure-alert dog, I'll have part of Sophie with me, too."

"I understand. That's why I'm so glad it turned out this way, that Bianca can give you what you need and that I'm able to offer her to you."

"Me, too." She was crying.

"I'm on my way to Sophie's now," I said. "I'm going to pick up Bianca's medical records for you and anything else I can think of that you might need—her pan, her brush, and the red cape."

"Blanche's cape?"

"Yes. She's staying with me and she won't need it, Ruth, but you and Bianca will. You'll be taking her to work with you. You'll be taking her everywhere."

"Oh."

"I'll bring it all tonight."

"And Bianca?"

"And Bianca."

"At seven?"

"Seven's fine. And, Ruth, I have something else for you, a gift for helping me."

"You don't have to do anything, Rachel. Truly. You've already done so much."

"No, I do. I'm going to work with you, to help you feel comfortable and in control with Bianca, for as long as you need me."

On my way down MacDougal Street, I thought about the time I'd seen Philips sitting in the run, the time the head count of dogs and people was off. I bet he'd been there before, watching the little clone play, awed by what he had accomplished. He could watch her in Sophie's garden, too, from the top floors of the main house or from that little window in the back of the cottage. I bet he did it often, spying on Sophie and Bianca, never able to get enough of all three of the cloned dogs he'd created, wishing he could tell the world what he'd done.

Elizabeth was in on it with her father and, apparently, involved with Philips. From what I had seen, they were a perfect couple, too. And Mel had been in on it from the start, pretending to be a dog walker so that he could keep an eye on Bianca and Sophie, so that they'd be sure they'd gotten what they were after, and once they were, then Philips could work on the real project, his hubris, and Madison's, getting full range. It must be nice to have money. You can be as crazy as you want to be, as long as you've got the bucks to pay for it.

But there were still a few things I didn't know. Who was the woman in the park who'd told me she knew Herbie? Was there another adopted kid around to do Madison's bidding, or was she his secretary or his personal assistant? And whom had I heard at the cottage? Was that also the woman from the park? Or did Madison have mice, really big ones?

I unlocked the door to Sophie's building, letting Dashiell in ahead of me, then walking down the short hall to Sophie's door and unlocking that. I looked around the living room for the last time, then began to gather the dogs' things and pile them into shopping bags to take with me. Even if Wexford decided he wanted some of Sophie's things, I was sure he wouldn't need a couple of used brushes, a red leather collar, a nail clipper, and the medical histories of dogs he didn't want.

When I finished, I straightened up the kitchen, packed up all the veggies and supplements, put away the blanket I'd left on the couch, put the towels I'd used in the hamper for someone else to wash or throw away. I smoothed the bed where Blanche had been, but left the dent in the pillow, her big head having rested where she could best smell the comforting odor of her lost mistress. I wondered about the windows, if I should leave them open or closed, but decided it didn't matter. In a day or two, Sophie's things would be taken out of here and the apartment would be painted and rented to someone else. I wondered who would empty the apartment and where her things would go, but I was dog tired, and it didn't really matter now. What difference could it possibly make what happened to her towels or her toaster, as long as her dogs would be safe and loved.

And then, just like that, one of my questions got answered in the Zen way I had been taught on another job. I had paid attention to what I was doing, cleaning up Sophie's apartment, letting my mind relax, not forcing anything, and the answer had come. JSB Realty and WAM Realty were branches of the same firm, both owned by Charles Madison, named for two of his favorite musicians. That's how the veterinary office had appeared and disappeared on a Sunday. And how his son, without a real job, had a space worth thousands a month. And a piano he probably couldn't play.

I thought about the music I'd heard over the phone and

in the garden, opening the door and walking out, thinking that this was the last time I'd do that, too, the last time I'd stand in Sophie's garden, protected by the ivy-covered wall I'd climbed, the building next door to the west and the fence to the east with the broken slat, the empty apartment, access for Madison when he was playing Joe and didn't feel like coming in the front door. Or perhaps he'd sat there and listened to her talk on the phone when she did that out in the garden, when she'd called me and told me why she needed a detective. About that, I could only guess. I'd never know everything.

I sat on the stone bench, Dashiell at my side, no bull terrier to play with this time. And then I heard it—not the piano. The man who played the piano so well that he wanted to make sure he had an offspring to do so when the time came that he no longer could. I heard something else coming from the main house. It sounded like a dog whining. And I remembered Sugar, there all alone.

And then I remembered, she wasn't alone.

I pulled out my cell phone and hit re-dial.

"Ruth, it's Rachel again. Do you by any chance know of anyone else who might need a seizure-alert dog?"

"I, well, no, not offhand. But my doctor would. Why?"

"There are two more clones I'd like to place and they might as well go where they can do some good. It would seem a shame to let talent like this go to waste."

Wasn't that how it all started, Madison feeling that way about his own talent?

"I'll call him. I'll find two people who need the dogs. I promise."

I told Dashiell I'd be right back and, leaving him in the garden, once again I hoisted myself up over the ivy-covered wall.

The door to the cottage was open this time so I just

walked in, without knocking. The lab was there, undis-
turbed, the man who'd worked there at the precinct now,
telling stories. The cottage was dead quiet, but I went upstairs anyway, to see what was there, finding a small bedroom with a pale blue blanket on the bed, a tiny bathroom
next to it with a tiled shower, a smaller than usual sink,
everything blue. The dog bed was blue, too, one of those
denim-covered round ones from L.L. Bean. Her name was
on it, so I had the answer to one more question now. It had
been Smitty who I'd heard on the stairs, not a person. Had
she been the surrogate? I wondered. And where was she
now?

I heard that sound again, the creaking of the stairs, and
whipped around to see who it was. It wasn't Smitty this
time. It was a dog far more clever and way more agile.

He cocked his head and wagged his tail.

"Great," I told him. "We'll be even more unobtrusive
than I planned."

I bent and kissed the top of his head. Then together we
headed out of the cottage and across the garden to the main
house to rescue Sugar and her sister the way I'd once lib-
erated Dashiell from people who didn't deserve to have
him.

Dashiell was looking up at me. What difference did it
make if he came along? There were only dogs in the main
house. Everyone else was either dead or in jail.

The French doors were latched but opened easily when
I shook them back and forth to loosen the lock. When we
stepped into the open living room, I heard the sound again,
that whining noise. Sugar and her sister were in the living
room to greet us and neither one was whining. Their tails
wagged rapidly from side to side. So what was that sound?
Was there another litter of clones?

I climbed the stairs, the two bullies running on ahead to

lead the way, Dashiell sticking with me. We continued on up, past a floor with a study and a small bedroom, to the next floor where there was a master bedroom suite. The sound got louder, and then I heard something else. A woman speaking. Well, crooning. After a moment, the whining sound stopped. I heard a dog bark. Then the whining started all over again.

I climbed the last staircase to see what it was, and there she was, the woman from the dog run, the one who'd told me the story about Herbie and sent me running off to New Jersey to try to find him. She'd just tiptoed out into the hall and looked startled to see me, but instead of acting frightened or indignant and asking why I was there—perhaps she knew—she lifted one finger to her lips, to stop me from speaking. But it was no use. The noise started up again, louder than ever.

I passed her and opened the door she'd just pulled closed, stopping in the doorway, Sugar and her sister at my right, Dashiell at my left, heads up, noses going. Smitty stood when the door opened but she didn't come toward us. She seemed not to know what to do, and so she did nothing. Would that human beings could be so wise.

He was in his crib, his face red, his small arms pumping, his legs, too. When I bent over the side, he reached for me, but I didn't pick him up. He was a cute baby, I'd give him that. Only time would tell what he'd become. I hoped like hell, in this case, nurture would win out over nature.

Without saying a word—what was there to say?—I turned and left, going back to Sophie's the way I'd come, the bullies pausing for only a moment before following Dashiell and me over the wall.

CHAPTER 35

He Tried to Pull Me Closer

On a crisp fall day at the end of September, two days after visiting Sophie's class and getting petted and hugged by all her kids, Blanche kissed me good morning, ate her breakfast, and walked slowly out into the garden, lying down in a sunny patch of grass between the cottage and the main house. After a moment, I heard her cough once. When I got to where she was and knelt to stroke her head, she sighed deeply. I told her I loved her and felt her let go and disappear, as peacefully as my father must have, his blanket as smooth in the morning as it had been when he'd shut off the light.

We buried her in that very spot and that weekend we invited Ruth, the young boy who had Sugar, the freelance editor who had her sister Snow, and Sophie's class to come. Some of the kids read poems they'd written for her. One sang a song. Everett, the tall boy who carried a purple backpack, had brought a flat stone to mark the grave. Chip had gotten a white dogwood tree to plant there and the boys helped him dig the hole and set the tree. After that, we ordered pizza for the kids and watched them play with each other and the dogs until it was time for them to go.

That night, the bed seemed much too big with just the two of us and Dash and Betty.

"She waited until the case was resolved," I said into the dark room, "and until she could say good-bye to the kids."

"Rach?"

"Mmm?"

"Do you think the baby is really a clone?"

"I don't know. Agoudian thinks it was a scam. He thinks Philips and that woman made the kid the old-fashioned way. I told him that was ridiculous, that Madison was crazy, but he wasn't stupid. He'd have the baby tested."

"What did Agoudian say about that?"

"That they'd get a court order and do exactly that."

"Test the baby's DNA?"

"And Madison's."

"And?"

"Look, Chip, whether the kid's a clone or not, it's inevitable, like no-iron cotton, the tangelo, the Doberman pinscher, the H-bomb—one day, it'll happen. Man is a tinkerer."

He tried to pull me closer but someone's rump was in the way and someone else's foreleg was pushing hard against my back. I closed my eyes and pictured the flat, white blossoms that would appear next spring, white like Blanche, and the words Everett had painted on that flat stone we'd pressed into the earth at the base of the tree.

"Here lies one good dog."

Then, despite myself, I pictured the baby's fat little fingers, reaching up to me as I bent over the crib.

They'd have the results any day now, but I'd told Agoudian not to call me. This was one answer I didn't want.

Turn the page for a glimpse of
WITHOUT A WORD,
the next suspenseful
Rachel Alexander Mystery
from Carol Lea Benjamin

One

Leon Spector had dead written all over him, not the kind where they put you in a box, say a few words and toss the earth back over you, not the ashes to ashes kind of dead, but the kind that lets the world know that whatever the battle was, you lost, the kind that says that sometime, a long time ago, you were beaten into the ground by circumstances beyond your control. I didn't know what those circumstances were in Leon's case, but on a particularly sunny afternoon at the Washington Square Park dog run the month I turned forty and my pit bull, Dashiell, turned five, Leon apparently planned to tell me.

He met me as I was closing the inner gate, a wide, multicolored camera strap slung around his neck, his Leica hanging low on his chest. I'd seen him at the run before, not with a dog but with his camera, and I'd seen him taking pictures on other occasions as well, the opening of the new park along the river, the annual outdoor art show, the

gay pride parade. Someone said he was a freelance pho-
tographer. Someone else said he was working on a book.
Until that afternoon, that was all I knew about Leon, but
not why he carried not only a camera everywhere he went
but the also the weight of the world. You could see it
pulling him toward the ground, as if the gravity under Leon
was working overtime.

"I've been looking all over for you," he said as I bent to
unhook Dashiell's leash. "I couldn't call you because . . ."

I looked up. Leon stopped and fiddled with the strap of
his camera.

"Because I'm not listed?" I asked.

Leon shook his head. "I never got that far," he said.
"The person who told me about you, who said what I
needed was a private investigator and that's what you . . ."
He stopped and shrugged. "It is, isn't it?"

I nodded.

Leon nodded back. "She just said she'd seen you here
and that your dog wore a red collar with his name on it and
that you had," he made a spiral with his left pointer, "long,
curly hair. She didn't know your last name."

I didn't know his last name either, at least not yet, but I
didn't say so. Leon didn't look in the mood for small talk.

"What's the problem?" I asked.

Instead of answering me, Leon put the camera up to his
face and looked through the viewfinder. I wondered if he
had a deadline of some sort or if he was just one of those
people who talked better if he was doing something else at
the same time.

I heard the shutter click and looked in the direction
Leon's camera was pointing. There was a little girl of
about nine or ten sitting alone on a bench, watching the
dogs. She was wearing dark glasses and a shirt that looked
three sizes too big. Next to her, on the bench, there was a

small, see-through plastic purse the shape of a lunch pail, with something colorful inside, but I was too far away to make out what it was.

I waited. Sometimes, doing something else or not, I let the other guy do the talking, see what comes out before adding my own two cents.

"I need you to find my wife," he said.

I guess that explained the sagging shoulders, the hang-dog look. He'd been a good looking man once, you could see that. But now he looked faded, used up, worn out. You could feel the effort it took for him to form sentences, as if he could barely muster the energy to speak.

"It's not for me," he said. "It's for my daughter. She's in trouble and she needs her mother."

Dashiell was busy digging a hole in the far corner of the run, a hole I'd have to fill in before I left. I turned to look at Leon now to see if his face might tell me what his words hadn't. But Leon's face wasn't talking either.

"Where is her mother?"

"That's the whole point. I don't know, not since she walked out on me and Madison."

I took out a small notepad and a pencil. I wrote down "Madison."

"Divorced you?" I asked.

He shook his head. "Nothing so . . ." He scratched at the dirt with the sole of his shoe. "Nothing as clear as that."

"Missing, you mean?"

Leon nodded. "I do," he said. "Every day."

I nodded. I knew what it was like to miss someone who was gone. I figured, one way or another, just about every-one did. But Leon had a bad case of it, not only being abandoned, but being abandoned with a kid.

"Come on," I said, "let's sit down."

We walked over to the closest bench.

"No clue as to why she left," I asked, "or where she went?"

"You ever notice the way things look one way, but they're not, they're another?"

"How did you think things were?"

"Permanent," he said.

I felt that little stab that sometimes comes along with an unexpected truth, simply stated.

Leon lifted the camera to his face again. But this time I didn't hear the shutter click. I wrote down, "How long is wife missing? How old is Madison?"

"After the initial shock of it, the police investigation, all of that," he moved the camera away from his face and turned to look at me, "everything just a dead end, I managed okay." He tilted his head left, then right, as if he were arguing with himself. "At least that's what I thought. Not perfect. Far from perfect. But okay. Considering." He shrugged. "But now." He shook his head. "I don't know how to handle this."

If his daughter was pregnant, I wondered if there might be some female relative who could help. Or a neighbor they were close to. Was this just an excuse to try to find his missing wife again? I was about to ask when Leon started talking again. Perhaps he was finally on a roll.

"She went out one night and never came back," he said, covering his face with the camera. He was pointing it at the southern end of the run where a Weimaraner had dropped his ball into the water bucket and was trying to fish it out with his front paws, but I had the feeling Leon wasn't actually looking through the lens this time.

"Your wife?"

Leon moved the camera away and nodded. He hadn't taken a picture this time either. "Just like that," he said. "Went for a walk. Didn't take a thing with her."

"No money, no passport, not even a change of clothes?"

"Just a change of heart, I guess. And Roy."

"That was the man she ran off with?" I asked quietly, sympathetically, finally getting it.

Leon shook his head. "That I could understand, if that's what she had done."

"But it wasn't, is that what you're saying?" Wanting to shake him by now. "Spit it out, Leon. I'm going to be a member of AARP before you get to the point."

"Roy was the dog," he said.

"The dog?"

Leon nodded, though it was sort of a rhetorical question. "See, what I don't get is that Sally never wanted him in the first place. She said, 'No matter what you say now, Leon, I'm going to be the one taking care of it. I already have more than I can handle with the kid, going to school at night and you, Leon. What the hell do I need a dog for?'" Leon shrugged again. "Guess I was the one who needed a dog. Guess that's what she was saying. So I said I'd take care of him. I figured that would take care of the problem, you know what I mean?"

"But it didn't?"

"One night she says, 'I think Roy needs a walk. I think he needs to go.' So I get up to take him out, but she flaps her hand at me, picks up the leash and walks out the door. That was the last time I saw either one of them." He scratched the side of his nose with his thumb. "I guess she was the one who had to go, not Roy."

"The police . . ."

He shook his head.

"What about Roy? Did he . . ." I stopped to consider how to word what I wanted to say. But was there anything I could say that Leon hadn't thought of a thousand times over? "Did he ever turn up?" I asked.

Leon shook his head again. For a while, we just sat there. Leon didn't say anything and neither did I.

"That's why I was looking for you," he finally said, "to ask if you could find her for us."

"How long has she been gone?"

"Five years, two months, eleven days." He looked at his watch but he didn't report back to me.

"That long?"

Leon nodded.

"Without a word?"

He nodded again.

"How do you know she's still alive?"

"I don't," he said.

"There was no credit card activity that night? Or afterwards?"

"She didn't have it with her." He shrugged. "She'd just gone out to walk Roy."

"Did she have a driver's license?"

"We didn't have a car." As if that answered the question.

"What about social security payments made under her name? Did the police follow up on that?" I asked, thinking she could have a new name, a new social security card, a new life.

Or not.

"They didn't come up with anything," he said. "No sign of . . ."

I nodded.

He was probably in his forties, but he could have easily passed for sixty, the hair sticking out from under his baseball cap a steely gray, his skin the color of honeysuckle, that yellowish white that looks great on a plant and really lousy on a person. But it was mostly his eyes that made him look so old, his sad, dead eyes.

"Look, someone gone that long," I shook my head from

side to side, "Leon, if your daughter's pregnant and that's, that's a problem, there are only a few choices that can be made. Why go through all this . . ."

"Pregnant? Wouldn't that be . . ." For a moment I thought he was going to laugh, but then he looked as if he was about to cry. "Madison's not pregnant," he said. "She's suspected of murder."

"Murder?" Why was he talking to me? His daughter didn't need her mother, she needed a good lawyer.

"They say she killed her doctor in a fit of rage. She gets them sometimes."

"Fits of rage?"

Leon nodded.

"And did she?"

Leon looked shocked. Then his old, sad eyes looked even older and sadder. "I don't think so."

"But you don't know?"

Leon shook his head.

"Did you ask her?"

"I did."

"Well, what did she say?"

"She didn't say anything. Madison doesn't speak. She stopped talking three days after her mother disappeared." He glanced around the run, as if to assess whether or not anyone might be listening, but there wasn't a soul near enough and besides, a Jack Russell had spotted a squirrel on a branch and was barking his fool head off. "I was hoping if you could find Sally for us," he whispered, "maybe Madison would start to talk again. Maybe she'd say what happened that day instead of letting people who weren't there say what was in her heart and what she did."

"Does she respond at all? Does she write things down? Does she nod for yes, shake her head for no?"

"Sometimes she draws pictures but even then, you can't always know for sure what she's thinking. There was a picture on the doctor's desk, a heart with a scraggly line going into it."

"Stabbing it?"

"It could look that way."

"And was she angry with her doctor?"

Leon nodded. "She has these tics and he was treating her with Botox, to paralyze the muscles so that she'd . . ."

"Look more normal?"

" 'Pass for normal' is what he said. Can you imagine saying that to a patient? To a kid?"

Pass for normal, I thought. Isn't that what we all tried to do?

"But the last shot he gave her, he screwed up." Leon looked straight at me. "He said it would go away, that it would wear off, but meanwhile it made one eyelid droop and she was really freaked out by it."

"So was the picture an expression of her anger, maybe a threat, is that what the thinking is?"

He nodded. "She was his last patient of the afternoon. The receptionist was there when Madison showed up but not when she left. When she went back to the office, she found him, Dr. Bechman, dead."

"Stabbed in the heart?"

"With the Botox injection that Madison had refused."

That did it for me. No way could I turn down the case now.

"Alexander," I said. "It's Rachel Alexander." I gave him a card with my land line and my cell phone numbers.

It took him a while to find his card. It was in the third pocket he checked. I explained my fees and the advance I required. I said there might be some expenses in a case like this and that he'd have to cover those, too. And finally

I told him I couldn't guarantee I'd find Sally after all these years, that there was only the slimmest chance of that, but if he still wanted me to try, I would. He said he did.

As for Madison, I hoped there'd be some other way to prove her innocence, if she were innocent, because even if I found her mother and even if the kid started talking again, told the cops what happened on that terrible day, said the blame wasn't hers, who says anyone would believe her?

Leon and I shook hands. Looking at his sad face, I wasn't sure who needed Sally more, the father or the daughter. And I had no idea at the time what I was committing myself to and how it would change my life.

"So the receptionist found the doctor when she got to work in the morning?" I asked, wondering why no one had called earlier to say he hadn't arrived home. "That must have been a shock."

"It wasn't in the morning. She went back that night."

"Why would she do that?"

Leon shrugged.

"You think maybe his wife called the receptionist—if he had a wife?"

"He did. He kept her picture on the desk. They all do that for some reason."

"So maybe she called the receptionist at home to ask where he was, if there was some meeting or conference or business dinner he'd neglected to mention?" Why call nine one one, I thought, when it might just be miscommunication, or a lack of communication?

"I wasn't told why she went back, just that she did."

"And the doctor was there, dead?"

"That's correct."

"What about Madison? Was she there?"

"No. Madison was at home. She came home right after her appointment."

"And did she seem upset?"

Leon didn't answer my question.

"Were you there when she arrived home, Leon?"

"What I say to you, what you say to me, it's confidential, right?"

"It is as far as I'm concerned."

He nodded. "Well, then," he said, "I wasn't at home when she got there, at least not right at that exact moment. I got home about an hour later."

"How do you know she was home an hour if she doesn't speak, if she doesn't communicate with you?"

"She always came straight home from . . ." Leon stopped and looked at me.

"So when you got home that day, did she seem upset? Was anything different, anything off?"

Leon shrugged.

"Not that you noticed?"

"No."

"And when did the police show up?"

"Late. After Madison had gone to bed."

"Were you asleep as well?"

"No."

"And when they came, they told you what had happened?"

"Yes."

"And they showed you the drawing?"

"No. They described it to me."

"And what else did they say?"

"That no one else was there, just Madison and Dr. Bechman. And then they said that the receptionist had gone back and that she'd found him."

"But they didn't tell you why? They didn't say she'd been called, nothing like that?"

"I never thought about it, about why she went back.

They were saying that Madison was the only one there and that Dr. Bechman was dead. That's what was on my mind."

"What else did they say?" Wondering if they'd gone beyond implying to accusing.

"One detective said they'd been told that Madison had a history of violence and that she'd been very angry at Dr. Bechman for the perceived harm he'd done to her. Can you imagine? 'The perceived harm.' Then the second detective, he said they were told the doctor had ruined her eye. You see how it was going?"

I nodded, wondering what the cops thought about Leon that night, first his wife had gone missing and now this, the man getting agitated just telling me about it.

"What happened next?" I asked him.

Leon rubbed the back of his neck, looking away, looking anywhere but at me.

"Leon? I'm on your side. Speak up."

"I kind of . . . I got angry. She's my daughter and . . ."

"So you said what?"

"That they should be ashamed of themselves implying that a child with a disability had committed murder."

"Good. That's good you said that. And what was their . . . ?"

"I was yelling—well, yelling softly, if you know what I mean. I didn't want to wake Madison. But they remained calm. Cool. It was almost spooky. They asked if I was there. You know how they do that? They knew I wasn't. Trying to trip me up, to make me out to be a liar, the way they did when Sally disappeared." Leon's lips tight for a moment, his hands balled into fists. "I told them I hadn't been there. So then they asked what time Madison got home." He stopped again, looking at me, then looking away.

"Confidential, Leon, straight down the line."

"I said she'd come straight home, that she was home by 5:45. Then they asked if she'd been upset when she'd gotten home, if anything was out of the ordinary and I said no," talking faster now, "that she was fine, that she did her homework before dinner, watched TV afterwards, went to bed on time, everything as usual."

"But you weren't home."

"No, I wasn't." Looking me in the eye now, letting me know he'd do anything to protect his kid.